THE LADY'S RISK

A MARRIAGE OF CONVENIENCE REGENCY ROMANCE

CONRAD LEGACY BOOK 4

C.K. MACKENZIE

The Lady's Risk
Marriage of Convenience, Partners in Crime Regency Romance
Conrad Legacy Book 4

Contact Information: ckmackenzieauthor@gmail.com

Cover Art by Graziana Masneri

Publishing History
First Edition, 2024
Paperback ISBN 979-8-9901599-0-7
Published in the United States of America

❀ Created with Vellum

ACKNOWLEDGMENT

For my darling soul dog, thank you for our amazing 13 years together.
I miss you every day.

CHAPTER 1

May 1816
Damietta, Egypt

"Captain!"

Philip Paul Conrad rolled from his bunk before his mind fully grasped the situation. Eyes barely open, dagger in hand, he crossed the small cabin. Argus stood at the door and didn't so much as growl. Philip wrenched open the door to stare at his first mate. Good thing he hadn't bothered to undress after they docked.

"Harry?" He stepped out of his room, letting the door latch heavily behind both him and Argus.

"Stowaway, Cap," his first mate and closest friend said.

Philip's eyebrows shot upward. The lanterns swayed gently as he and Harry hurried down the darkened corridor. Fully awake now, he snorted. "A stowaway? Already? We made port two hours ago." If that.

"If I'd known there was a time limit, I'd have told her to wait." Harry chuckled and climbed up the steps onto the deck.

The sun hadn't even crested the horizon, and it barely lit the sea in beautiful jewel tones that promised an equally beautiful day.

"Her?" Maybe not as awake as he'd believed.

Navigating the Mediterranean Sea had been trickier than Philip thought, despite the maps he'd acquired from their ships' captains who had long sailed this route. It didn't help that a storm had blown through, making the waters choppy and keeping the port shrouded behind the driving rain.

His shoulders still ached from when he and Reeves held the wheel steady.

But the morning was a far cry from that. The rain had passed over, leaving the air warm and fresh, even at their location on the wharves. The sky remained cloudless and the wind just steady enough to fill the sails. Not that they were going anywhere anytime soon.

"I am not a stowaway," the woman insisted in clear, precise English. She glared at the crewmen who stood beside her. One tried grabbing her arm, and she slapped his hand, much to his companion's amusement. "Do not touch me."

"Listen, your highness," Hutton sneered and reached for her again.

"Don't touch her," Philip ordered. The men stood at attention, and the woman looked surprised. Either at his appearance or his order, he couldn't tell. "Go on, then. Back to your duties."

"Aye, Captain."

They did as ordered, leaving only Harry and Argus at his side. Philip nodded at the woman. She was of average height, with dark hair slipping from beneath her headscarf and wide, frightened eyes. She was modestly dressed. Even in the dawn light he saw hints of wear on the hem of her skirts. The ends of her hijab were frayed as well. The wind blew gently over the deck, catching the frays. She ignored it and held his gaze, defiant.

Except her fingers gripped her skirts as if they were her only lifeline.

"If you aren't a stowaway, then I presume you have a good reason for being on my ship?"

Her eyes dropped, and she stepped back. Not noticeably, just a fraction, as if keeping out of arm's reach. He didn't think it was because of Argus. "I thought this was *The Clement*," she said, her voice dropping as well. "I boarded the wrong ship."

He didn't know what he'd expected, but it wasn't that. "This was a mistake? An accident?" He had a dozen other questions but settled for, "At which berth is *The Clement* docked?"

"I don't know," she admitted. Her English was tinged with a slight accent, but the words sounded clear enough. She spoke slow and exact. "I counted the ships. I'm looking for Saied el-Nebi and Saied Bartley. They were conducting business with *The Clement.*"

At a loss, Philip merely nodded. He'd never encountered a stowaway before. Technically, he supposed she wasn't one. Settling on common courtesy, he said, "All right. Would you like to come below deck for breakfast, Miss…?"

Her gaze shot upward and met his for a fraction of a breath before skittering away. She looked torn between frightened and exhausted. He had a feeling he'd made a breach of etiquette. In the next breath, her shoulders drooped, and exhaustion won out. "Thank you, Captain."

"Harry?" Philip tore his gaze from hers and met the amused look of his first mate.

"Aye, I'll find it." Shaking his head, Harry slapped on his hat and headed toward the gangplank.

The woman looked over her shoulder, onto the wharves below. Philip didn't know what she saw, but before he could ask, she shook herself and stepped forward. She kept her chin raised, her eyes straight ahead. Something about her mannerisms set off warning bells, but Philip couldn't figure out why.

Probably just a cultural difference. Though he didn't quite believe that.

"My crew won't harm you," he promised as they crossed the deck to the steps that led below. "I'm sorry you were accosted when you boarded, but we didn't expect passengers."

"I told them I was looking for *The Clement*." She sniffed in obvious disdain at his crew's listening abilities, but she didn't raise her voice. "They did not believe me."

Frowning as he held out his hand for her to descend first, he glanced around the deck. He knew these men. They had sailed with his family's company for years, many of them on this route since relative peace spread over the lands.

"I apologize on their behalf," he said, still not certain why they'd treat a woman with such callousness, even one they believed was a stowaway. "I'll have coffee brought out," he said, gesturing toward the captain's dining room rather than his quarters. He wasn't getting any more sleep today. "Unless you prefer tea?"

She studied him for a long moment. The room was dim; there'd been no need for any lanterns in there. She didn't look around at the furnishings but watched as if expecting him to disappear. An odd sensation he couldn't name slithered down his spine.

"Coffee, please." She paused again. "Thank you, Captain."

"You , you don't have to call me that." He offered a small smile, not at all certain what had happened in the last twenty or so minutes. This wasn't how he thought he'd start his day. "Laska, coffee, please."

The cook didn't say a word—he rarely did. He leaned to the side and eyed the woman, who sat stiffly at the table, hands folded neatly in front of her. Laska, who had been with the family for years, snorted.

"Kaz!" he called. "*Śniadanie!*"

Philip merely nodded. He waited as Laska set about making

coffee with the long-handled copper kanaka. Argus settled beneath the table, not in his normal place on Philip's feet, but closer to their guest.

Their guest, who hadn't moved. If Philip didn't know better, he'd have wondered if she breathed. Her hands remained folded, and she looked at the table before her as if it fascinated her.

The movement of the ship hadn't seemed to bother her, but upon closer inspection he noticed that her knuckles were white with the force of her grip. Fear? Seasickness?

"Captain."

He turned, accepted the small tray of two coffee cups, and nodded in thanks. He'd bet fear, and a rush of anger swamped him at whatever—or whoever—so terrified her.

"Here you are," he said softly as he set the tray carefully on the table. She didn't jump but stiffened. "It's traditional Egyptian coffee," he offered for lack of any other polite opening.

"Thank you," she said again. Then she took a sip. "It's been a trying morning." Her lips pressed hard together, and she closed her eyes. "What is the name of this ship?"

"*The Lady Kaya,*" Philip said, letting the coffee move through his own system. Though being woken so suddenly was energizing enough. Argus huffed at his own lack of food, but Kaz soon appeared with a bowl of meat.

"Where do you sail?" She held his gaze, a steady look so at odds with the nervousness of her movements.

"Here." He gestured in the general direction of the port of Damietta. "We made port a few hours ago." He waited, but she watched her cup so intently, Philip wondered if it spoke to her. Perhaps she was reading the grounds like some read tea leaves. "I didn't fully introduce myself. Captain Philip Conrad."

She paused, her movements still and small, as if afraid to draw attention. Unwanted attention. "Layla," she eventually whispered. She licked her lips. "Layla Braithwaite. And I'm sorry I disturbed you so early in the day."

"It's all right." He grinned and raised his cup in salute. "I had to get up anyway."

* * *

Miss Layla Dahah Braithwaite watched the English captain with a boldness she hadn't felt in far, far too long—not that sneaking out of the house and running from what remained of her family wasn't bold.

It had been a risk, and one worth taking.

His humor confused her, but she felt the tension in her shoulders ease just the slightest. After years of living with her uncle's unpredictable temper, she knew how a man might lash out. She didn't feel that from Captain Conrad. However much she might not understand his jest, she appreciated the effort.

"I was looking for *The Clement*." She loosened her fingers from around her cup, lest she shatter it. "For Saied—ah, *Mr. Josiah Bartley*. Do you know him?" Her heart pounded so hard, she wondered if Captain Conrad could hear it from across the table. It'd been years since she spoke to anyone, let alone a man, even within her own family.

No one spoke much in that household.

He paused, as if thinking, but once again he shook his head. "I'm sorry, the name doesn't sound familiar."

"How about Mr. Muhammad el-Nebi?" She didn't expect an English captain who'd just docked to know an Egyptian merchant, but she'd run out of options. Options? Ha. Whatever options she thought she had dwindled with every passing moment. Her desperation to escape Damietta relied on finding one or both men.

Again he paused, as if thinking on it, only to shake his head. Layla slowly released a long breath and swallowed hard.

"I was told they could be found on *The Clement*." Careful of the captain's dog, she pressed her toes against the floor until she thought the floorboards might crack. A small but necessary means for keeping her emotions under control.

"Has the ship recently docked?"

"I don't know. The customs officer didn't say." She finished her coffee, the first thing she'd had since escaping before sunset last night. By now the household, who rarely paid her any attention unless something was misplaced or they suspected she hadn't worked fast enough, knew she'd disappeared.

So did her would-be groom.

Her hand shook at the thought, and Layla set her cup on the tray, careful to make no sound.

Don't make a sound. Don't remind them you're here.

"When Harry returns with word on the ship, we can search then." The captain watched her with dark, hooded eyes. She kept her face carefully blank of all emotion, something she'd perfected years ago, and forced herself to breathe evenly as she met his gaze. "Are they ships' captains?" he asked. "You said they had business on *The Clement.*"

Layla shook her head, a minute movement, and cleared her throat. "No, merchants."

He brightened and gathered the tray. "Perfect. I don't believe they're on my list; however, we're always looking for new contacts. We'll breakfast while we wait."

Whistling, he swept away back to the kitchens and spoke with the man there. Layla couldn't hear what they said, but it didn't matter. She had her own plans to make.

"Plans," of course, being a strong word that didn't apply to her current situation. When her uncle had announced that he'd arranged her marriage, Layla hadn't planned anything more than her escape from the house that stifled her because of her mother's actions and the circumstances of her own birth.

When he said she'd marry Yusif al-Najjar, even her aunt balked. The man was seventy, at the very youngest. His previous wives—all six of them—were known to have met tragic, slow deaths. If he had daughters, no one had ever heard of them. His sons, however, were just as ruthless and greedy as he was.

After that announcement, Layla's only thought was that before the wedding she'd escape and never return. She had a little money saved—all right, stolen—but not so much anyone would notice. Enough for a steerage-class cabin on a ship headed for England. Or Upper Canada. Or one of the islands in the Caribbean. Or even America. All the places she remembered wondering about in her youth.

It didn't matter where, as long as she escaped Egypt.

She released a breath just as Captain Conrad returned with another tray, this one overflowing with fresh foods.

"I thought you said you arrived only hours ago." She eyed the bowls, piled high with eggs, cheeses, and fresh fruits. Foods that wouldn't survive a long voyage.

"We did." He sighed and added fruit to his yogurt. "While I was sleeping, my cook went shopping."

Her lips twitched, and it shocked her down to her very soul. Layla couldn't remember the last time she felt any joy, let alone laughed. A sound escaped her, hoarse and rough, and she covered her mouth to smother it. Still, she thought it might've been a laugh.

Captain Conrad also smiled, his deep, rich laugh sliding between them like a song. "It's all right, go ahead and laugh at my expense."

The sound caught in her throat and refused to break free, but Layla grinned, a wide pull of her lips that felt just as good as laughter.

When she'd slipped past the women's gardens, she thought that was it. That her freedom lay before her. Head down, hajib covering her face, she had hurried through the streets of Damietta, skirting the souk she frequented and keeping well away from both the street guards and the thieves. Only when she set foot onto the wharves, long after night prayers, had she allowed herself a moment's relaxation.

Unfortunately, she'd been so turned around that by the time she'd arrived, the customhouses and merchant offices had closed. The rain hadn't helped matters. She'd sheltered in a doorway for most of the night, too afraid to sleep lest someone find her and drag her back.

"Thank you," she said, hiding her emotions deep inside her. She even hid her momentary joy, though to do so hurt more than she'd imagined it would. "Your hospitality is most welcome." She counted her breaths and maintained her control. Hands steady, she speared a piece of fresh mango and met the captain's gaze.

"You said you counted berths to find *The Clement.*"

She'd expected that question, though he hadn't phrased it as such. "It was dark, and I've never been to the wharves."

A small lie, but the truth lay deep in her heart. That life was long ago and long over.

"I don't suppose you have," he agreed readily enough and let the silence settle.

Layla searched for anything else, any small means of conversation, but it had been years since she'd spoken freely to anyone, let alone a stranger. And a male stranger at that. Her hand shook again, and she gripped her spoon tighter.

No one knew her on this ship. No one could find her, either. She'd boarded the wrong ship on accident, but it seemed like fate had intervened. If her uncle searched for her—and he would, out of fury and wounded pride but not much else—he wouldn't find her on an English ship.

He couldn't. She had to believe that.

If she didn't find Bartley or el-Nebi before sunset, she'd need another means of securing passage. But right now, she had relative safety and peace. Right now, she believed her desperate means of escape had worked. The dog nudged her toes, and

Layla startled, pulling them back beneath her chair. Scrambling for conversation lest the silence drive her mad, she grasped the first thing that came to mind.

"What brings you to Damietta? You are English, are you not?" A strange look crossed his face, there and gone in a breath. Layla couldn't figure it out. She had so little experience with such things.

"I'm sailing with my family's company. We're merchants." His lips moved again, into something not quite a grin. "English merchants."

Oh. Yes, he had mentioned that. Layla nodded and finished her breakfast. She was afraid she'd eaten too much, more than her typical small portion, but the captain said nothing as he finished his eggs. Quite at a loss, she cautiously relaxed against the back of the chair and looked around the room.

Her heart pounded too hard in her chest, and her ears rang with the fear of discovery, though she reassured herself she wouldn't be found on this ship. Her hands shook again, and she folded them tight against each other, her toes digging into the floorboards until she swore a splinter worked its way through her thin-soled shoes.

"I've never seen so much wood," she admitted into the uncomfortable silence. Her cheeks heated at the inane comment, one even she knew sounded silly.

"I don't suppose you've—"

Whatever polite comment he was about to give her rather strange observation disappeared into the hearty greeting of his friend. Layla couldn't remember what title he'd given the man, only that his name was Harry.

Harry. Her father's name.

The memory struck her out of nowhere, a vicious knife straight into her heart. It'd been ten years since his death and three since her mother's. She'd locked those memories in her heart so deep she'd forgotten them.

Until now.

"Good news, Miss Braithwaite." Captain Conrad grinned again, that wide-open grin that looked so natural as to be unnatural. In Layla's eyes, at least. Perhaps all Englishmen smiled like that. Perhaps most people did.

"You found *The Clement*?" She stood, hands braced on the table in both relief and to steady herself. Her knees trembled. She looked between the men and waited, heart pounding so hard it hurt.

"Aye. Well, no."

She frowned. All her hopes, her single dream that sustained her, vanished with Harry's words. Her chest felt as if it had caved in on itself, and she struggled to breathe. "I do not under-stand." *Keep your emotions hidden. No one must know.* "How is that good news?"

"*The Clement* sailed. However, in asking after it, I found a Mr. Muhammad el-Nebi."

Layla's heart skidded to a stop, and her knees buckled.

"I didn't know your name, and for that I apologize." Harry looked sorry, but his blue eyes danced with excitement. "When I described you, Mr. el-Nebi seemed most surprised."

Surprised that she'd asked about him after all this time? That she was so desperately hopeless that he was her only hope?

"Where is he?" Her voice scratched along her throat, but she didn't care.

"He was finding his partner, a Mr. Bartlett?"

"Bartley," Captain Conrad corrected.

Layla met his gaze. Its steadiness eased some of her nervous excitement. He'd listened. When she told her story, he'd listened. How unusual.

"He'll be here shortly."

Layla opened her mouth, but nothing emerged. Instead, she sat heavily on the chair and stared at the captain. "Thank you."

Philip watched Miss Braithwaite collapse onto the chair in obvious relief. It was the most overt emotion he'd seen from her all morning, and it only convinced him further that her past was far more difficult than he could've imagined.

"Thanks, Harry." Philip clasped his friend's shoulder and nodded. He waited until Harry left before approaching Layla. "Did you want to wait here? Or above deck? You'll be safe here. Safe on this ship, I promise."

She hesitated, and he swore he saw her willpower gather around her like a cloak as she debated the answer. "Here, please. It's a lovely day, but I think I'd rather wait here."

Where no one could see her—he didn't need her confirmation, and he certainly wouldn't push. "Would you prefer company while you wait?"

Her head tilted to one side just slightly. Slowly, she shook her head. "*La shukran.*" She hesitated, lips pressed together, then offered a slight smile. "No, thank you."

"*Kama chaa.*" He bowed slightly and left.

He stopped at the galley and motioned for Laska. The cook

eyed him, but his gaze trailed to where Miss Braithwaite sat, ramrod straight, her fingers digging into the table.

"What's she running from?" Laska demanded, his voice low and hard, the Polish of his native tongue coloring the words.

"I don't know," Philip admitted. "She's scared. The men she was searching for are on their way; she'll meet them here."

Laska's gaze flicked from him to Miss Braithwaite and back again. He gave a short nod. "No one will disturb her."

"Thank you, my friend."

Laska called for Kaz again, but Philip turned back around.

"Laska, when did you shop for supplies?"

He snorted. "Not everyone sleeps away their morning. Some must eat."

"I wasn't…I wasn't sleeping away the morning," Philip grumbled as he left the room. He'd had a scant two-hour rest. He could not sleep away a morning that hadn't even properly dawned.

Now, however, the day had brightened while he'd been belowdecks with Miss Braithwaite. The promise of the beautiful day lay spread out before him, but the anticipation of docking in Egypt had dimmed. Perhaps "dimmed" was the wrong word. Changed.

Philip looked south, toward Cairo, but that journey could wait. He hadn't anticipated Miss Braithwaite's appearance. Now that she had, quite literally, landed on his doorstep, he'd help her. It hadn't even occurred to him to do otherwise. Tearing his gaze from the horizon, he scanned the wharves instead. He'd spent a good portion of his life on the wharves, traveling around London's docks with his parents as they conducted Conrad Shipping business.

He knew a swindle when he saw one.

Miss Braithwaite wasn't out to swindle him. He kept an eye on the wharves below, looking for anyone suspicious. They moved smoothly, unloading or loading cargo, shouting orders.

No one looked out of place, as if they were watching his ship, waiting for his unexpected visitor.

Philip checked in with the boatswain, but no customs agent had arrived. More importantly, no one had asked after Miss Braithwaite. Before he could decide whether to return to the dining room or remain above deck, he heard the commotion he'd been waiting for.

"Is this *The Lady Kaya?*" a man asked in English.

"Aye. And you are?" one of the sailors responded. Philip's lips twitched. Harry had already spread the word about the men's impending arrival.

"I'm Mr. Bartley, and this is my partner, Mr. el-Nebi. We've been told you have a, ah, passenger on board."

Philip snorted at the wording but noted neither man used Miss Braithwaite's name. Not when shouting it along the wharves might draw attention. Did they have reasons for such subterfuge? Given the discretion of their movements, their words, he'd say yes. If Philip were to bet—not that he did that anymore—he'd lay odds that they were naturally cautious.

He nodded for the guard to allow them on board and watched the two men hurry onto the ship. Both were well-dressed, one in modest western clothing, the other in a traditional Egyptian jellabiya.

"Misters Bartley and el-Nebi?"

The taller one nodded, not as out of breath as his companion but clearly eager. "I am Saied Muhammad el-Nebi." He bowed a quick greeting, which Philip returned. "Is it true you have a woman on board? Medium height, dark hair and eyes? She speaks English."

"Aye."

"Is she Miss Layla Braithwaite?"

Philip paused at the odd inflection in his tone, but Layla was waiting for them. "Aye," he said again.

El-Nebi's eyes slid over the crew, and his voice lowered. "She is safe?"

Philip stiffened, ready to defend his crew. What kind of sailors did these men think he employed? But before he said a word, he realized that wasn't what el-Nebi meant. He meant was she safe from whatever she ran from.

A chill slid down his spine. Perhaps fate had intervened for Miss Braithwaite.

"Yes." Gesturing toward the stairs, Philip fell in step with the men. "She's in the captain's dining room. She's been here since dawn and is quite safe."

El-Nebi nodded, while Bartley caught his breath. They descended the stairs, Philip leading the way. Miss Braithwaite sat in the same place at the table, her hands folded tightly before her, staring into the room as if she didn't see it at all. Laska stood off to the side, silent and watching.

Guarding.

Philip nodded, and Laska slipped back into the galley. Miss Braithwaite didn't seem to notice.

"Layla?" El-Nebi's hesitant question buzzed through the room like a thunderstorm, crackling with electricity and intent. He stepped inside, closely followed by Bartley, who had finally regained his breath.

"Uncle Muhammad?" Her voice, a slip of sound, echoed like a clap of thunder.

"You're alive, child." El-Nebi's words surprised Philip. But then, since Harry had woken him, he'd faced one surprise after another. It'd been a busy morning.

Miss Braithwaite hesitated. "Yes," she said, as if she hadn't expected that statement. "Why would you think I was not?"

"Omar, well..." Bartley grumbled uncomplimentary sentiments beneath his breath. "Clearly, he lied to us. To all of us."

Instantly the mood shifted. All the breath rushed out of Miss Braithwaite, and her limbs loosened in obvious relief.

Stepping aside as she raced around the table, Philip watched as she transformed. No longer was she the terrified, unaccompanied woman of an hour ago. As she embraced the men, her voice steady as she repeated their names, he saw the woman beneath the closed-off exterior.

He recognized a new appearance around her. Safety.

* * *

LAYLA HUGGED the two men she'd thought had abandoned her. She'd believed she might need to beg for their help, but everything she thought she knew had been wrong. It'd been so long since she'd felt the touch of another, she nearly cried, but she wouldn't embarrass either them or herself. Stepping back, she swallowed against the relief that choked her and drew her control around her once more.

"I'm sorry," she whispered. Her voice broke. "I didn't mean to show such emotion."

Uncle Muhammad pulled her close again. "We thought you died," he whispered. "When your captain's man found us..." He trailed off and shook his head.

Layla almost argued that Captain Conrad wasn't her anything, but the distinction seemed trivial given the circumstances. Peering around the men, she didn't see him in the room. Even the cook had disappeared, giving her privacy for this reunion.

A new emotion swamped her, and it took her a moment to identify it. Gratitude.

"What happened, *najmat saghira?*" Uncle Josiah asked.

Little star. She hadn't heard that endearment in so long. Until he spoke it, she'd forgotten about it. Layla felt tears well in her eyes, but she refused to let them fall. *Don't let them see your weakness.*

Words she'd lived by for ten years.

They spoke in Egyptian, which set her more at ease. She'd forgotten so much of her English; it'd been a decade since she spoke it. Over the years, she'd tried thinking in English, whispering the English word for everyday objects as she cared for her sickly mother. She'd tried to remember other things outside her small world. But that had grown harder and harder the more time passed.

As she had many times over the last few hours, she pulled memories from deep inside her, that place where she'd buried everything from before her father died. It was safer that way.

"After Papa," she said slowly, those long-suppressed memories rising up like whales from the water. They swamped her, pulling her under as if she'd thrown herself over the side of this ship and into the depths of the sea. "After he died, Mama contacted Aunt Heba." Layla didn't remember that part, she'd been young and grieving herself.

"Come, sit, child." Uncle Muhammad led her back to the table, where three cups of fresh coffee waited.

She looked around, but neither Captain Conrad nor the cook—she didn't recall his name—stood in the room. Layla frowned; she hadn't even thanked the captain for his kindness in finding her father's business partners. In offering her, however unknowingly, a new start.

"I don't know what happened. She was ill. Aunt Heba took us in, but I don't think—" she broke off, the words trapped. She felt as if her uncle stood before her, that thunderous look on his face, the one he often wore right before his hand shot out like a snake and slapped her.

"Omar never liked that your mother—" Josiah shook his head. He didn't have to say it; Omar had repeated it often enough over the years. He didn't like that Layla's mother had married an Englishman. A foreigner. "Why didn't she come to us?"

Layla didn't know. She wondered that, in the beginning.

Mama had been so ill, and whenever Layla had asked to go home, her mother only looked away. After she died, Layla hadn't been allowed to leave the house except for her morning errands in the souk. She had been so tightly controlled, only recently did anyone speak to her again. Even then, it'd been in fearful whispers that Omar might discover them.

"She never said, but she was very sick." Neither man looked surprised, which only twisted the knife deeper into her heart. They knew Mama had been sick and yet...But then, Omar had also lied. She nodded slowly, trying to absorb all this new information. But it still hurt, the abandonment. "I don't know if she wished to make amends with Aunt Heba or something else, but we stayed."

"I'm sorry, Layla," Muhammad whispered. "We had no idea. Did...how long...?"

The grief she'd buried along with everything else welled up, and she took a moment. "She died three years ago." Layla had spent every minute since in pain, and she hadn't been able to ease it no matter how she tried.

"After your father's funeral," Josiah started then stopped. He glanced at Muhammad, and after whatever silent communication they shared, he started again. "We searched for you and Seyda Mariam. We searched everywhere, even Omar's home. Omar made it seem like the plague took you."

Layla stilled. Ten years of anger at them faded. Little by little, it seeped out of her at the shock of these revelations. Of course Omar lied. Of course they had searched for her. She swallowed her rage against the man who had tortured and berated her for years. He'd kept her from her real family. For now, Layla packed that up and set it aside. She'd think on the reasons why later.

"Mama didn't have the plague," she shot back. The emotion burst from her so forcefully, it physically ached. The words rang in the air with all the strength of her conviction. "She was sick for years."

"No, she did not," Muhammad murmured. She met his gaze, but his dark eyes only held quiet sympathy and sorrow. His words tingled down her spine, though Layla couldn't say why. "Why did you leave now?"

He sat tall, with his shoulders back, and Layla was struck by a memory of being carried on his shoulders along these very wharves. Mostafa, Muhammad's oldest son, and Charlie, Josiah's eldest, walked beside them. She wondered where they were now.

"I…" Words failed her, and she shrank into herself. She didn't want to admit the truth, that she'd run away from an arranged marriage, but she didn't wish to lie, either.

"No matter." Josiah stood, hands slapping the table as he did so.

She startled at the unexpected sound. One did not make unnecessary noise in her uncle's house. In the next moment, she remembered that Josiah had always done that. A sort of signal, she recalled, that whatever they discussed had concluded and they were moving on to other, more pleasant topics.

"Luncheon." The cook, medium height with round cheeks and light eyes, held a tray piled high with food. He set it in the middle of the table. "Miss Layla must eat."

He glanced at Muhammad and Josiah as if they might protest. When none was forthcoming, he nodded once and disappeared. Layla stared after him.

"We just ate breakfast," she protested, but the smell of fresh fish tempted her.

At home, she wasn't allowed more than a small plate of food. If that. One of Omar's favorite punishments was withholding her dinner. When he was in a particularly foul mood, he'd slap her until her lip bled then withhold her small meal so she went to bed hungry, bruised, and bleeding.

Layla couldn't remember the last time she'd seen so much food all at once.

"Your captain is very generous," Josiah said, taking one of the plates of *sayadeya*.

He wasn't her captain; she didn't know him at all. Well, she knew he was sympathetic to strange women who'd accidently boarded the wrong ship and were in need of help. That was a kindness in his favor, she'd grant him that. And she couldn't fault his generosity. Despite her hesitation, she took one of the plates from the tray.

"You'll stay with us," Muhammad agreed as they ate. "Jomana will be so pleased. Amirah, too. I haven't sent word home that we—" He looked at Josiah, but Layla couldn't decipher either of their expressions. "We weren't sure what your captain's man said was true."

"We haven't heard a word since your father died," Josiah added in a sympathetic voice. "If this mysterious stowaway wasn't you…" He trailed off with a quick shake of his head. "The chances were so slim, but we hoped."

"And we're very happy, *abna mahboubeh*."

Beloved niece.

The unease that had banded around her chest since she first learned about her impending marriage loosened. It didn't completely disappear—Layla wasn't certain it ever would—but she breathed easier. For the first time in years, she took a deep breath and looked forward to her future.

"I've missed her," Layla admitted. "Both of them." She'd missed all of them, though she hadn't let herself feel any emotion since long before her mother died. Now that she'd escaped that house, so many things she'd long suppressed came to light.

"Augusta, too," Josiah added. "And Evelyn…well, that's all for later. We've all missed you, *najmat saghira*."

His sincerity warmed her almost as much as the endearment. This was her family. These people her true uncles, their wives the aunts who made her laugh and taught her about the world. Their children those cousins she'd played with.

"I've missed you all so much." Too much to have let herself feel such longing over the years.

When she was finished with her meal, though she only ate a few bites after the filling breakfast, she stood. Her knees didn't wobble, and her lungs didn't feel as if someone had crushed them with a boulder. She no longer knew the etiquette of mealtimes, whether she should stay until everyone had finished, or even if eating together at all was proper.

The sooner she found Captain Conrad, the sooner she could begin her new life. Perhaps not in a new country. All her vague plans for leaving Damietta fell before her. But at least she could relearn what Omar had taken from her.

"Let me thank the captain."

With a renewed spring in her step, she left the room and headed up the steps onto the deck of the ship. She hadn't asked who the ship was named after, but that polite inquiry could wait. Not that Layla planned on seeing the handsome Englishman again after this. Handsome, an odd compliment to think. Not that she had ever seen a comparison, but she enjoyed looking at his face.

He was more than pleasant looking. With his sharp nose and dark eyes that seemed to laugh at himself, the curl of his hair against his collar. Yes, she found him most attractive.

She didn't know what her future held now. Her plans for leaving had changed. No longer did she believe she'd be forced to beg for passage from people who had abandoned her. Instead, she felt as if she whirled, uncontrolled, in a haboob, uncertain where her life might take her next.

It didn't matter. Being back amongst family who cared for her, who didn't treat her like a servant—or, worse, a burden— lightened her mood.

The sunlight surprised her, and she took several moments to

adjust. Securing her hijab over her face, she watched the open sky for longer than she probably should have. Birds she didn't know the name of swooped down, gliding on the wind with such grace, she envied them.

"They're swifts," Captain Conrad said from beside her.

Layla jumped. She usually paid much closer attention to her surroundings, especially when anyone stood near her. "Swifts?" she asked, unfamiliar with the English word.

"Hmm, I'm afraid I don't know the word in Egyptian." He frowned, his dark eyes holding hers.

Yes, very pleasing to look at.

She stared a bit too long as she stood beside him in the sunlight, watching the birds fly overhead. His dark hair was hidden beneath a hat, now that the sun had risen, but his curls still brushed the collar of his coat.

Curious to see if his hair felt as soft as it looked, Layla nearly reached up and touched it. Scandalized, she stepped backward until she bumped the railing.

"I wanted to thank you," she stammered, looking down into the water. It wasn't as clear as she'd imagined, but she supposed that was because of the congestion of the wharves. She remembered them being busy. "For your generosity. And your cook; I'm afraid I don't remember his name."

"Laska." Captain Conrad frowned. It didn't look natural on him. "You're leaving? I mean—yes. Yes, of course." He leaned closer, his gaze intent. Layla didn't back away—she couldn't— but she didn't feel threatened, either. "Are you certain? I'm more than happy to offer sanctuary if you need."

"Sanctuary?" She didn't remember that word.

"*Malja,*" he added in Egyptian.

Narrowing her eyes, Layla eased further along the railing. The sun shone too brightly now, and she longed for the shadows of the dining room below. The safety of people she trusted. "How do you know Egyptian?"

He looked surprised. "I'm here to forge connections with merchants. Shouldn't I know the language?"

Flushing, she looked away. "My apologies. Yes, of course."

Her father knew the language, as did Uncle Josiah. Of course Captain Conrad would learn the language, out of necessity for doing business. Layla berated her own suspiciousness; she'd spent the last ten years trusting no one but herself.

Not even her mother. She hadn't known what Mama might say after the sickness took hold of her.

"I mean it, Miss Braithwaite." His voice held that note of sincerity again. "If for any reason you feel you must stay here, I won't ask questions. You're safe on board my ship."

"Thank you," she repeated, her voice soft with her own sincerity. "I—your offer is as generous as the table you set."

He blinked, and that half smile reappeared. "Breakfast? I'm glad you enjoyed it."

"And the luncheon your Laska offered."

Captain Conrad laughed. It was a boisterous, honest sound that tingled along her skin. Bemused, Layla merely watched him.

"He disappeared again. Gone shopping, he said." Conrad shook his head. "He likes you." He paused, and when he shook his head this time, it seemed more so at himself. "Though it might be more accurate to say he's protective."

"Oh." Something settled in her chest, a warmth she only vaguely remembered feeling but couldn't put a name to. "Please thank him."

"Cap!" Harry hurried across the deck, glancing at Layla, then at Captain Conrad. "You better see this. Miss." He nodded and tugged at his hat. "You best stay here."

Despite the warmth of the beautiful, sunny day, Layla felt a cold shiver race down her spine. Before she could figure out what to do, Muhammad and Josiah appeared, as if they'd heard the commotion below deck.

Foreboding. That's what the shiver was.

She inched closer to the men but stopped after only a few steps. She'd escaped Omar's house. His abusive ways, his cruelty, his plan to marry her off to a man more than three times her age. Straightening her shoulders, Layla turned toward the commotion.

Her stomach clenched around her meal, but she stood tall in the face of whatever might happen next. Options. After her disappointing morning, she hadn't believed she had any, but now she knew better. Even if Muhammad and Josiah turned their backs on her, though she no longer believed they would, she had options.

Breathing slowly and willing her luncheon to stay down, Layla raised her chin. Her fingers might have been bunched into her skirts, and behind her hijab her lips trembled, but she stood tall.

The man beside Omar scowled. She didn't know him, but she hadn't seen anyone outside of that home for years. It didn't matter; he could only be one person. He wasn't old enough to be al-Najjar, but one of his sons, sent as the force behind Omar to drag her back.

She didn't hear what he said, but whatever it was, Omar's face flushed an angrier red.

"Promised the half-English bitch." Omar was in a truly rare fury. The fact he spoke in English stunned Layla, who hadn't even known he knew the language. "Her betrothed's son is here to claim her."

Her heart stuttered, and her breath heaved. She'd left for her own safety, but she'd left her aunts and cousins behind. They'd surely taken the brunt of Omar's fury, and the thought sickened her. They weren't cruel, not in the way Omar was. Just dismissive. Layla always knew they looked out for themselves. In that household, doing so was necessary.

"You're on my ship," Conrad was saying over the ringing in

her ears. His voice was far more composed than she'd have thought, but around him, the air sat heavy with anticipation. Conrad wasn't a man to trifle with, though his words were agreeable in a menacing way. "And we have certain rules here. If you can't follow them, I'll happily toss you overboard."

Josiah snickered, though he and Muhammad stood closer, and she accepted their protection. Her fingers refused to release her skirts, and her toes pressed hard into the deck boards, but she kept still even when Omar spotted her. Proud of the fact that she didn't shrink from his attention, Layla lifted her chin, just the slightest defiance.

She'd risked everything in leaving. She wouldn't back down now.

"Ah ah," Conrad said, one hand easily restraining her furious uncle. "You have one minute."

"She ran away from my house after I contracted her in marriage." The words rang far too loudly for any sort of privacy. "Now I find her here, on board this ship, and looking very cozy with you."

"*Abna akhat al-habib?*" Muhammad asked.

"Yusif al-Najjar," Layla said around a dry throat. "Or his son." Her gaze returned to the furious man beside Omar. Her entire body shook, and she hated that she shrank further back, between Muhammad and Josiah.

"The wool merchant?" Muhammad hissed.

"He's old enough to be your grandfather," Josiah added.

Probably even older than that, but she hadn't the strength nor calmness to answer him. She missed what Omar and Captain Conrad were saying. Before she realized it, al-Najjar's son, looking angry and belligerent, as if he planned to fight each man on this ship, stepped back.

Al-Najjar himself confidently boarded the ship, as if he hadn't expected his son to properly execute the job of kidnapping her. Terror chilled her veins as his cold laugh flitted over the deck.

"We won't let him take you," Josiah promised.

"I'll marry her." She heard the exasperation in Conrad's voice clear enough.

CHAPTER 3

"Philip," Harry muttered just as Argus appeared from wherever he'd been hiding and growled at Omar Shadi and the two men with him. Neither had offered a name, but clearly the older man was Layla's supposed betrothed.

They spoke in rapid Egyptian, which they thought Philip wouldn't understand. The anger he suppressed ignited with each disparagement against Miss Braithwaite. Hands curling into fists at his sides, he held himself still. Barely.

He didn't see Harry's eye roll or hear his sigh, but he knew well enough what his friend was thinking. It came through clearly in his exasperation. *Impetuous*, Harry would say. Always had been, and it seemed he hadn't outgrown it as much as he claimed. Or would've liked.

The wind blew over the deck in the stunned silence that followed his pronouncement. So much for that hard-won control.

Philip held Shadi's gaze even as he felt the astonishment of his crew. Shadi looked stunned also, as if this was as far from whatever he'd expected as he imagined. The son merely scowled.

"You want the girl?" Shadi sneered, a truly ugly look on his face. "Bah, I knew she was a whore. Just like her mother."

Philip punched him.

His control snapped. One moment Shadi spoke ill of Miss Braithwaite and her mother, the next Philip didn't even have time to berate himself for his impetuousness. The loss of his valued control.

One moment Shadi belittled Miss Braithwaite, the next he lay on the deck.

"*La tuthurc,*" Philip spat in warning. The other man narrowed his eyes, but al-Najjar held him back with a swift word of warning himself. Fighting for his control, Philip waited. The man didn't utter a word but deferred to al-Najjar. He didn't understand any of this.

The old man laughed. "I like you, Captain Conrad," he said in clear English. The wisps of his white hair blew merrily in the wind. "If you can pay for her, you can have her."

Philip nodded once in acknowledgement. Argus barked, and its echo was the only sound on the deck for a long moment. Philip didn't bother quieting him.

"You have a way with people," Harry muttered.

"It's a gift." Philip ran a hand down his face and looked over his shoulder. "Clear my deck, Harry. I think we've had enough visitors for one day."

Harry snorted again but did as Philip asked.

Miss Braithwaite stared in wide-eyed shock, and the two men beside her watched with interest, all emotions carefully hidden. Though there might've been a snicker concealed behind a carefully raised hand.

He would never live this down.

Nonetheless, he meant it. As spontaneous as his words had been, no one should be spoken of the way Shadi spoke of his niece. Philip wouldn't go back on his word…no matter that he'd spent all of an hour with her.

Crossing the deck, he bowed to a still wide-eyed Miss Braithwaite. "I apologize. I realize my actions were, ah…hasty."

Her eyebrows shot up at his understatement. At least she appreciated that. "I don't even know you," she whispered. She paused, a drawn-out hesitation in which she seemed to wrestle with her next words. Peering around him, her shoulders sagged. "At least you aren't seventy."

She flushed and closed her eyes, but Philip laughed. It didn't feel like a laughing matter, of course, and she couldn't know he laughed mostly at himself and his own reckless ways. Still, he hoped it had diffused the situation. Slightly.

"Seventy? No, not even close. Is that how old al-Najjar is?" He paused. So that was the older man, then. He'd sent a lackey— or his son, Philip didn't much care—but didn't trust either him or Shadi, and so he'd come himself.

"At least." She stopped and held his gaze, as if reading his mind. If she asked, he'd tell her he didn't have a reason, that the words just slipped out. Which didn't happen very often. Not anymore. Nowadays, he kept a tight rein on his feelings. Except, apparently, this morning. She didn't ask, however, merely studied him for a drawn-out moment.

He couldn't read her, didn't know what she thought. Then again, she'd lived under Shadi's roof. Given the five minutes he'd spent with the man, Philip didn't blame her for keeping her emotions closed up tight. He understood that all too well.

The birds called out again, echoing over the wind as his crew remembered themselves and their duties. Philip didn't know what Harry was doing (hopefully moving the crew away from this conversation), but he kept all his attention on Miss Braithwaite and her pretty brown eyes.

"Before you accept, would you like to ask me anything?"

Her gaze slid to her companions, both of whom watched her with concern. Philip didn't look over his shoulder—he knew Shadi had already stood up and was glaring at them. The wool merchant's laughter echoed over the day and sent a chill down his spine. Philip shifted until Miss Braithwaite's gaze met his again. Whatever dowry her uncle demanded, it'd be worth it to see the fear on her face disappear.

The bastard had abused her, and Philip fully believed Shadi would contract her to a man with the same tendencies. His cruelty shone through clearly in both his words and her reactions. Philip would bet he abused his wife and children, too. He had seen it far too often in the women and children who sought refuge on his family's estate.

Granted, he'd never offered any of them marriage. But then, he'd never been in this particular position, either.

First time for everything.

"Will you allow me to see my family?"

Surprised, his head jerked back, and he blinked. "You want to return?"

"No!" The word shot from her like a musket ball, and she flushed again. "I meant my real family." She nodded at both men, still flanking her as if they were her protectors. Philip supposed they were. "I haven't seen them in nearly ten years."

"I won't take you from them, I promise." He was making a lot of promises, wasn't he?

"Why?" The word barely dented the silence on the deck. Even though they'd wandered back toward whatever duties they had, his crew still watched him. "Why offer such a thing?"

Because deep inside, he was still that wild, impetuous boy who spoke before he thought things through. Because he had no other idea about how to stop her repulsive uncle from taking her back to the house she'd escaped from. Because he really didn't like the merchant's smile.

Marriage—not exactly the adventure he'd planned while in Egypt.

"You needed help."

"I cannot disagree with that, but it doesn't explain why you proposed such a momentous offering."

"No. No, it doesn't." He wiped a hand down his face again, but it didn't help. He didn't really have an answer for her, though he'd have dearly loved to hear one himself.

"Perhaps you'd like to retire belowdecks?" Bartley asked, stepping into what had to be the world's most awkward conversation. "Muhammad and I shall negotiate." He peered at Philip with a hard scrutiny that would've frozen another man. Philip didn't blame him, but his own circumstances weren't ordinary. "Unless you've changed your mind?"

"Go ahead." He nodded. He'd stand by his word.

"Layla?"

She turned her head just enough to meet Bartley's gaze. "Yes." She might've nodded, but it was such a small, tight move, Philip wasn't certain.

Bartley frowned and stepped closer. "We can find another way," he whispered in Egyptian.

"Don't be hasty, *abna akhat al-habib*. Josiah is correct."

"Thank you, but this is a safer way."

Philip didn't interrupt the conversation, which was clearly well-meaning and heartfelt between the three of them. When she looked back at him, he offered his arm. Did one require a chaperone after the proposal had been accepted? He had no idea how this worked; no one in his family did anything the usual way.

"We'll retire below, in the dining room, Miss Braithwaite," he offered. "We'll have more privacy there." He whistled for Argus, who growled once more at the men being forcibly shown off his ship. Good boy, Argus, who growled once more then trotted toward them. "Have you met Argus?"

"This has been a very strange morning," she admitted as they descended the steps. "I have no idea what might happen next."

Philip snorted. He'd love to know, too.

* * *

LAYLA FELT MORE adrift now than she had when she sneaked out of Omar's house and into the night. Then, she shook from fear of the unknown, the terror of being seen when she hadn't been in a decade. Of capture and being returned to that house where she'd be beaten and starved.

Now, once more seated at the table, the sun streaming through the panes at the rear of the ship and a glass of carob juice in front of her from the ever-thoughtful Laska, she thought maybe she'd reacted too hastily. Maybe she'd managed to escape from one marriage straight into the arms of another.

Protection lured her, however. The promise of safety.

She was safe from Omar and al-Najjar, perhaps, but she knew nothing of Captain Conrad.

Folding her hands tight in front of her, she watched the light shift over the room. No matter how she tried, she couldn't think of one question. Her mind had blanked, and the only thing she could think was that this wasn't at all the life she'd envisioned so many years ago. Not what her parents had planned for her, either.

Finally, she met his gaze and watched him pet Argus.

"I didn't realize Englishmen sailed with their animals." It wasn't anything she'd wanted to say, but at the moment it sounded the easiest.

"Some do, I suppose. Argus is the offspring of my sister's dog, Lady Michaela." His hand lay on Argus's head, but his entire attention rested on her. "The runt of the litter, poor thing. I nursed him day and night with Yara." He looked fondly at Argus. "He's been mine ever since."

A shiver raced down her spine, and Layla didn't understand it. Perhaps it was being at the center of his focus. Being seen, actually, truly seen, as herself for herself, for the first time in years. Her fingers tightened around each other, as if to hold her still in the middle of a haboob.

"I apologize again," the captain said. Should she call him Philip? Layla had no idea about the decorum of this particular situation. "I'm…well, 'impetuous' is a good word. Rash, impulsive, hotheaded. All good words you can use to describe me." He sighed and picked up a piece of mango Laska had left in a bowl. "I thought I had all that under control—you can't be any of those things and expect the obedience of your crew. Nor any hope of coming out safely on the other side of a voyage."

"I still don't understand," she admitted. She felt as if she ought to understand. As if she was being deliberately thickheaded over something that should have been obvious. "Because you're rash, you thought you'd offer marriage?"

"No. Well, yes." He shook his head.

"That doesn't make anything clear," she snapped. The temper she thought she'd long ago wrestled into nonexistence cracked back into being. Layla had a feeling that temper shocked her more than it did him. "A clear answer, if you please. Why did you offer marriage?"

"I know the kind of man Shadi is," he said slowly, voice low and even and soothing despite the nature of the words. "I know the kind of men he knows, too. Men like al-Najjar. I may be too impulsive, might not think everything all the way through in any given situation, but I know his kind. He's…not nice."

With her lips pressed together so tightly they tingled, Layla grappled for a reply. Her toes dug into the floorboards so hard they'd gone numb, and she wasn't certain she'd ever be able to unlock her fingers from each other. Argus once more moved beneath the table, settling between her and Philip, just close enough she could feel the heat from his body.

The runt? If the word meant what she remembered it meaning, she strongly disagreed. The dog was huge.

"How?" The word scratched her throat, but she forced out the rest. "How do you know?"

He was like Omar. She'd agreed to this marriage in an effort to escape Omar and Yusif al-Najjar, and she had leaped into the arms of a man who was just as bad. How else would he know what Omar was like?

"I won't hurt you, Miss Braithwaite." He looked so sincere, so open in that moment, that Layla believed him.

"I haven't trusted another person in over ten years." She swallowed and gathered that same strength and courage that had helped her escape Omar's house just last night. It felt like a lifetime ago, as if the woman in that house were nothing more than a dim dream, that the one from this morning was the real Layla. "Why should I trust you?"

"I'm not asking you to trust me without knowing me." He leaned across the table, his dark eyes even darker as he sat with his back toward the windows. "If you wish to back out of this marriage, you'll still have sanctuary here."

"Do you have any siblings?" She didn't know why that was her question, nor what difference it might make, but then, she hadn't expected this situation at all. She certainly hadn't prepared for it. "Other than your sister and her Lady Michaela."

He grinned. It was such an open, happy smile that a stab of jealousy pierced her and stole her breath. She hadn't expected that, either. His smile was as honest as she'd ever seen; he couldn't fake the love and admiration he felt for his family after her small, innocent question.

"I have four siblings altogether. Two older sisters, an older brother, and a younger brother." He laughed, that lovely sound she thought she could listen to for hours. "And a great many animals."

"Why did you sail here?" Also not exactly what she wanted to ask, but apparently something in her wanted an answer.

"We used to have contacts here. We import a lot of things

from all over the world, but with the wars, so much has been lost. I'm here to reconnect with our merchants."

"All right." She accepted that, even if she sensed it was only part of the truth. She had no idea what made her suspect that. Maybe because it was such a short, neat answer. Or perhaps she'd grown so suspicious over the years, she didn't believe anyone.

"Do you mind if I ask you a question?"

Her breath caught, but she managed a quick nod. "All right."

"Bartley and el-Nebi, how do you know them?"

Layla eased her fingers slightly apart. She didn't believe he'd hit her if she didn't answer, though she'd been trained the hard way. In the past, if she didn't, she'd face the consequences. Her mind raced, but she didn't feel that tense anticipation she had in Omar's house. Answering would cause no real harm.

"They're my father's business partners. Were. He died ten years ago." She still felt a stab of pain at the memory of her father, but over the hard years since his death, his face had dimmed, the memory of his laugh had faded. She'd even forgotten his name until she heard Philip Conrad speak with his friend. "I grew up with their children, called them 'Uncle' and their wives 'Aunt,' though there is no blood relation between us."

"I have several aunts and uncles like that," he said softly, as if it tugged at a memory. "Both of my parents were only children, so any relations are all close friends. None are blood relations, but that doesn't matter. I love them all dearly." He nodded, but his gaze remained on hers, so direct that she shivered again. "It's nice, having that connection."

Layla swallowed, but her fingers loosened a fraction more at his admission. Her toes didn't press quite so hard into the floorboards. "It's been over ten years since I've seen them. But when I needed them most, they were here." She closed her eyes and felt her cheeks flush again. "I didn't mean to say that."

"There's no need for any embarrassment. Family is family, whether they're related by blood or not."

Something in his voice made her head tilt in consideration. Not because of his family that wasn't blood—she knew all too well the difference there. But because of his understanding. Layla had spent so long hiding her every emotion, every thought, that nothing could slip out without her careful consideration.

Family. Yes. She'd seen what Omar had done to Aunt Heba, her mother's sister. Layla didn't know what kind of person she'd be after suffering years of violence and cruelty and depravation.

"You still haven't answered my question." But her fingers had loosened almost completely, and her jaw didn't clench quite so hard. "Why marriage?"

"I suppose you didn't hear all of our conversation." He scowled, and even that looked handsome on him. Another observation that surprised her. He hadn't moved, but something in him changed. He was coiled tight, yet so carefully controlled she didn't believe he'd snap. Not at her, at least.

"No," she admitted. "I did not."

"Your uncle isn't a nice man. In addition to disparaging you, he spit out quite a bit of vitriol about your father, his business partners, your mother, and the woman I presume is his wife, your aunt?" She nodded, fingers cold now at the mere thought of what Omar might have said. "While he didn't say it outright, something al-Najjar said makes me suspect he's owed a significant sum of money."

"Oh." Layla stilled. Head tilted as she watched the captain, she realized what he'd said was true. She hadn't realized it until now. Rather, hadn't realized that the suspicions she'd gathered over the years were true.

"Many things that Aunt Heba whispered make sense now. I doubt she knew, not really, and she never would've said anything aloud. Not within range of my hearing, at least. But deep in her heart, she knew."

Layla pressed a hand against her chest and released a long breath. Even Omar taking away her food now made sense, though she couldn't forgive him for the many nights she'd gone hungry. She'd never forgive him for anything he'd done.

"That still doesn't answer my question."

He chuckled, a short sound. The sun had moved, slipping between the docked ships, highlighting the side of his face. She couldn't tell if the upward tick in his cheek was a trick of the light, or if he held himself utterly still with only that as a sign of his restraint.

"He, or al-Najjar's lackey, saw us on deck. They jumped to conclusions about the nature of our conversation." He sighed and shook his head. "After his accusations, I didn't know what else to do that might save your reputation."

CHAPTER 4

"You could've done nothing. No one would blame you for not getting involved." Layla wanted to snatch the words back and stuff them beneath the floorboards, but of course it was far too late for that. Had she learned nothing in the past few years?

She waited for his reaction, but he only snorted and shook his head. Argus whined beneath the table, and she frowned. They never had dogs, not in Omar's house, and not that she remembered from before. Having one here, so close, made her more aware of the creature than she'd realized.

"I suppose, yes." He shook his head again, that smile playing around his lips. "That honestly never occurred to me."

It bubbled up inside her, an answering laugh. She didn't release it, but she did smile, a wide pull of her lips that hurt her cheeks. They weren't used to such exercise. Her heart wasn't used to such openness, either. "I believe you."

He ran a hand down his face and chuckled again. He did that often, and she wondered why. Did it help, his hand over his face? She never moved in so obvious a way.

"What do you expect of me?" Layla forced the words from

her throat, though they wanted to remain stopped up inside. The less she said, the safer she would be.

"Miss Braithwaite—"

"I suppose…" She remained still. Her heart beat wildly in her chest, and she pushed aside her fears. She felt safer in this ship's dining room than she had since her mother fell ill. "I suppose you should call me Layla."

"Layla." His smile softened, and his eyes lit up as if she'd gifted him something precious. "That's a lovely name. Thank you." He offered a half bow from his chair. "Philip. Philip Paul Conrad."

Layla might've imagined it, but could've sworn he paused after "Paul." She shook her head; she was being foolish. Looking for secrets and hidden meanings in everything. Her toes finally relaxed, and she stretched her ankles, careful of Argus beneath the table.

Sipping the carob juice, she allowed herself another moment in this wonderful, blissful silence.

"I'm a little unclear about how marriage works," he confessed, as if they were sharing intimacies over a lamp and not where anyone might interrupt. No one did—she supposed they wouldn't dare, not after that display above deck. "It's my first marriage."

That laugh caught her off guard again, and a small sound slipped out before she could stop it. Layla gripped the delicate glass hard, looking into its depths as if it might have an answer for her wild emotions. It did not.

"Mine as well," she whispered. "Though I hadn't expected this one." She shook her head. "I didn't expect the previous one, either. I'm afraid of what might happen next."

"I promise you." He placed his hand over hers, and she jolted at the touch. Philip stilled but didn't point it out, merely rested his hand beside hers instead. His thoughtfulness touched something inside her she'd thought long dead. "I promise you, I'll stand beside you no matter what Omar does—or the wool merchant, for that matter." He paused and added softly, "Or anyone else."

"That's a lot of promises." Her fingers shook again, but rather than press them into the tabletop as she normally would, Layla inched them toward his hand. She didn't touch him—that was beyond her. But she wanted to make an effort.

"I'm impulsive, rash, hotheaded, and hasty." He didn't laugh or smile as she expected. "But I don't break my promises."

Layla lifted her carob juice, but her hand shook, and she immediately set the glass back on the table. "All right."

"You don't have to believe me after only a few hours' acquaintance."

She didn't but wouldn't voice that. It would sound rude and provoking. No matter what he said, she knew very little about Philip Conrad. Even less about herself after being trapped so long in a house that closed in on her.

"Layla." Muhammad entered the room with a nod toward Laska, who she hadn't realized stood in the doorway, and Philip. "It is concluded, Captain." He offered her a soft smile. "I'm afraid we were most generous toward our beloved niece."

Philip only nodded. She wanted to ask what she was worth. How much her new husband must pay a man she'd never considered her uncle. She was uncertain how it might work, and she wondered if some of the money might be given to Aunt Heba. Then again, Omar would only steal it back.

"And the bride's gift?" Philip asked, surprising both her and Muhammad. Philip reached into an inner pocket of his coat and withdrew a small pouch. Then he pulled out an uncut emerald and held it in his palm.

Layla forgot how to breathe. The room spun, and she wondered if she might faint. How embarrassing. Her ears rang —or perhaps that was Argus's insistent barking. Suddenly, the room she felt safest in closed in on her, too stifling, too dense, too much. Her breath stopped in her chest, and no matter what she tried, she couldn't breathe.

All she'd wanted was freedom. But this wasn't at all what she'd envisioned.

* * *

PHILIP CAUGHT her before she hit the floor. Muhammad frowned, deep lines bracketing his mouth, but didn't say anything. Laska merely stepped aside and held open the door as Philip carried Layla next door to his own cabin.

She stirred before he opened the door, blinking up at him with wide, confused eyes. "The seas are very rough."

He grinned, the worry that gripped his heart easing. "You're in my arms; I'm carrying you from the dining room into my own chambers."

He set her on her feet, then crouched slightly and watched her. Beneath his hands, her shoulders were thin and bony. Laska was right, she hadn't eaten well in who knew how long. One stiff breeze and he was afraid she'd break.

No, she wouldn't break. Not ever. She stood straight, chin lifted just enough to signify defiance. Will. Strength.

"I apologize." She gripped her skirts, her fingers holding them tight enough he thought she'd rend the fabric. "I am not usually so..." She trailed off and looked around the room. "It's been a strange day."

"I can't argue with that." Philip snorted and looked around, wondering what she saw in the dark wood and brass of the captain's cabin. "We can set up your own room. Your own space. I'm sure there's a seamstress in town; we can visit her if you wish." Then he remembered she'd said she had family, aunts who would take her shopping. "Or you and your aunts can go shopping."

"Shopping," she repeated, as if it were a foreign word. Her

fingers tightened. "I'm sure it's an added expense, having someone come in, but I am uncertain if I can…"

Oh. Oh, yes, that made sense. After everything, she'd rather stay indoors, where no one could touch her. He nodded. "We can find someone. I'll speak with Bartley and el-Nebi." He stopped. "I'm certain you'd prefer to visit with your aunts, to see them again after so long, before the marriage?"

She had stopped shaking, and her fingers even loosened somewhat from her skirts. "Yes." Then she slowly tilted her head. "No. I think I'd rather have the contracts signed before I leave this ship."

In case Shadi or al-Najjar came looking for her. If she had the added protection of a husband, they'd have less of a legal standing. Philip refrained from adding that the protection of marriage only counted in polite society. He doubted either man operated in such open areas.

"As you wish." He gestured for his chair, the only place for her to sit other than his bed. He eyed it. He'd rolled out of the thing before the sun rose, but that had only been a few hours ago. Felt like a month.

"Ah." She shook her head. "I had forgotten the furnishings were bolted to the deck. It's been a while since I set foot on a ship."

He had so many questions about her past. Before she lived in Omar's house. The tidbits she'd mentioned only teased at a happier childhood. But he wouldn't ask now. They had time.

"When I left the house, I only wanted freedom," she said softly. "Freedom from Omar and his cruelty. Freedom to make my own choices."

"I'm sorry. I've taken that away from you." He hated that he had, that the only solution he'd thought of was replacing one marriage with another.

"I thought so, yes." She pulled her gaze from her hands, which were once more gripping each other tightly. "However, I now see that this is the safest, ah, route for me." She frowned and shook her head, that small, tight movement he'd noticed earlier. "Thank you. I've said that many times today, but I meant it every time. Without your promise, I'm uncertain what might've happened to me."

Philip didn't have an answer, and "you're welcome" sounded trite and insincere. Still, he'd learned his lesson, and he kept quiet for a moment before he blurted out another random promise. "I'm not certain of the protocol here. Should I escort you to visit your aunts? Or will your uncles be sufficient?"

A small, breathless noise that sounded almost like a laugh escaped her. "I've no idea. I'm positive I've broken every rule and etiquette imaginable today." She looked out the small port window. The captain's cabin boasted three, but they still only showed a small bit of the endless blue sky. "When I was young, I remember my mother scolding me for being a—I forget the English word. Wild, I think she meant."

"Still, you survived." He waited until she met his gaze. "That's more than most people can say in life."

"I'd like to remember how to live."

"That, my dear fiancée, is something I can help you with." He grinned, certain that staying in his room without a chaperone broke more rules than even he was used to breaking. He held out a hand and watched her contemplate it before slowly taking it in hers.

Her hand was small, rough, and calloused. Used to hard work, though his wasn't much better. Just as quickly as she'd taken his hand she released it, though she didn't look down but held his gaze. He was right. She was strong.

"I have a luncheon meeting with a ceramics exporter." He didn't need to consult any calendar. He'd planned these meetings months ago, before they sailed. "He's one of the merchants we traded with before the wars."

She merely nodded, but Philip had a feeling she heard every

word he said. Outside the door, he heard the faint whining of Argus, who must've grown tired of the closed door. He had the run of the ship and didn't like doors between him and his destination.

"Tomorrow I'm meeting with a date and fig merchant." He opened the door, and Argus bounded in, sniffing the air before plopping himself in front of Layla. She eyed him suspiciously. "I'd love to import mango, but I'm afraid the fruits won't last as long as the return voyage."

"England doesn't have mangoes?" She shook her head. "How do they survive?"

Grinning, he accepted her small bit of humor and gestured for the open door. They'd been absent long enough. "It's a hardship. My mother has extensive greenhouses where she grows them. Bergamot, too. Other fruits not native to England."

Layla sniffed, but her eyes danced with humor as she stood in the small square of sunlight from the stair opening. "I'm not sure I'll enjoy it there."

"It takes getting used to." He climbed the stairs, though he supposed he ought to have allowed her to go first. He didn't want her accosted, lest Shadi or al-Najjar had somehow managed to slip by every one of his crew, Harry, and Argus.

Improbable, yes. But yesterday he would've said the same about offering marriage to a complete stranger so he could rescue her from her uncle.

"Ah, there you are, Conrad." Bartley nodded from where he and el-Nebi stood by the railing. "A word, if you please."

He nodded, hesitated, then said softly, "Take as much time with your family as you wish. You said it's been years; we'll sign the contracts before you leave. You're safe." She clearly didn't believe that, and Philip only partly did as well. "Also, it's probably more proper to sleep under their roof than here."

He couldn't see her smile, but he hoped she cracked a small

one. "Thank you. Again. And please thank Laska; he's been most kind and generous."

"I'll pass it along," he promised. He wanted a talk with his suddenly generous cook. "Send word when you're settled."

She nodded again and stepped toward el-Nebi. Philip turned toward Bartley and watched the man. Slightly shorter than he, and thin, with a full head of graying hair and dancing blue eyes, Josiah Bartley eyed Philip as if he couldn't decide whether to shake his hand or stab him with a dagger. He didn't look like the dagger type, but one never knew.

"I asked around," he said, his voice too even to give away his thoughts. "Several merchants knew of the Conrads. Not personally, but by their shipping company. You have a far reach here, Philip Conrad."

Philip didn't feel the need to explain anything. His family wasn't anyone's concern, nor was their business here. However, he'd proposed to the man's niece; clearly, Bartley was worried about his character. Couldn't blame him for that. Scrambling for a piece of information that might appease Bartley, he offered an easy smile.

"My parents met in Egypt," he finally said. "They still hold an affinity for the country." He grinned. "And its coffee."

"Hmm." Bartley waited, but Philip said nothing more. "Those I've spoken with all say the company is honest, generous with their terms."

"Are you angling for a partnership?" Philip's lips twitched. Of course, he knew that wasn't Bartley's motive.

"I'm angling for your promise that you won't hurt Layla." His gaze hardened, as did his voice, though he didn't move. "She's been through enough."

"I'll protect her," Philip repeated what he'd told her. "Everything else is between us."

Bartley waited, as if weighing that answer, then nodded

once. "She might not have had us for years. We thought she and her mother died after Harry's death."

Philip started at the name. It took him a moment, but then he realized Bartley meant Layla's father, not his own first mate. Bartley didn't expand on that sentence, but his ashen face told Philip the man felt sickened by that absence.

"We won't let anything happen to her again."

"Neither will I."

Bartley eyed him, then nodded and crossed the deck. With Argus at his side, Philip waited as the trio left the ship.

The sun shone overhead—nearly time for his first appointment, then. After all the excitement of the morning, he couldn't be late. Philip bet the entire port knew of his arrival by now. As well as his hasty marriage proposal.

No, he was never living this one down.

"Ready for your meeting with Abdel Saeed?" Harry appeared at his side, a knowing smirk on his face, his blue eyes dancing with laughter at Philip's expense. "And here you thought you'd make connections and watch the birds."

"Clearly, I was mistaken. Miss Braithwaite needed help." He shrugged and looked upward, but the sky overhead remained empty. "No birds, either."

Layla. A beautiful name that matched the warmth in her gaze when she let herself relax. Philip promised, both to her and to himself, that he'd do everything in his power to help her relax and remember what safety felt like.

"I'm not disputing that all too real fact." Harry crouched down and scratched Argus's head, grinning up at him. "Great way to start your first day here. What have you planned for the rest of it?"

"It'll be hard to top that," Philip agreed. "But first I need to speak with Laska."

Harry's laughter followed him back down into the galley. Laska and Kaz were hard at work, doing whatever they did there. One job Philip never had on board a ship was that of cook. No one wanted him to have that job.

"Miss Layla needs food." Laska looked at him defiantly, as if Philip was going to steal a meal right out from under her. "She is as skinny as a leaf."

"I know." He sighed and leaned against the doorjamb. He needed another hour or two of sleep, but he had meetings. He eyed the katana, but Laska shoved a chunk of bread smothered in fig preserves into his hand.

"You must eat, too." A fierce frown settled over his features, and, not for the first time, Philip wondered what happened in Laska's past.

"She'll need protecting," he heard himself say as he bit into the bread. "Her uncle wanted to marry her off to a seventy-year-old wool merchant."

"Bah." Laska folded his arms over his broad chest, and Kaz mimicked him. "Nothing will happen to Miss Layla on this ship."

Kaz nodded fiercely in agreement. Philip wondered what the two had spoken of while he and Layla had sat mere feet away. Whatever it was, they'd obviously concluded that they'd be her protectors.

"You secure your contracts." Laska jerked his head toward the door in clear dismissal. "We prepare the wedding feast."

"I'm sure her family will—" Philip broke off at the glares they fired at him. "Thank you," he said instead. Then he added, "Miss Layla also thanks you for your understanding and generosity."

They beamed as if he'd offered them a princess's hand in marriage. Shaking his head, Philip retreated onto deck. Staring toward the south, though he barely saw past the warehouses, he wondered if his new bride might fancy a voyage down the Nile.

CHAPTER 5

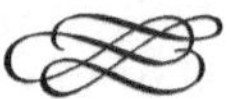

That night, for the first time in a decade, Layla slept in a soft bed, in a noisy room, full of family who treated her like a long-lost daughter. The longer the sheer joy of her family surrounded her, the more a decade's worth of anger and resentment disappeared. Perhaps not truly, entirely gone, but diminished.

They laughed and talked, and nobody asked intrusive questions about the previous years. Reminisced, yes. They told Layla of marriages and children. Even of tragedies, in the case of her cousin Evelyn's husband.

All those stories made her feel like part of a distant family. They didn't entirely bridge the gap between them, but they helped Layla feel not quite so isolated. It warmed her deep inside, where she thought she'd never feel warmth again. Slowly, over time, she breathed easier. Moved more smoothly, even laughed, surprising herself with the sound.

It was a small step. However, it was one she held tightly against her heart, treasuring it even more deeply than she treasured the emerald Philip had offered.

She pulled the plush blanket over her arms; it also covered

her toes, so she didn't have to choose. The pillow was luxurious and soft and clean, and she closed her eyes in bliss.

"Do you require anything, *azizi wahid?*" Aunt Jomana placed a small oil lamp on the table and sat on the bed beside her. "I'm sorry we overwhelmed you, but we're so very happy you're back with us."

Jomana brushed her fingertips over Layla's forehead. The memory of her doing that, of her mother doing it as well, bolted through her. Caught off guard, Layla stiffened, pulling back slightly as she stared blindly at Jomana.

"I apologize." Jomana paused and removed her fingers. "I—"

"No." Layla swallowed.

It had taken her all day to remember her manners, how to act with others who wanted her in the same room, in their lives. Forcing her arm into careful, slow movements so she didn't give away her nervousness, Layla touched Jomana's hand. When her aunt didn't move, Layla deliberately brought her fingers back against her forehead.

"I'm unused to the touch." She swallowed again, uncurling her toes from their clenched position beneath the blanket. "It's been a long time, and I'd forgotten..."

"*Azizi wahid.*" Jomana leaned over and kissed her forehead. "Do not apologize. It is we who should apologize. Your uncles are correct; when your father died, we believed Omar and his lies. We thought you and your mother had died as well. Before that, we searched Damietta, but there was no word about either of you, and things were...chaotic."

In the darkness, with her cousins only now falling asleep, all of them crammed into one room so they could stay with her, Layla thought her aunt hesitated. Dismissing that as a product of her own general suspiciousness, she gently loosened her grip on Jomana's hand, but she didn't release it.

"I don't remember everything that happened," Layla confessed. "Mama was grieving. I'm not sure if she intended to visit with Aunt Heba or something more, but she was very sick." Layla frowned at Jomana's frown. "She was sick before then, wasn't she?"

"Yes, *azizi wahid*." Jomana smiled then, a soft, sad one that tugged at Layla. "We'll talk more in the morning. Sleep now; it's been a long day." She pressed a kiss against Layla's forehead again and stood, taking the lamp with her. "We'll plan your wedding then, too."

"Wedding," Layla repeated, the word faint—not from tiredness, though exhaustion settled on her chest like a weight. From disbelief. "I hadn't expected that."

Jomana smiled, a wider grin now. "Better than the wool merchant." She wrinkled her nose in disgust. "Or one of his sons. Augusta said Josiah asked every ship's captain, customs official, and dockworker what they knew about Conrad Shipping. If even a portion of what he discovered is true, the family has a fine reputation."

Layla offered a smile, but her stomach rolled at the thought of what tomorrow might bring. A fine family reputation was all well and good, but it might mean little against a single person. Still, that was welcome news. She doubted anyone would've said anything nice about al-Najjar. Not with his cruel smile and vicious laugh.

"He offered me an uncut emerald."

"I heard." Jomana nodded decisively. "We shall have some of it made into beautiful jewelry and hide the rest." She leaned over and touched Layla's hand again. "As a precaution only."

A precaution. Philip's promise rang clearly in her memory. Safety. Protection. She believed him. Still, Jomana was right. Having provisions was always a good idea.

"Good night, Aunt Jomana." The words flowed over her tongue as she imagined the sea flowed against the shoreline. "Thank you for...everything."

"Sleep well, Layla."

Her aunt left, and Layla heard her admonish the others to sleep. They had a big day with the seamstress tomorrow, as Layla was to be fitted with both English gowns and new traditional Egyptian ones for her wedding. Mind whirling despite her own tiredness, Layla stared at the ceiling. The sounds were different here, quieter than on the other side of Damietta where Aunt Heba lived.

Though she was grateful down to her very soul that she'd escaped, Layla felt a twinge of guilt for leaving her aunt and cousins behind. Not that Heba would've come. If Layla thought she would've, they'd have escaped years ago, before Mama died.

Mama. Why had she stayed with Aunt Heba when she had Aunt Jomana and the rest? Why leave them? Had she truly planned for only a short stay, but her illness debilitated her? Had she stayed here, would she have been able to find proper medicine?

Layla wouldn't have left, of course not. She'd never desert her mother. Knowing she'd had options, however, made her ill. She had so many questions. Questions he mother would never be able to answer now.

Slowly, the house quieted from the excitement of the day, but Layla couldn't sleep. Closing her eyes, she pretended she once more stood on the deck of Philip's ship. The sun shone down on her as she tilted her face toward the sky, letting the warmth and openness and freedom seep into her bones.

As she finally drifted off, warm and safe and happy for the first time in years, she heard Aunt Jomana's endearment—except it echoed in Philip's voice.

Azizi wahid. Dear one.

* * *

LASKA WASN'T AS generous with Philip's breakfast as he had been with Layla's. Philip didn't blame his cook, but he was hungry.

Just as he took his first sip of coffee, Harry sat down opposite him. He looked bright-eyed and cheery, wearing a wide smile as he popped a date into his mouth.

"Coffee?"

"Never touch the stuff." Harry ate another date.

"Why are you so awake?"

"Spite, my dear Philip. Spite and pettiness." He saluted with Philip's own cup of carob juice and drained it. Laska hadn't used the fancy glasses today. Apparently, only Layla was worthy of those. Eyeing Philip over the rim, Harry narrowed his gaze. "Why do you look like you're on the verge of falling over?"

Philip hadn't slept well. Too many thoughts about his actions having consequences, as if his mother's voice echoed through his cabin. It'd taken him years to manage his reckless behavior, but he thought he'd put those days behind him long before he gained captaincy of this ship.

Apparently, he'd been mistaken.

No matter its means, he couldn't regret his proposal. Still, there were probably at least a dozen other ways he could've helped Layla Braithwaite aside from offering marriage. But he couldn't think of one, and it was far too late now, anyway.

"Numbers," he told Harry instead. "The merchants I met with yesterday, I'm not certain they can deliver on their promises." Which was only part of his concern. The other part was the continuing conflict and the number of political exiles in the area. But there was another part, too.

He'd planned a formal meeting with Layla's family this morning.

"The terms are good. Better than I expected."

"Good enough to support your new wife?" Harry grinned, but his eyes watched Philip all too seriously.

"That isn't funny, Harry," he snapped.

"Oh, I agree. I've known you for, what, five years now?" Philip didn't say anything but held Harry's glare. He wrestled with his own temper, a battle he fought daily. "I know how rash you can be, but this takes the prize. You know nothing about her, other than she ran away from her uncle's house and mistakenly boarded this ship."

"I know she needed help."

"Philip." Harry sighed and leaned across the table.

"I won't abandon her. Not now." Not ever. There would be vows, no matter the language or custom. "I may have spoken in haste," Philip admitted, stabbing a chunk of mango with his knife. "However, Layla isn't a charlatan, swindling ship's captains into marrying her."

The emerald held sentimental value, but he didn't tell Harry that. For as long as he'd known the man, Philip had never divulged his family's history. Whatever Harry suspected, whatever he thought he knew, Philip doubted it was the truth. Not the entire truth, at least.

"I never said she was." Harry held up a hand, forestalling any further argument. "I merely wish you weren't so… impulsive."

Philip snorted and held his friend's gaze. "Me too." He finished his breakfast, not any more awake than he had been, and stood. "Laska, I believe Miss Layla will be joining us for a late luncheon."

"*Tak, tak,*" he said then called to Kaz in Polish, but Philip only caught part of that conversation.

"Are we speaking with Bartley and el-Nebi?"

"About the wedding?" Philip frowned as they ascended the stairs. "Is there something more we should be doing?"

Harry grunted and shook his head. "Philip, Philip, Philip." He clapped him on the shoulder. "About importing whatever they export."

Ah, yes, that made much more sense. Philip definitely wasn't as awake as he hoped. "I had thought of it," he said, rather than admit his difficulty in keeping his thoughts on business in the wake of his impending nuptials. "I didn't catch what they trade in."

"You were rather busy yesterday." Harry eyed him again but thankfully refrained from adding another comment about his rashness. Philip would rather his crew talk about almost anything else. "Ceramics and nuts to France and Britain. I believe they also export melons and other fruits to the Ottomans."

"How did you find out all this?"

"While you were speaking with Miss Braithwaite below, I asked questions."

Laughing, Philip headed for the railing and looked out over the wharves. He didn't see Bartley or el-Nebi, or Layla, but he supposed it was still early. "Hilton said you always asked the right questions."

"I'm not asking questions on his behalf." Harry watched him for a moment, frowning. "You know that, right? I didn't join your crew because I'm on a mission for the colonel."

"I know," Philip said, surprised. Surprised that Harry realized that about him. "Hilton retired when Napoleon was defeated." He paused and waved a hand in dismissal. "The first time."

"Just so you know." Harry nodded decisively and gestured toward Damietta.

"Why did you join?" Philip watched him carefully, not sure what answer he expected. "I never asked. Not that I'm not grateful."

"The import/export business aside, you clearly need someone to save you from yourself."

Philip's eyebrows shot up, and he admitted a twinge of hurt at his friend's statement. "You agreed to sail for Egypt because you think I need protecting?"

"Nah." Harry laughed and clapped him on the shoulder again. "I've seen you fight. You can hold your own, I've no doubt. I agreed because I've never been to Egypt, and it sounded fascinating."

Though Philip only half believed him, he grinned. He'd accept that answer, though he was a little annoyed that Harry's first one involved saving Philip from himself.

"In your questioning yesterday, did you discover why Bartley came here? Or stayed?"

"No, why? You suspect him?" Harry frowned. "Of what?" He sighed. "I've worked for Hilton for too long."

Philip snorted and looked out over the brightening day. The sun was slipping between the docked ships and over customs buildings and warehouses. A light breeze blew across the deck, bringing with it the less-than-pleasant smells of the wharves.

"No," Philip admitted. "I don't suspect anyone of anything." *Yet*—though he had no idea why he felt the need to add that clarifier. "But there aren't a lot of British merchants anymore. Before Napoleon's invasion, maybe." He waved it away. "Maybe he arrived back then and stayed."

Maybe it was easier to stay in Damietta than it was to return home. Everyone had something they needed to prove—Philip knew that better than most. He watched the swifts sail overhead, the gulls that flew over the sea as if they might never land. There were times he envied them that freedom, the freedom from expectations and one's own hopes.

"*Sade!*" a voice called from below, and Philip looked over the side of the ship and onto the wharves. "*Sade, captan!*"

"*Nim?*"

A boy waved a missive in the air, as if it might float upward if he didn't hold on to it. Before Philip had the chance to descend onto the wharves, Hutton clambered down, took the missive in exchange for a coin, and scrambled back up.

"Captain." Hutton nodded and handed it to Philip. He didn't apologize for his actions toward Layla yesterday, but then Philip hadn't truly expected that. Still, he seemed more attentive today, as if that might make up for yesterday.

"Hutton." Philip nodded and took the rolled-up parchment. It was written in English, which he supposed he should've expected. It contained only a few lines about meeting Bartley and el-Nebi for breakfast and a mention of marriage preparations.

"Harry." He glanced toward the horizon, where barely a cloud covered the sky. "See if you can find out anything about Darwish, the coffee grower."

"Where are you going?" Harry didn't sound very trusting. Philip didn't exactly blame him, given the events of yesterday.

"Looks like I have a meeting with our two new exporters."

Harry only sighed. "Don't propose to any more women."

"I didn't exactly propose to Miss Layla." Philip shrugged and strode across the deck, whistling for Argus. "You be a good boy for Kaz." He ran a hand down Argus's neck and let the dog nuzzle his hand. "Stay here."

It wasn't a far walk to the partners' offices, the *al-tajir*. Philip enjoyed the stroll, the stretch of his legs. The array of birds like kites soaring overhead. The warmth of the Egyptian sun. How had his mother gone from this endlessly blue sky to the dreary spring rain of Hertfordshire?

Shaking his head, he slowed down and took a moment. The view from the wharves wasn't much, but the birds overhead didn't mind. Philip watched the gray and white swifts swoop along the wind, uncaring about life down below. He'd been cramped up on his ship for far too long, and he missed the simple sight of the birds soaring along the sky.

Even with his meetings yesterday, he hadn't had the chance to explore Damietta. It moved much like the ports he'd grown up around, London and Blackpool. Norwich on the few occasions he'd visited. It was constant, and he liked that.

Marriage proposal aside.

He found the offices easily enough. Well-appointed and orderly, even their interiors reminded him of those he'd visited in London.

"Ah, Captain Conrad."

"Saied el-Nebi." Philip bowed in greeting. "I trust all is well with Miss Braithwaite?" It amazed him that even after such a short time, calling her "Miss Braithwaite" sounded foreign. "Layla" flowed much more smoothly off his tongue.

"She is with my wife and daughters and is quite well. I believe they're fitting her with new gowns today." El-Nebi gestured toward a small alcove just off the main room, which held only a single table and three chairs. "Josiah will join us momentarily, but let's sit. Will next week work for the ceremony?"

Next week? Philip blinked. That quickly? He supposed they wanted her safely married before anyone protested. Anyone *else*, that was. He'd planned to sail south toward Cairo early next week. His plan had been to meet with their former trade partners, then sail south while the shipments were loaded.

"That should work," he said instead.

Cairo could wait.

"You plan to leave Egypt." It wasn't a question.

"I—yes. I'm here only to reestablish trade with some of our previous partners, though several are…no longer with us."

"Yes." El-Nebi nodded, small, short movements. "The wars have been hard on all of us. The French invasion, the resurgence of plague, famine, then the coup, if one could call it that. However, now that we are stabilized, it's easier to form trade partnerships."

Philip suspected the coffee grower, Darwish, had perished along with thousands of others. Rather than voice that, he said, "My family has had long alliances with many people here. I'm sure Saied Bartley told you that my parents met in Egypt."

It was the story they'd told everyone, and it wasn't a lie. They had met in Cairo, when his father crossed the Sinai in a state of drunken blindness on the fate of a single letter that promised atonement. His mother, however, had other ideas about her future, and none of them had included an English husband.

Fate, it truly was a strange entity.

El-Nebi nodded, but he didn't seem overly interested in that story. "If Layla asks, will you allow her to remain in Damietta?"

Was living apart normal in an Egyptian marriage? Philip had no idea, though he'd heard of several English marriages where the couple lived distant, separate lives in separate houses.

"If that's what she wants." He paused, not certain if that was the correct answer. Pressing his fingers into his thigh, he forced himself to wait a beat. However, the question remained. "Is that what she wants?"

"I do not know. However, given the unusual circumstances of your marriage—"

"Muhammad?" Josiah Bartley's voice echoed through the offices as he strode in with a wide smile. "Ah, Captain Conrad." He settled in the third chair, a sheaf of papers in his hands, which he spread out. "I've sent for breakfast; I hope you like shakshuka?"

Philip nodded. "Very much."

Both men looked at him in surprise. *Damn it.* He pressed his fingers harder into his thigh and held his tongue, ignoring their looks. The space between his shoulder blades itched. Philip didn't know if it was because of those unusual circumstances el-Nebi mentioned or because of the quickness of a marriage he'd never really thought about.

Bartley shrugged and gestured to the papers. "Let's talk trade, shall we?"

CHAPTER 6

"*H*arry." Philip waited until one of his crew walked past, then scanned the deck. He didn't need anyone overhearing their conversation. It wasn't that he didn't trust his men. But since the rather public announcement of his betrothal five days ago, they'd been acting strange.

He couldn't figure out why, only that his crew had taken it upon themselves to keep Layla safe. She'd visited only once since leaving with her family, to discuss the ceremony itself. He hadn't even threatened his crew. But in the days since docking, something had changed on board the ship.

"What do you know about the wool merchant, Yusif al-Najjar?" he asked Harry. "Other than what everyone's already heard."

"Only what the ship whispers." Harry shook his head, eyes darting around the deck. "Several of the men have asked around, and no one had anything kind to say about him or his sons."

"That doesn't surprise me, given that Layla's uncle contracted marriage between them." Philip held on to his temper. Harry wasn't his target. Rationale and control would prevail here. Two things he struggled with. "It does surprise me that he hasn't visited again."

"Visited?" Harry snorted. "You doubled the guards, and no one leaves the ship alone."

"You think I'm being too overbearing?"

"No," Harry said seriously. "I think it's been an odd week of silence from a man who had probably never heard the word 'no,' let alone in front of one of his minions and a clearly deferential son."

Philip thought that, too. Al-Najjar's laugh still haunted him despite the reassurances Layla's family had offered about her safety. Reassurances she'd offered, too, on her visit. But that wasn't the laugh of a man who accepted defeat. Why had he now, the money Shadi owed aside?

"You wouldn't happen to know where his offices are?"

"Purely by chance, happenstance, if you will"—Harry's hand gestured vaguely toward the east— "I overheard several of the men talking about just that."

"A coincidence, to be sure." Philip nodded sagely. He couldn't have said why he felt that a visit to al-Najjar was important, only that he didn't trust the man. Five days of silence worried him.

He was surprised al-Najjar hadn't come calling again, this time with a small army of blackjacks. He hadn't heard from Shadi, either, not for more money or any other bribe, something Philip had expected. Given the contract el-Nebi and Bartley had negotiated, Shadi owed al-Najjar a great deal of money.

"Care for a walking tour of the wharves?"

Harry grinned. It wasn't a kind smile but a sharp, hard one that, from what Philip had heard, had sent shivers of fear down more than one man's spine. "I hear they're lovely this time of year." Harry bowed low, one arm stretched out in an elaborate gesture, and Philip swallowed a grin. "After you"

"And in the morning sunlight, too." Philip set his hat more firmly on his head and led the way. "Should add a certain tinge to the scene."

"And what scene are we hoping for?" Harry stepped onto the wharves with him, brushing the sleeves of his coat as if they were walking to a musical recital and not the offices of the so-called former fiancé of Philip's own fiancée.

Philip looked at his friend in surprise. "I'm hoping for a simple talk," he insisted with far too much sincerity to make anything he said believable. "I only wish to ensure Saied al-Najjar understands the…situation?"

"Plan?" Harry offered. Philip shook his head. "You're right, too strong a word for anything you do."

"I beg your pardon!"

"Arrangement?" Harry offered thoughtfully, ignoring Philip's indignant outburst.

"Circumstances, perhaps," Philip concluded with another grumble. They walked along the wharves, dodging workers, horses, and carts as they made their way toward the far end of the port.

He couldn't say it was seedy, not as such. But the air changed. Even the sun seemed dimmer, colder, though May in Northern Egypt was anything but. More men stood around this area, watching them carefully.

"Before we enter." Harry stopped him out of earshot from the door. A quick look around showed no one stepped closer toward them. "What do you hope to gain from this meeting?"

"I don't know," Philip answered honestly. Ensure the man wouldn't contact Layla. That was top of the list. Ensure he had no contact at all, and perhaps ensure that the debt was fully settled. "It's one thing to owe money, even a lot of it." He shook his head and clearly saw Shadi's face, contorted in rage and fear as al-Najjar stood beside him on the deck of *The Lady Kaya*. Omar Shadi had been terrified, even while he'd belittled Layla and her mother so thoroughly. Yusif al-Najjar had been calm and collected.

"You think there's more?" Harry's voice held no inflection, merely a polite kind of curiosity.

"I have no proof," Philip admitted slowly. "Only a suspicion that in order to settle his debt, Shadi agreed to marry Layla off in return for—I don't know," he said again. "It seems a stretch that al-Najjar would forgive all he owed."

Harry's eyes narrowed. "I'm not disagreeing, but what makes you say that? Pretty bold statement."

Philip turned for the door. "The amount Shadi demanded."

He pushed open the door, a surprisingly quiet movement given the age of the building. If this place hadn't been ancient when either of the grandfathers he'd never met were boys, Philip would give up his ship. Luckily, he'd given up betting during his later school days after the hard-won realization that his tendency to act before thinking only led to badly placed bets.

Now, he kept that tendency under control. Except when it came to women in distress, apparently. Though given Layla's resilience and her ability to sneak out of the house alone, at night, during a storm, perhaps "distress" was too forceful a word. She'd definitely needed his help, though perhaps not his hand in marriage.

"Ah, the English captain." The darkness of the interior did nothing for al-Najjar, whose wrinkles looked even deeper than they had five days ago. He eyed Philip as if he were the day's luncheon as he ran a hand over his head, where wisps of white hair refused any sort of taming. "Still intent on marrying the English chit after all."

Control. Jaw clenched, Philip kept his hands loose at his side so as not to give himself away. Philip didn't see anyone else in the room, not even the son who'd accompanied Shadi.

"Word spreads, I see." Philip didn't offer a greeting.

"There's very little in this port town that I don't know," he rasped.

A threat, right off. Al-Najjar wasn't playing around, but Philip hadn't expected he would be. His contacts must've been how he knew where Layla was and how Shadi found her. Information was al-Najjar's currency.

Feigning nonchalance, Philip glanced around the office. Well organized, nearly bare of all papers, the only sign of any sort of wealth was the furniture. Philip had grown up around money, learned what it could and could not purchase. Either al-Najjar didn't know what else to spend his money on, or he liked the spectacle of gold-inlaid desks.

If Philip were still a betting man, he'd have bet on the latter. Show-off.

"Then I've made this trip for nothing." He met the old man's eyes. Despite his frail body, his gaze shone back with malicious intelligence. "Miss Braithwaite and I are marrying in mere days. Nothing can stop that."

He'd check on the guards around her house on their way back. Possibly add his own men. He didn't trust al-Najjar, or his son, as far as his two-year-old niece could throw him.

He'd stand guard himself if need be.

"My congratulations." Al-Najjar didn't sound very congratulatory. More dismissive, though whatever else he felt he kept tightly under wraps. Perhaps Philip had the man all wrong, but he doubted that. "May your marriage be blessed for many happy years."

For a long moment, Philip only watched the man. Suddenly, he smiled and offered a bow, keeping his gaze on al-Najjar. "We won't take up any more of your time."

On their way out, al-Najjar sneered at him and said something in Egyptian. Philip ignored it and kept walking.

"What did he say?" Harry asked once they were clear of the door.

"I'll stand guard tonight," Philip said instead of answering. "You'll take care of Argus?"

"Aye, of course." Harry stepped in front of him, forcing Philip to stop his long, angry strides. "I'll send a couple men round. Don't do anything stupid."

Rage boiled through him. No amount of pressing his fingers into his thigh could stop that. Jaw clenched, hands in tight fists, Philip didn't release the hold he kept on his emotions. "Thank you, Harry."

Pretty little thing. Looks delicious, too.

Rash and impulsive or not, this marriage would protect Layla from that man. That was all that mattered.

* * *

THE NOISE from the henna party pierced Layla's head like a knife. She closed her eyes even as her cousins laughed and ate as they painted her feet and ankles. Her stomach rolled from so much food, but mostly from nerves. Uncertainty settled around her more heavily than her new clothing. After some discussion with her aunts, Evelyn, and Amirah, they decided on English wedding attire. The better to show the port who she was now, lest anyone—Omar, al-Najjar, whoever—come after her.

"Are you feeling all right?" Evelyn asked.

"It's been an interesting week." Layla blinked rapidly, hoping her stomach would settle and her head would stop pounding. Alas, it wasn't meant to be. She forced her lips into a smile, but from the look on her older cousin's face, she knew she wasn't successful. "It is...new," she said, not wishing to offend anyone. She couldn't bring herself to admit she'd thought they'd all purposely abandoned her. "I hadn't expected any of this."

Evelyn waved off one of the children with a soft, wistful smile and a kiss on the head. "Do you remember when we were young? You, me, Amirah? How we played in the gardens?"

Amirah laughed, looking radiant. "Oh, those gardens where we visited so many wonderous places."

Uncertain how to explain what had happened in the last years, Layla let their words pull the memory from the depths of her mind. The gardens were lush, vibrant places that she only vaguely remembered. Looking from Evelyn to Amirah, she tried to envision them as children.

The children's laughter here in the room wound through her, and in a flash Layla saw them, all three of them.

"Yes," she said slowly. "We were loud—louder than anyone else around." She tried to remember more, but then a servant came around with a tray of sweets.

"No thank you, Nour." Evelyn shook her head and steered the girl back toward the main group. Layla was grateful for the reprieve.

"Do you need a moment, Layla?" Amirah reached out and took her hand. It closed warm and confident around hers.

"I need—the memories," she heard herself say. "This week has been wonderful, but busy. It's been a long time, and I—" She broke off, the words not there in either English or Egyptian. "Remind me?"

"Of the time the three of us climbed onto the roof?"

Layla laughed as that memory resurfaced. Like a pop it appeared, the feel of the brick beneath her hands, scraping her palms, the three of them quieting their giggles though they were loud enough the whole street heard them.

"We thought we could see the ships from the house." This house, she remembered. Where the three families lived. A large compound, she supposed. Estate, her father would've called it. "I forgot so much," she whispered as Amirah retrieved them glasses of juice.

"What have you forgotten, *akhat?*" she asked softly as she passed the cups around. Layla gratefully drank the carob juice.

"Many things," she whispered into her cup. "It was safer to forget."

Evelyn took her hand. "You survived."

"And you found your way back to us," Amirah added. "Whatever you forgot, we shall help you remember."

"Amirah is right." Evelyn's words flowed over her, soft and comforting. "The important thing is that you've returned."

"I've missed you," Layla admitted. "I'd forgotten what it's like, having family."

"Will your English husband steal you away so soon?" Amirah's voice lowered even as the singing rose around her.

"No, not yet, I don't think. He only just arrived and has business here."

Plus, he'd promised she could visit with her family. He hadn't put a time limit on that visit, and Layla hadn't asked. However, in the last few days, he'd visited only a couple times, brief calls that didn't delve too deeply into their future. He'd posted guards, too. She found herself more grateful than suspicious over that. She trusted neither Omar nor al-Najjar.

So much had happened in the last week—new clothes, all the food she could eat, family she'd thought had abandoned her welcoming her with open arms. Her head spun as if she rode the sands of a haboob.

"Perhaps you can stay here while he sails back to England. Many women do when their husbands are on a voyage." Amirah hummed, but there was a faint wrinkle between her eyes. Her hand fluttered over her belly, as she was several months pregnant with her first child.

Layla hadn't met Amirah's husband yet; apparently, he was traveling to Cairo with Charlie, Evelyn's brother. The business had opened another *al-tajir* in the capital, and they ran it there.

Layla nodded slightly. She didn't think Philip would leave her alone. Not after he'd so rashly promised to marry her to keep her safe from Omar's threats. On the other hand, he'd also kept his distance, and she wondered if that was because of Omar's revelation that she was half English and half Egyptian.

"We'll talk later," Evelyn promised as the women gathered back around. She kissed Layla's cheek. "I know it's been an exciting week, and I don't care how often I've said it before: I'm so glad you're here."

"As am I." Her smile might've been faint, but it was real and honest, and she once again subjected herself to the henna party.

It lasted hours. Long after she wished for her bed, with the plush pillows and luxurious sheets, the women danced and sang and wished her well. They painted her hands and arms, her feet and ankles. For a little while, she joined in the singing, though she'd forgotten all the songs.

"Layla, dear, before you retire, your aunt and I would like a word." Aunt Augusta beckoned her into a sitting room, where a single oil lamp offered minimal light.

"I don't know how to thank you for the henna party," Layla said, smothering a yawn. She'd spent the last week thanking people. Still, she was grateful for their generosity, for remembering her when she'd forced so many of her own memories deep into her heart. For accepting her back into their lives as if nothing had happened.

"It's the least we can do to keep with our traditions." Jomana sat beside Augusta, and they shared a look that banished all Layla's tiredness.

She sat upright, hands pressed into the tops of her thighs, her intricate henna designs a stunning motif against her sudden trepidation. It slithered down her spine, that foreboding. In the week since leaving Omar's house, she'd hoped never to feel that again.

"What's wrong?"

They were going to make her pay back the cost of everything, the clothes, the food, all of it. They'd discovered something in Philip's past. Philip had changed his mind.

"It's nothing about the wedding," Augusta hurried to say. "Please don't think that."

"And from what your uncles have learned, it's nothing about Captain Conrad, either; we promise," Jomana added.

"All right." Their reassurances did nothing to ease her sudden nausea. Layla swallowed. She wouldn't have to return to Omar's house. He couldn't touch her anymore. Even if her future husband changed his mind, she had family here, a home and safety. "Then why do you look as if you've come to tell me this is all a dream and none of the last five days have happened?"

"Nothing like that, *azizi wahid*," Jomana promised. She reached over and took Layla's hand, which was cool and trembled slightly. "It's—" She looked at Augusta.

"What do you remember of your mother's illness?" Augusta's voice was low and quavered only the slightest. Enough that Layla heard it, but she had long ago learned that even the slightest change in pitch was cause for concern.

"She was ill," Layla started slowly, the memories of those early days at Omar's a blur. "I don't know why." She closed her eyes, hoping she could recall arriving at the house, but she only saw Heba as she looked now, older and worn; the gaze that looked back at her deadened. "Uncle Josiah said Omar told him Mama died from plague."

"Mariam didn't," Augusta said.

Layla's eyes snapped open. Augusta stated it so firmly, so finally, that all Layla could do was meet her aunt's gaze, surprised at the harshness in her words. "No. She did not." In a flash, the memory of those long days returned. The fear, the loneliness. "Aunt Heba brought medicines." Her hands shook, and she pressed her fingers tighter into her thighs, her toes hard against the floor. "I don't think Omar knew about the medicines."

"Nothing helped, did it?" Augusta shook her head. "It was nothing you did, my dear. Nothing you could've done."

"She had no strength. For a while, Omar let us be." She'd forgotten that, too, those moments of peace, and now she wondered if Heba had a say in that. If she did, she paid the price in those following years. "Nothing worked." Layla swallowed again. Despite the food and drink from the henna party, her throat had dried up, and the words ached.

"Was she..." Augusta's voice caught, and she paused. "She was sick for a long while?"

"Mama never got better, no matter what I did. Some days, for weeks, she could sit up on her own, eat by herself." Those were the days Heba sent her to the souk or forced her to clean the kitchens. To earn her keep, she'd said. "It never lasted. Over the years, I thought I might find a pattern. That she would be better in spring or autumn, mornings or evenings, but no. Her body simply gave up. Some days she'd be stronger, but never like she was before. In the end, she couldn't keep anything down except a little mulukhiyah." The soup hadn't helped. Nothing had. "I don't know why she died. Every day she grew weaker and weaker."

"You remember nothing more, Layla?" Jomana leaned forward. "Nothing about her illness?"

How could she explain that in the intervening years she'd concealed everything? Her parents, her family, the happier times she only now had begun to partly remember in snippets of memory. She never spoke of that time before. She rarely spoke at all in that house.

The darkness had crept into her soul until it concealed everything that had once shone with light.

Layla shook her head. "I'm sorry."

"No, no." Jomana's hand squeezed hers, and only then did Layla realize how tightly she held on. Her fingers, however, refused to loosen their grip. "It's not your fault. It's been years."

"It's *our* fault." Augusta's voice wavered. "We should've searched harder."

"I don't understand." Layla's own voice trembled, but she steadied it. Her hard-learned control exerted itself again. "What does Mama's illness have to do with…anything?"

She knew. Something in her knew it was the beginning. That everything she'd survived these last years had started with Mama's illness. Straightening her back, she eased her hand from Jomana's, her breath even as she gathered her courage around her. Even her toes didn't press so hard into the floor.

"We believe," Jomana began then stopped. "I'm sorry, *azizi wahid*. We have spent the last ten years hiding from the truth. It was safer that way."

"We hid everything, buried every last shred of evidence and never spoke of it, not even here in the house." Augusta paused and looked around, but no one disturbed them. "We believe your mother was poisoned."

Layla stilled. Part of her had expected that. Their questions, their hesitation. Another part of her blinked in disbelief. "By whom?" She licked her lips, her mind racing. "Omar?"

"No, no, we do not think so." Jomana made a rude sound. "He isn't smart enough, the coward."

Layla's lips twitched at that very accurate observation, but the revelation about her mother rooted her to her seat. "You've had ten years to think about this. You have no ideas?"

"We have a list of suspects," Augusta corrected softly. "Some have died since. War, plague, disease." She shifted in her chair and unlocked a desk drawer. Layla hadn't even realized it held a drawer. Handing her a paper, Augusta added, "One or two have been crossed off because we've discovered their innocence through other means. Some your uncles proved innocent. Either they weren't in port during those months or possessed another viable alibi."

"Why?" Layla glanced at the paper, but it'd been years since she'd read anything in any language. Her entire body heated with shame. She looked up again rather than admit that. "Why poison her?"

"Not only her. Your father." Augusta looked away. "Mostafa, too."

Breath stuttering in her chest, Layla's gaze swung to Jomana. "Mostafa?"

No one had mentioned him, but then, so much had happened, and she hadn't thought too much about it. She'd thought Mostafa traveled to Cairo with Charlie and Amirah's husband, though no one had said so outright. This was why.

Jomana's eyes closed, and her head bowed. "We realized too late."

"I'm sorry, Auntie." Layla stood and hugged her. Ignoring her own initial twinge of discomfort at the contact, she held her aunt close. "I'm so sorry."

For all the horrors she'd endured these last ten years, she wasn't the only one. Layla didn't know why that made her feel less alone.

"How?" She pulled back and looked between her aunts. "How could someone poison so many without anyone realizing it?"

"War, my dear." Augusta looked tired, exhausted to the bone. Whatever their fears and suspicions, they'd weighed heavy on her aunts since her own disappearance. "It's easier to create chaos when chaos already exists."

"Why tell me now?"

"We're hoping your captain might help us solve the murders."

CHAPTER 7

$\mathcal{L}$ ayla didn't remember much about the wedding ceremony. It'd been a turbulent week. Between escaping Omar's house, finding Philip, and learning about her parents, all she wanted was a long sleep.

However, nightmares plagued her. Images of her mother, sick in a darkened room, though her sickbed had sat beneath a window. Layla had looked out it often, wondering why they were so alone.

Nightmares of Mostafa's silent face watching her. Of Amirah's, though Layla couldn't decipher the look her cousin gave her. Of Evelyn's nameless, faceless husband.

She found herself back in Philip's cabin, the well-wishes of his crew echoing in her ears. Argus snored in a corner, apparently equally exhausted. She envied him his rest.

"Laska left us drinks." Philip offered her one. Her husband.

Husband. It rang oddly in her ears and didn't sound real at all. She could honestly say she didn't feel changed after the ceremony. She breathed easier, but otherwise felt the same as she always had.

Philip stood before her, holding out one of those delicate glasses.

Then again, the odd tingling over her skin whenever he stood before her was definitely new.

Accepting the glass, she peered inside suspiciously, but she could see little in the dim cabin.

"It's not wine," he promised in a quiet voice, even though they were alone in the room.

"Oh." She cautiously sniffed the contents. "It smells like hibiscus tea."

"Laska likes you." Philip chuckled and sipped from his own glass. He tried to hide a grimace at the taste. "I understand he ensured a breakfast feast for us in the morning."

"I don't even know him," she protested. "Why would he show such kindness for a stranger?"

Philip studied his glass as if it held the answer. He didn't drink again, but instead set it on the table. "I don't know his story," he admitted. At her confused look, he added, "What happened to him before we met. He sailed with a Polish captain, one we knew. Well, one my family knew. This was—oh, eight, nine years ago. They were exiled from their homeland."

"Exiled," she whispered. "It must be hard, not having that connection, being alone."

"He's not alone. He's sailed with this crew for years; they're family." He paused and gave her a brief, quiet smile, there and gone. "That's all I know of him from before. I do know that he adopted Kaz before he left Percy's crew. There are far too many orphans because of the wars. Kaz was one. They found him on their last run to what they considered Poland."

She understood the—what was the word? That need for a bond with someone. Anyone. Standing in a ship's cabin, a life she never thought she'd have spread out before her, Layla's heart hurt for the cook.

"You know all your company's captains?" She sat, grateful for the chance to do so after the long day. "The way you spoke made it sound as if you know all your captains by name."

He held her gaze, and she wondered what he thought. She'd believed it a simple question, but perhaps she just didn't know much about merchants.

Without a word, he sat on the bed, still watching her.

"Is something wrong?"

"No, no." He shook his head and offered a slight smile. "Just figuring out where to start. A few hours' acquaintance spread out over a week isn't much for a marriage." He huffed a breath and ran a hand down his face. She noticed he did that often and wondered why.

"I thought you were rash and impulsive. Not the figuring out sort," she teased, quite unsure where that impulse came from.

He let out a startled chuckle. "It's a quality I worked long and hard to suppress." Even in the dimness of the cabin, he looked pensive. His tone nagged at her, as if he held a part of himself back despite his joking.

"I understand that." She sipped her tea again but truly didn't want any more. Setting it quietly on the table, she thought about his words. "You know nothing about me except that I needed help. Is that why you offered marriage?"

"Yes." He shook his head. "Believe it or not, that's exactly why. I'm sure we could've come to another arrangement, offered everyone a nice, tidy sum, but that would've taken time. And it didn't feel as if you had much time."

"Feel?" She tilted her head. Stretching her legs before her, she rotated her ankles. "You *feel* time?"

"Not like I can feel the deck of the ship or the skin of your hand." He reached out, his fingers grazing the back of her hand, tracing the swirls of the henna. His touch shivered over her, and she forcibly kept herself from pulling back. "I meant that al-

Najjar didn't seem like the negotiating sort. Marriage offered protection."

"Omar isn't the negotiating sort." Her skin tingled where he'd touched her, shooting up her arm and making her crave more. "He's the angry kind, taking because he can." Layla paused. "Though I think now, maybe he only did so with people he had control over." She waved a hand, tired of talking about herself. "Why do you suppress it? Your rashness."

"Why do you?" he asked, though it wasn't in a rude or mean way. "Because it gets us into trouble."

"Nothing I did mattered, whether I was rash or not." Had she been rash? Layla thought perhaps, before, but those memories weren't yet there. They teased her, as if maybe if she thought long enough or focused intently, they'd slot back into place. "What trouble did you find?"

"Let's just say my mouth ran faster than my brain." He shook his head and offered a small smile. His eyes, however, remained serious and steady in the dimly lit cabin. "Multiple times."

Curious about that, she worked through several variations, but she didn't have the words—the polite words, at least—to ask. Perhaps after they'd been married longer than a few hours.

"Leaving that house was the most impulsive thing I can remember doing." She paused. Except for when she and her cousins had stood on the roof, but that seemed trivial in comparison.

"Why did you?" He leaned forward, his hands clasped before him. "I—I don't mean that you shouldn't have, and I don't mean to sound rude. But why now?"

"I've thought about that. As I walked through the night streets, hiding and getting lost." She stood, but there was very little room for walking. Taking a couple steps toward the door, she turned and walked back, past a snoring Argus, who opened one eye to watch her.

"You chose to leave at night?" He watched her, that steady look that felt like a caress.

"I had no choice."

"No, I suppose not," he murmured.

"When Omar told me he'd contracted my marriage to al-Najjar, all I could think was to run away. We all have a choice. I had forgotten that, over the years. My father died, and my mother was ill for so many years. After she died, I simply… stayed."

That wasn't exactly true. She had nowhere else to go. No one had visited, no one mourned her mother but she and Heba. Only she and her two female cousins performed the burial rites. Only she mourned the woman who had once been Mariam. She'd thought herself alone and abandoned, and she'd needed a place to sleep.

"One day Mama was there, the next she wasn't, and Aunt Heba put me to work in the kitchens."

"I'm sorry. It's a small, trite consolation, but that doesn't make it any less true." He stood and took her hands, a gentle hold that warmed her more than the spring sunlight on deck. "When Shadi told you about al-Najjar, something in you snapped."

"Almost like a pepper, snapped in half." She shook her head, but her voice didn't shake. It remained steady and strong. "I had a choice, though I'm certain Omar didn't believe so. I could stay, marry al-Najjar, and no doubt die within a year. Just like his other wives."

Philip hissed, his fingers running lightly over the backs of her hands. His touch helped her words flow more easily. It also sent shivers over her arms and down her spine.

"Or I could leave. Before, I thought everyone had abandoned me. My family—my real family—never contacted me, never tried to see me." That lingering hurt still ached, but she understood now that Omar had lied to everyone so thoroughly, the entire town believed it.

"Shadi told you they didn't want you." Philip still held her hands. "Made it easier to keep you there."

"Yes." She tightened her fingers around his. "How did you know?"

"I told you my family owns a shipping business with a great many captains. We also employ people who might not have any other place to go, who need another chance. My sister, she owns a beauty creams business where the women of the county can work with other women. Many of them are widowed and have nowhere else they can go."

"Truly?" She felt alert then. As if her mind had switched from her own troubles to something far more interesting. "How many women? What kinds of beauty creams? How do they sell them? Is it only in your county?"

He laughed, and Layla only then realized her storm of questions. She stepped back, pulling her hands from his, but Philip held firm. "Don't be embarrassed. There's nothing to be embarrassed about."

"I—when I was young, I planned to take over Papa's third of the partnership." She remembered Papa's smile now, though the rest of his facial features, especially his eyes, remained indistinct. "He used to sit me beside him as he tallied his ledgers."

"Truly?"

"Do you not believe a woman can tally numbers?" Where had her audacity come from?

"Oh, I know for a fact they can." He shook his head and led her the few steps back to the chair. "My mother and sisters would skin me alive if they thought I believed otherwise."

"What are they like?" She sat back down, not entirely certain where the conversation was heading. "You sound as if you respect them very much."

"They're vivacious. Headstrong." He looked down at her, and Layla had a feeling he didn't see her but the women in his life. "The whole family is, which is why I've tried not to be so impulsive."

"They're impulsive, too? Even in their businesses?"

"No, not—not all, not to my extent." He shook his head and began to pace.

Layla watched him for a few moments, certain there was more than what he'd divulged. She searched for the words to ask more about his family.

"Are we supposed to consummate the marriage?" she heard herself ask instead.

Why had she opened her mouth? And Philip thought he was the rash one.

* * *

STARTLED, Philip stepped back. He swallowed a laugh, certain that was the absolute last thing he should utter. He might not regret marrying Layla, but he certainly didn't know what step came next.

Crouching before her, he took her hands. He'd never really had a romance. None of the county's women appealed to him and his need for adventure. They'd wanted to settle down, to be a part of the richest family in the county and not worry about their future. He couldn't blame them, but that didn't make them any more appealing.

"You've just escaped a house where you were treated like a slave." He caressed her hands, once more tracing the swirling henna. Her fingers moved against his, the barest touch, and he noticed she didn't tremble as she had only a week before.

He also noticed he enjoyed touching her, but he pushed that aside. He meant to promise he wouldn't push her. He wasn't going to seduce her now. No matter how badly he wanted to taste her.

"I won't abandon you," he promised. "Those aren't merely words; they're a promise. We'll figure out this marriage." He kissed her fingertips. "Until then, we can wait until you're comfortable."

"Not all men are like you." Her voice came out soft and slightly disbelieving.

"No," he agreed. Then he stood, bringing her up with him. "More's the pity." He winked and grinned. She laughed, a small sound, but a real one, and his grin widened.

"Will you take me on a tour of *The Lady Kaya?*" She sounded more awake than she had all day, but what caught his attention was the eagerness in her tone. "It's been years since I knew the layout of a ship."

"Let's start on the deck. It's my favorite part." He opened the door, and Argus woofed softly. "You stay here." He crouched down and petted beneath his chin, Argus's preferred scratching spot. "It's all right. I won't be long."

"Is it your favorite part because you can see everything?" They climbed up, and the stars shone over the deck, casting everything in an otherworldly light.

"Yes." He looked at her in surprise. "How did you know?"

"Memories I had long forgotten," she admitted as they crossed to the poop deck. He acknowledged the night guards, who offered them privacy. "I pushed them down so far that when I see something again—like the deck of a ship at night— it's like a lamp is lit, and the memory returns."

He took her hand and squeezed in understanding. "When we're out at sea, far from port, with nothing but stars and sky for miles—there's nothing like it."

"My father used to take us sailing." She paused, head tilted upward as she turned in a small circle and watched the sky.

He watched her, fascinated by the way she'd opened up. By the joy on her face, the way she spread her arms out, as if embracing the stars.

"I don't remember where we sailed, but I remember sitting on his shoulders, looking up at the sky." She stopped and met Philip's gaze. "I thought it was the most beautiful thing in the world. The sky at night over the vast sea, with no land in sight. It stole my breath."

Capturing her hand, he tugged her toward the railing. He swallowed the words he wanted to say, about her beauty, about the way she drew him in. He resisted his sudden need to kiss her. Instead, he turned so they faced the horizon.

"When I was young, my father taught me to sail. He taught all of us." Behind them, the sun didn't even dent the horizon, and he had no idea of the time. "My mother suffers from terrible seasickness, so she stayed in the offices and oversaw our books. I think they wanted to see if anyone took after her on the water. Luckily, none of us did." He chuckled and patted the railing. "I named this ship after her. I thought I was so clever, calling the ship after my mother who would never sail on it."

"Did she think you were clever?" Layla turned in her red and gold wedding gown and watched him. He wondered how she knew.

"She indulged me," he admitted.

His mother had other concerns then. He hadn't been the easiest child, Philip admitted that now. When he told Layla he'd been rash and impulsive, those was the simplest and mildest terms he could've used. "Wild" was a better word. "Undisciplined," even. Not in the sense of simple disobedience.

None of his siblings blindly obeyed anything or anyone. Somehow, he'd been worse. Gambling, fighting…drinking. Even after he knew of his father's past, that hadn't stopped him. Compulsion, his parents had called it. It'd taken him years to overcome all that.

Layla watched him in the darkness of the port, the water lapping along the ship with only the calls of the watchmen keeping them company. The air had cooled despite the warmth of the day, and the sky remained cloudless.

Slowly, she nodded, as if she understood he wasn't ready to reveal anything more. He'd made a promise to his siblings long before he'd left for school, and he'd discovered on his own just how difficult it was to maintain any sort of equilibrium.

"Tell me of your sisters?" she asked, stepping closer.

"Esme, my oldest sister, is married to a marquess. That caused quite the scandal when they returned from Upper Canada." He chuckled, remembering when she and Landon had returned. "She's wicked good at cards, so don't bet against her."

"I don't believe I've ever played," Layla admitted. "But I shall keep that in mind. And your other sister? The one with the business?"

"Yara." He nodded, shifting toward the east so he could watch the sunrise. "She has an affinity for animals, and she and Alec, her husband, own a vast estate teeming with all sorts." He paused and realized something he should have long before this moment. "They both know how to use a dagger." He slipped his khanjar from its sheath and held it out. Layla didn't take it, but he hadn't expected her to. "My mother made sure my sisters knew how to defend themselves."

"Truly?" The breathless word drifted across the short space between them. Her fingers grazed his wrist rather than the hilt of the khanjar. "I should like to learn."

"I'll teach you." He returned the dagger to its sheath and turned her toward the horizon, where the sunlight only now barely touched the sky. "My mother believes everyone should know how to defend themselves."

"She's right," Layla said, watching him over her shoulder. Her voice shifted low as she turned back toward the east. "Not everyone is kind in this world."

"No." He cleared his throat as the birds awakened. Somehow, he thought they should end their first night as a married couple talking about anything other than a past he promised he'd never repeat, her safety, or either of their families. "When I was young, I followed Yara around day and night. She and one of the older farmhands would scour the countryside. George, he knew all the birds, how to keep away predators during the spring hatching, how to help with a broken wing. He and Yara roamed constantly, looking out for our animals, helping the wild ones."

Layla stepped back, closer to him as the sun hinted at another bright day. "Is that where you learned about the swifts?" She didn't look at him, but carefully, gently set her hand over his.

Philip was completely unprepared for the shock of that touch. It wound through him, sharp and arousing, straight to his cock. "Yes." He cleared his throat. "I was obsessed with birds. When I was young, they were all I cared about. The different kinds, the way they glided on the wind. I sketched hundreds of them. I wanted to understand them so I, too, could fly. Everyone I met knew about my obsession."

"And now?"

Now he wanted his sketchbook so he could draw Layla in the inky night sky. Her head tilted just enough that the sunrise highlighted her hair, still in intricate braids from the wedding. Philip cleared his throat again, scrambling for words.

Turning her just the slightest, he pointed toward a lone bird soaring in the predawn. The warmth of her body pressed close against him, tempting his control. With her hand in his, he followed the bird's movements.

"That's a gray heron; see how its wings move?"

"It's very graceful," she breathed, leaning her head back against his chest.

"They're freshwater birds, living along the banks of the Nile."

"And that one?" She pointed farther west. "Is that a swift?"

"No, a kite. It's larger than a swift." He glanced down at her, and the look of wonder on her face made his heart skip. "Kites are birds of prey; no doubt they're hunting the swifts."

"And that?"

He looked where she pointed and thought he could stay like this forever, watching the sunrise with Layla in his arms.

CHAPTER 8

*P*hilip left his new wife asleep in the single bed in his cabin. As they'd watched the sunrise, Layla had grown quieter, sleepy despite her obvious desire to stay awake. He didn't mind sleeping in the chair. It wasn't the most uncomfortable place he'd ever slept, and he managed a few hours' rest before seeing to his duties.

It wasn't a typical wedding night, but he thought she needed the comfort of companionship first. It'd been a trying week for her.

Now, as he splashed cold water on his face and washed the night away, he realized Kaz would have to shave him in the captain's room this morning. Argus stretched, ready for breakfast and his morning walk about the ship. He yipped at Philip to hurry.

"Hush," he whispered with a quick scratch under Argus's chin. "Layla is still asleep."

Easing open the door, he let Argus loose and looked back at Layla. She hadn't moved, curled beneath the blanket, back against the wall. He understood that. Protecting your center with your back against the wall so no one sneaked up on you.

Fury shot through him that she'd been forced to experience such fear. That his beautiful, witty Layla had learned that sleeping that way was safest.

He'd pay a visit to that so-called uncle of hers. Not yet, not with his temptation sparking so dangerously close to the surface. His father's voice echoed in his memory.

Don't let the need for instant satisfaction overwhelm you.

Crouching beside the bed, Philip let temptation overcome him, and he reached for her. He brushed her hair from her cheeks, and that simple touch grounded his temper, at least somewhat.

Her eyes shot open. "No, no." He stilled his hand, sorry he'd let his impulses disturb her sleep. "I didn't mean to wake you."

"I'm awake." She stretched, and Philip kept his gaze on her. Her body moved long and elegant as she unfolded from her tight coil. His mouth went dry.

"You don't need to wake yet, I promise." Giving into temptation once more, he kissed her forehead. She blinked at him but didn't flinch away. "I'll return in a few hours, and we can enjoy Laska's breakfast feast with your family."

She watched him silently for several moments. Then she nodded, tugging the blanket back around her. She didn't curl back into that tight ball but stretched over the bed, wiggling her toes beneath the blanket. "I ate more yesterday than I have in years; I shouldn't be hungry."

"Don't say that to Laska." He stood, just barely resisting the urge to touch her again. It was becoming a compulsion, feeling her skin against his. Its smooth slide against his fingertips. "He's most insistent on feeding you."

"And I'm grateful. I shall never take any food for granted ever again." She reached out and caught his hand. Despite the heaviness of the blanket, her hand was cool as her fingers wrapped around his. "I promise you; I can do more than sleep and eat."

He understood all too well that need, the driving desire to prove oneself, so he didn't dismiss her words with a quick laugh or a shrug. Instead, Philip raised her hand and kissed her fingers. The move felt as natural as breathing.

"For this morning, sleep." He held her hand for another moment. "No one will disturb you."

He felt her gaze on him as he left, latching the door securely behind him. Harry awaited him in the dining room. Argus abandoned him for the galley just as Kaz brought out a cup of coffee, as if he knew exactly when Philip would arrive.

"How does he know?" Philip asked as the boy retreated to fetch breakfast and the shaving kit.

"Know?" Harry looked up from his papers. "Know what?"

"Nothing." Philip dismissed it with a wave of his coffee cup. "What are you studying so intently?"

"The contracts our potential merchants sent over." He frowned, lifting one and sliding it across the table. "You're right; they can't possibly supply this much in a season."

"They're desperate. Trade isn't what it used to be, not since Napoleon's invasion and the subsequent coup by Muhammad Ali." Philip glanced at the numbers and handed it back. Pressing his fingers against his eyes, he shook his head. "Have el-Nebi and Bartley sent over anything?"

"I think they were waiting until after the wedding." Harry grinned, looking far more awake and alert than Philip felt. "I was approached by a Mr. Bingham. The name didn't sound familiar."

Philip went over his mental list of former contacts and shook his head. "No, I don't recall that name."

Harry shrugged and waved at the pile of papers before him. "He wasn't listed, but he left his card. I'll ask around for more information."

"I'll speak with el-Nebi and Bartley about these other potential partners." Philip frowned at the stack of papers, but there was little he could do now, half awake and still feeling out the country's situation. "Any word on Darwish?"

"Aye, I found him. Well, his son. Didn't want to disturb the wedding festivities with bad news, but Darwish himself died about eight years ago."

Frowning, Philip finished his coffee just as Kaz returned. "Is the son still in the coffee business?"

"You and your coffee habit will be happy to know that he is, indeed."

"Good morning." Layla's bright voice echoed throughout the room.

Argus woofed and bounded out from the galley, skidding to a halt right before her. Kaz bowed and retreated, while Laska poked his head out and retracted it just as silently. Harry stood and offered his seat.

"Oh, thank you." Layla was awkwardly petting Argus's head as he stared up at her adoringly. "I'm afraid I couldn't sleep anymore." She smiled, a beautiful, sunny smile that punched Philip in the gut.

He'd give so much to see that smile every morning. Preferably after he tasted her lush lips.

"It's a beautiful day, too nice to spend inside." She watched him from across the table, her back ramrod straight, her eyes uncertain.

"Mrs. Layla." Laska appeared just then with two plates piled high with fruits and nuts.

"I'll leave you two alone." Harry bowed, hiding his smile, but his amusement came through clearly.

"I'm sorry to have interrupted." She ate a date, her eyes half closing.

"No, no." Philip shook himself out of his trance even as he called himself all sorts of a fool. "You—you didn't interrupt. We were discussing our contacts here in Damietta." He pushed the papers aside before Laska buried them beneath their breakfast

—not the feast he'd planned for Layla's family, but the one he'd planned for just the two of them. "I'm eager to speak with your uncles, see if an arrangement can be made between us."

She paused, a slice of mango halfway to her mouth. Setting it back on the plate, she watched him. "How long do you plan to stay in Damietta?"

He'd planned only long enough to find their former contacts and settle the business, then sail the Nile south to Cairo. He'd almost forgotten his second, secret reason for claiming Egypt as his first solo voyage with his own crew. Layla had occupied so many of his thoughts.

"We have time," he assured her. "I—or do you want to stay here? With your family?"

"I'd like to spend time with them," she admitted. "Visit for a little while longer. A week isn't enough, given how much time we lost."

"Of course." He stopped to spread fig preserves over a piece of bread.

"Is something wrong?" Her voice washed over him, quiet and even as Kaz set a cup of hot coffee before her.

He met her gaze, surprised. "No, I was planning my day."

Her lips quirked. "I thought you weren't the planning sort."

"I should never have told you that." He groaned but shared her smile. "You'll be safe enough at the house. They have several guards already, and the compound looks secure enough. Some of my men have also volunteered as guards. I'll escort you there after our breakfast feast and return before supper, if you prefer."

"That sounds lovely, thank you." She nodded at the stack of papers. "Are those from your merchants?"

Distracted, he watched the graceful movement of her hand as she waved at the papers. She had lovely hands.

"Philip?"

He paused, staring at her as if he'd never seen her before. That was the first time she'd called him that. And damn him if he couldn't get used to hearing his name in her soft, gentle voice.

"Yes." He cleared his throat and finished his coffee in a single gulp. It burned down his throat. "I need to contact the coffee merchant. The previous owner's son has taken over the business, and I'd like to reestablish trade."

"Cap." Harry had returned, looking tense. "Sorry to interrupt, but el-Nebi is looking for you." He nodded at Layla. "Both of you."

Given the timing and the look on Harry's face, Philip knew that whatever he'd planned for the day had taken a turn. He doubted he'd get that shave any time soon. Holding out his hand for Layla's, he led her above deck and into the warm midmorning sun.

"Uncle Muhammad." Layla nodded, a cautious smile on her face. "You're alone?"

"Ah, good, you're both here." He didn't look pleased. For one wild moment, Philip thought the marriage wasn't valid.

Prepared to fight that, he braced himself, holding Layla's hand in what he hoped was a reassuring gesture. Given the way her fingers tightened around his, he thought maybe she, too, worried about the legalities.

"I just received word, Layla." El-Nebi's voice was low though the crew had given them privacy. "Omar is dead."

* * *

LAYLA STARED in shock as Muhammad announced Omar's death. The news hung over the festivities of just yesterday, where she'd laughed more than she had in so long, it felt like a different life. Now, despite the sun shining brightly down upon them, she felt the darkness like a pall.

Beside her, Philip held her hand, and she let the comfort of his touch steady her. Questions raced through her mind, but the only one that seemed relevant was, "How?"

Muhammad shook his head. "Your aunt doesn't know; she found him in the kitchens."

"Kitchens?" she repeated, feeling foolish. "He never entered them."

The truth was that Omar only entered the kitchens when he wished to berate her. The kitchens were where he'd hit her until her lips bled before stealing her meager meal. Her fingers tightened around Philip's, and she wondered if he thought the same as she. That this death had cast a shadow over their marriage.

"This isn't an omen," he whispered, as if he knew her thoughts.

Layla jerked her head up and met his gaze. Her toes grew cold and stiff as she pressed them onto the deck. With a start, she realized she hadn't tensed up like this since the marriage papers had been signed. Safe with Philip or even her family, she hadn't felt the need for such restraint. Now, though he was dead, she held herself still, as if Omar stood before her.

"It's not," he insisted. "Only we make our fate."

"I'm not sorry he died," she admitted, the truth difficult to speak. She forced the words out anyway. "He was a cruel monster."

Aunt Jomana's words echoed back to her. Aunt Augusta's pale face as they warned her. Layla hadn't told Philip about the secret her aunts had shared, the fear they'd carried for ten years.

It wasn't he who'd poisoned her parents. He was only a few years older than she, and this was his first voyage to Egypt. Plus, that would have been odd, him returning to offer marriage when it was she who'd accidentally boarded the wrong ship. Layla shook her head. She saw treacheries where there were none.

She dismissed her suspicions, baseless as they were. Swallowing, she searched for her aunts but saw only Muhammad on the deck. Clearly he'd come first, before the rest of the family.

"Was Aunt Heba harmed?" she managed.

"She was not, from what I learned." He cleared his throat. "Her son, Malik, found me."

"Why you?" Philip asked before Layla could form the words. Even her throat had frozen in shock. "Why did they seek you out?"

Muhammad looked uncomfortable but held her gaze, his eyes soft. "Omar was not discreet about your marriage, *abna mahboubeh.*"

"Of course not." She nodded, trying to feel anything other than relief over his death. "Was it al-Najjar?" The words hurt as she voiced them, but she forced them around her tight throat.

"I'm sorry, *abna mahboubeh.* I have no more information. I suspect it might've been. If what we believe is true and Omar owed al-Najjar money, and then he didn't pay despite the generosity your captain settled on..." He shook his head. "I do not know."

For an instant, she wanted to protest that he wasn't her captain. Except he was now. They'd married just yesterday, though they'd spent the night talking. For which she appreciated his restraint—that wasn't the right word, but Layla hadn't any other. Not now, not with the news of Omar's death and Jomana and Augusta's words echoing in her head and her heart.

"Please—" She broke off and swallowed before trying again. "Please convey my condolences."

"Of course, Layla." Muhammad bowed and held her close, kissing her cheeks. "Have you told him?"

"Not yet," she whispered back.

He nodded and stepped back, looking at Philip. "You are correct, Captain. This is not an omen. I'm afraid it might be far worse. Keep our beloved niece safe with you."

Gone was the man who'd made her laugh and put her at

ease. Who spent half the night telling her stories of his family and his love of birds, stories of racing through meadows—a scene she only partially understood, having never seen a meadow before. The man who'd stood on this very deck and pointed out the rising sun.

In his place stood a man she hadn't realized she wanted by her side. Strong, tall, unafraid. The khanjar at his hip wasn't merely for display. Even Argus now sat in front of her, an added layer of protection.

"I'll protect her with my life."

Philip's words didn't send a chill over her arms or down her spine. He meant it. His words enveloped her in a cushion of safety she'd often dreamed about.

"Layla, Jomana wished me to tell you that she and Augusta will meet you here this afternoon rather than at the house."

"Thank you, Uncle." She forced her lips into a small smile, but her fingers couldn't loosen from around Philip's. Even her blood was frozen, it seemed. "Please ensure they are safe traveling the streets."

"I'll escort her." Philip's clipped words, what some might call hasty, were honest. True, she supposed. He meant every word. "And I'll post my men around the house, if that's all right with you."

"*Shukra, captan.*" Muhammad bowed. "Josiah is already seeing to extra protection." He stepped closer and whispered, "Stay safe, Layla. Until we know what happened to Omar, I fear you're in danger."

"I only just found my freedom, Uncle. Nothing will jeopardize it."

His gaze held hers, as if he were assessing that truth. Then, with a slight nod and a small smile, he left, leaving Layla cold in the midmorning sun.

"He could've simply died," Philip finally said. He picked up her hand and ran his thumb over her knuckles. The touch sparked through her, a shiver of wanting more. "Apoplexy, or maybe his heart gave out."

"Do you believe that?" Layla peered up at him, the sun warm against her back though her fingers were still chilled.

"No." He gave her a smile, there and gone in a heartbeat. "But it's possible."

"I don't mourn him," she said, looking out over the wharves, where hundreds of people went about the business of loading and unloading the dozens of ships at port. "He was a mean, cruel man who did not treat anyone well."

"I will protect you." His fingers grazed her cheek, sure and firm. He tilted up her chin. "Not only because I'm hotheaded and rash." He gave her that mischievous smile again, the one that made her skin tingle. "And not only because I promised I would. I'll protect you from Omar's enemies, al-Najjar, and whoever else wants you harmed."

Gratitude blossomed through her again, but now she thought it was more than that. Layla hadn't the word for it, but the feeling helped her shoulders relax and made her smile easier and more natural.

"Thank you" seemed banal, no matter how much she appreciated his promises. "Can you really teach me how to protect myself?"

That wasn't what she'd planned to say, but since he'd offered, it was all she could think of. That and kissing him.

"Yes. But it takes time," he warned. "You won't be ready within a day or two. Until you are, I'll be with you."

Embarrassed by her weakness, her fears real or imagined, Layla nodded. It didn't banish her thoughts about kissing him. Or what a true wedding night might feel like. "Who are you meeting with after the feast?"

"Darwish, the coffee merchant." He slanted her a grin. "As Harry jokes, have to keep the coffee flowing."

She nodded sagely. "I am most grateful for that." Layla

laughed. Despite Omar's death and its repercussions, her fear that whatever her aunts believed had happened to her parents was true, Philip's expression wiped all that away.

He bowed low, a sweeping movement she thought she'd seen before, when she was young and playing—something.

"As my lady commands."

CHAPTER 9

"Have you asked for his help?" Jomana whispered later that day, once they were back in their home.

Augusta was seeing to a question by the household staff, leaving Jomana and Layla alone in the cool antechamber. They'd lit no lamp; only the midafternoon sun slotted through the windows and illuminated the room.

She liked that, the intimacy the daylight offered. The confidences it helped her share. Layla had been reluctant to divulge any of her past, but she found herself recalling the long years of her mother's illness. The heartache and despair, the choking loneliness.

Jomana and Augusta had listened with heartbreak in their eyes. They'd shared memories of her and Mariam, which eased Layla's pain and helped her remember what life had been like… before.

"I haven't," she admitted. "It's been a busy day, with news of Omar and the wedding feast." When Augusta left, the door had closed securely behind her, but Layla knew Philip was guarding the room.

True to his word, he'd stayed close by during her afternoon visit. He'd brought the contracts from earlier, and when Augusta left, Layla glimpsed him stretched out in the chair. Arms folded over his chest, head tilted back against the wall, ankles crossed at his boots, he watched her. It struck her again, how very handsome he was.

"He's protective of you." Her aunt grinned and winked. "Does this mean you had a successful wedding night?"

Layla's cheeks heated, and before she could stop them, her eyes widened. She supposed she should've anticipated that question. It was only natural. Scrambling for an answer, she only debated the truth for a moment. What had happened between them lay between them.

"You could say that," she said, her cheeks heating all the more. Her gaze slid back to the door as Augusta opened it, but she couldn't see Philip. She hadn't lied, she just hadn't voiced the whole truth. They'd had a successful night. Perhaps not in the way Jomana meant, but Layla considered their closeness an accomplishment.

"I apologize." Augusta returned and settled back in beside them. "The staff is in an uproar about the additional guards, and, well—" She waved a hand toward the door. "About your husband's presence, Layla."

"Bah," Jomana said. "We are most proper. There is nothing for them to worry over or gossip about."

"Given everything, I prefer his presence," Layla said softly. She cleared her throat, but her conviction remained strong. "Even outside the door."

"He is very protective," Augusta agreed with a sly smile, echoing Jomana's observations. "I've never seen anyone move so quickly. And his dagger…it's Egyptian, did you see?"

Layla merely nodded. "He's very, ah, strong." She settled on "strong" and hoped it was enough to move the conversation away from their wedding night.

Away from Philip's dagger as well. He'd told her about his parents, but she wouldn't share that piece of him with anyone. She felt the secrets they told each other were between them, no matter how wonderful it felt to have others she could confide in.

"When Papa died, who inherited his third of the business?"

"It was absorbed by Muhammad and Josiah," Augusta admitted. "I believe you were set to inherit it, but, well…" She sighed and took Layla's hand. "I'm sorry—so sorry, Layla. We truly believed you had died."

"I don't blame you for that."

A part of her did, of course. Years of believing that they had dismissed her and Mama after Papa's death were hard to set behind her. However, Layla knew it was Omar's lies that had caused these painful years, and she fought her instincts to pull back and nurse that hurt, that resentment. Instead, she reminded herself that Omar had deliberately told them she'd died, though for what reason Layla couldn't say.

"And now? Is it possible that Papa's original will can be confirmed?"

"I'm certain the paperwork can be drawn up," Jomana added, standing from their small table. "That we can give you your proper inheritance."

"Good. I shall like that." It seemed a small point in all this, but it also felt important. A way she might reclaim her life. She stood as well, feeling awkward in her new English gown and sturdy new shoes. She had much to get used to again, and she was eager to begin. "And I'll speak with Philip about Mama." Her eyes slid to the closed door. "I believe he'll help me."

"Careful, Layla." Jomana embraced her in a warm, quick hug. "We just found you again."

"I will be," she promised, kissing each woman's cheeks. "But I have many unanswered questions about my past. About my parents and what happened after Papa died."

"Any help you need," Augusta offered, "you've only to ask." She unlocked a small chest that sat innocently on a side table. Layla hadn't realized it was more than ornamental. Now, Augusta handed her a small sheaf of papers, carefully folded and tied with a ribbon. "We kept everything."

"We documented every conversation, every hint we discovered. The list of names is here, too."

She carefully placed the folded packet in her pocket. Its weight might've been negligent, but it felt like she'd placed a stone around her waist. At the door, Layla paused. "What made you suspect anything in the first place?"

"Mariam did," Jomana whispered, her gaze flitting to the door and back again. "She thought Harry was acting oddly, but he rebuffed all her questions."

Frowning, Layla laid a hand against her pocket. "So she thought it must be—what? Illegal? Worthy of poisoning someone?"

"No, of course not." Augusta shook her head, but they both kept their voices low. Her aunts had stepped closer together, Layla noted with a start. As if they'd long grown used to whispering about this in secret.

"She thought it was a business deal gone wrong, but neither Muhammad nor Josiah said anything, and they weren't acting odd." Jomana shook her head. "Not like Mariam described Harry."

Layla didn't want to ask. She dreaded the answer as much as she had dreaded waking in Omar's house. "Was Papa...was he involved in something illegal?"

"No, *azizi wahid*. Not that Mariam believed." Jomana's voice barely drifted over the short distance between them. "And not that either of your uncles knew about."

Whatever they believed, it still terrified them ten years later. Layla stepped closer, so her voice wouldn't drift outside this room.

"You still don't know what it was?" Her own voice had lowered considerably, matching their tone in fear in discovery.

"We tried. For years, we tried, even after your father died and your mother disappeared..." Augusta trailed off and shook her head. "Neither of your uncles could discover anything from Harry, and nothing seemed out of place. Charlie discovered nothing, either. We're hoping fresh eyes might help." She sighed and hugged Layla tight. "No matter what happened a decade ago, whoever it was clearly targeted your family. They'll be after you."

"Is that why you told me?"

"We wanted you prepared," Jomana confirmed. "Your return from the dead has caused quite a stir in the community. People have talked about it up and down the wharves. We've had more visitors the last few days than we have in years."

She hadn't realized any of that, though of course it all made sense. People wanted to know everything they could. Word would spread about her reappearance—*had* spread, it seemed. If whoever murdered her parents, and Mostafa, still lived, he'd discover her presence soon enough.

"More business requests, too," Augusta added with a rueful smile. "Which is good, but worrisome, given what happened."

"I understand several business acquaintances have contacted both your uncles and your husband." Jomana leaned closer. "Be wary, my dear. Augusta is right. Given what happened to your mother, we worry."

"I'll speak with Philip," she promised, her mind racing. She had no idea where to begin this decade-old search, but hopefully he did.

Her fingers grazed the papers in her pocket. Hopefully he could help her read the letters. Layla was loath to admit she couldn't do it on her own.

* * *

Philip and Layla walked back to the ship in silence. Layla seemed relaxed but pensive. She easily kept pace but didn't look around, as if whatever she and her aunts had talked about during her tea remained with her.

The midafternoon sun baked the city and Philip pulled his hat lower against the glare. He couldn't imagine what the afternoons felt like in summer, given the heat of May. The sun highlighted everything, washing the street in a bronze light that nearly blinded him.

Lucky for him, it didn't, though he suspected whoever followed them hoped it would.

"Layla." He slowed her, taking her hand and steering her around a random corner.

"Is this the way back to the ship?" She frowned at him but moved closer, and he kept his voice low.

"No, we're taking a detour." Her hand tightened around his, and she looked around, her head barely moving as she did so. "I'm not sure. It's just a feeling, but let's take a tour of the city."

"Is this feeling telling you someone is following us?"

He looked around again, but other than that itch between his shoulder blades, he didn't see any sign that anyone was purposefully after them. Still, he held her hand tight as he turned down a side street and slowed their pace.

"It's telling me something isn't right," he admitted. "Which way are the wharves from here?"

"I have no idea." She made a sound in the back of her throat and offered a brief smile. "I rarely left that house before the other night. And remember." They turned down another street, and Philip had a feeling they were moving in the exact opposite direction they needed to go. "I got lost walking from Omar's house."

"I do remember that." He turned again, back toward the main street. "Which is no help. One of us should know the city."

"What makes you think someone is following us?" She was

breathless now, though they'd kept their pace even. Still, he thought he heard a thread of fear beneath that.

"Don't worry; this could be nothing." But he didn't think it was, and he turned down another random street.

"Do not lie," she snapped. Whatever fear he thought he heard disappeared. "I have lived my life in fear and lack. I've barely spoken with anyone in years." She jerked her hand from his and glared up at him, though she still kept pace with his long strides. "I won't do so any longer. If you truly believe someone follows us, then say so."

Philip hadn't expected that, the fierce surge of anger, though he supposed he ought to have. She'd been lied to about too much. "All right. I won't lie, I promise."

"Good." She pouted, only for a moment, and the way her lips moved made him want to kiss her.

He pushed down the hunger to taste her, to feel her skin beneath his hands. Her fingers tugged against his, and Philip jolted. "Sorry," he muttered, taking her hand once again.

At the next corner he stopped, looking around as if lost—which he admitted they were. That was the least of his problems. For a man who'd never thought much about marriage, he not only stood on a corner in the middle of the afternoon with his wife, but he very much wanted to toss out all his restraint—and his common sense—and kiss her.

On the corner, in broad daylight, and he honestly didn't care who saw. She looked up at him, her dark eyes curious and piercing as she watched him steadily. She licked her lips, parting them just the slightest.

He was rapidly losing all reason as to why he shouldn't kiss her.

"Followed?"

Philip shook himself. "No," he said, scrambling for the threads of their conversation. "Not anymore, if we were at all."

Once more she looked around, her head moving only the

slightest. Like a punch to the gut, he realized she'd learned such discretion because she'd spent years in a household that treated her like she was less than the sand on their shoes.

"I think we should return to the ship." Her voice thinned at the end of that sentence, and she took a deep breath. Clearing her throat, she met his gaze. "There are things we must discuss."

He had a feeling none of what they'd discuss involved kissing. More was the pity.

Philip nodded. "All right. Today's also a good day for your first lesson."

"Lesson?" She tilted her head, her voice rising in interest.

It twisted through him, that inquisitiveness. Perhaps a kiss wouldn't be amiss.

"Why do I think this discussion won't make me any less paranoid?" He sighed and turned back toward the main street. Sure enough, the moment he did, he spotted a dozen ship's masts in the distance. This port was a maze.

"I'm sorry to say it will only make you more so," she grumbled. Her fingers flexed against his. "I thought I'd stepped into a new life when I sneaked out of Omar's house. No more fear, no more worries. I could live as I wished, and nothing and no one could stop me. It was as if I'd stepped into the light of a new day."

Curious, Philip glanced down at her, but she resolutely looked ahead. Pausing only long enough for a glance behind them, he didn't see the man he'd sworn was following them. Maybe he was too paranoid. "How did you wish to live?"

"I hadn't much thought about it. Not in detail, at least. I thought about how things once were, though of course that could never be."

"And now?"

"Now I'd very much like to live to see the end of the month," she said grimly. When she met his gaze, Philip saw that hint of fear.

Even that first day, on the deck of *The Lady Kaya*, she hadn't shown fear. Annoyance, determination, uncertainty, yes. But not fear. The fact that she showed it now sent a shiver down his spine.

Maybe he wasn't too paranoid.

"Hutton." He nodded to the sailor on guard duty. "Where's Harry?"

"Still at the meeting with the coffee grower." Hutton jerked his head in the general direction of Darwish's offices. "Said he'd be most of the day."

"All right."

"Ma'am." Hutton gave a small bow and tugged his hat in respect.

"Do you want luncheon?" Philip paused at the top of the steps, looking over his deck. Nothing seemed amiss, but that feeling of being followed hadn't abated.

"I'd very much like a cup of coffee. The tea ceremony was lovely, and I enjoyed spending time with my aunts, but I prefer coffee."

"Go on below, then. I'm sure Laska already has a cup ready for you." Philip offered a smile, as naturally as he could, though he doubted it fooled her. "I'll join you in the day cabin in a moment."

She reached out, her fingers grazing his. "Be careful."

Her words rang in his ears, even on the open deck of his beloved ship. He looked around again, but the crew went about their duties with barely a glance in his direction. Turning back for Hutton, Philip whistled for Argus.

"Hutton." He waited while Argus bounded out from whatever shade he'd found. His black and white coat gleamed in the sunlight as he raced over. Bracing himself, Philip knelt on the deck as Argus jumped up and placed his front paws on his chest and gave him enthusiastic nips on his chin.

"All's quiet, Captain," Hutton said, just loud enough that

Philip heard him over Argus's whines. "No one suspicious, no one asking unwanted questions. Rogers spent time eavesdropping on the wharves but heard only the normal chatter."

"Aye." Philip scratched Argus beneath the chin. "I missed you, too, Argus, I promise." He looked up and met Hutton's gaze. "Mrs. Layla and I were followed from her family residence."

Hutton's face darkened, and he stiffened. For having treated Layla so callously on their first meeting, he looked ready to fight to the death for her now. "I'll double the guards," he said, stepping toward the bow. He looked back. "She's unharmed?"

"Yes."

"Good." Hutton nodded and called for a pair of sailors.

Satisfied that Hutton would oversee the guards, Philip crossed the deck for the steps. Argus raced down first, stopping not in the galley but at the open cabin door.

Layla stood in the room, a tray of coffee and fruits on the table. She'd unwrapped her headscarf, and her hair shone darkly in the shifting afternoon light. As it had on their first meeting, her beauty punched him in the gut.

Before he'd realized his intent, Philip crossed the room and cupped her face. Her lips parted again, her fingers brushing his wrists. He grasped for a witty joke, anything that might break the tension winding through him, but his mouth had gone dry, and the only word he seemed to know was her name.

"Layla."

Her fingers tightened around his wrists, and she slowly blinked, as if wrestling with her own control.

"Will you kiss me?" Her voice came out husky and low, winding around him and pulling him closer.

"If you want." His own tone was strangled, but he held himself still.

"Yes, please."

Her lips were cool against his, soft. Philip held himself in check, moving his lips gently over hers until she kissed him back. Hesitant, her hands sliding up his arms until they gripped his shoulders, she returned his kiss.

Hunger clawed through him. Her taste saturated his senses. He'd backed them up until she hit the table, and still he wanted more. Wanted all. Breathing heavily, he pulled back.

"That was very nice," she whispered, her words a warm caress over his skin. "It was my first kiss."

A possessive groan escaped him, and Philip dropped his hands. He instantly missed the feel of her skin beneath his touch. She was a temptation he knew he couldn't resist. "It won't be your last."

"Good." She nodded decisively. "I look forward to additional kisses." Her lips curled into a seductive smile that slammed through him. "And more than that." Then she gestured for the tray, as if she hadn't just stolen his breath. "First, I have a story about my parents. I'll start at the end because I don't know the beginning or the middle."

"All right." Confused, he latched the door. Argus demanded Layla's attention then, which she happily provided before he settled into his corner to watch them intently.

How had they gone from a truly exceptional kiss to talking about her parents? He could think of a dozen, a hundred, more interesting ways to spend their afternoon.

"They were murdered."

CHAPTER 10

"On the other hand," Philip muttered.

"Pardon?"

He waved away his mutterings and made a small gesture for her to continue. Layla paused, not entirely certain how to continue, and picked up a slice of mango instead. She stepped around Philip and walked toward Argus, who perked up and sniffed her offering. He was clearly an important member of the crew, and now that she and Philip were married, she felt she ought to get to know Argus as well.

Of course, she had no idea how to get to know him; she'd never been near a dog before. Or any animal. But Argus seemed friendly enough, greeting Philip like a long-lost friend and standing guard in front of her when he didn't even know her. At the very least, he deserved a slice of fruit.

Argus took the mango with a careful delicacy she hadn't expected. Not that Layla knew exactly what she'd expected, but he was so gentle, she found herself patting his head in affection.

"He's easy to like." She stood and faced Philip, who watched her with a strange look on his face. "I see why you wanted him with you while you sailed."

"Your parents were murdered?" he prompted.

Ah, yes. That. She nodded, a fresh stab of loss at the realization. "I didn't know until the night of my henna party."

He offered her the chair, but she waved it off. Nerves danced in her belly, and the packet of papers in her pocket weighed heavier than she imagined it should.

"I think you'd better start at the beginning." He sat, absently reaching for a slice of mango.

"I can't," she reminded him, a small bite in her words. Layla wasn't sure what to do with her hands. She folded them before her, but that felt too formal, so she slipped them into her pockets. That only made her feel awkward and uncomfortable, so she ended up tapping at her waist. "I only know the ending, which is what Augusta and Jomana told me the other night."

"All right." He nodded, his elbows on his knees, his hands clasped before him. His gaze, those dark eyes that drew her toward him, focused entirely on her. It rooted her to the spot, yet also enveloped her in a warmth she didn't understand. "Murdered. How?"

"Poison, they believe." She licked her lips and wished for the openness of above deck, but of course that lacked the privacy she wanted. The cabin was suddenly stuffy and far too closed in. She looked out the porthole at the afternoon sky, but the view didn't settle her nerves. "I only remember Papa's death, not that he was ill. Then Mama was sick, and we went to live with Aunt Heba. I didn't realize anything at the time; poison never occurred to me."

Should it have? She had no idea. She'd been ten years old when her father died, not at all acquainted with poisons. Not that she knew anything more about them now; Layla didn't even know what sort of poison whoever was responsible had used.

"What makes them think it was poison?" Philip didn't sound

dismissive, merely curious, and her shoulders relaxed. "A lot of upheaval has happened here in the last twenty years."

"My mother suspected it, and she shared her suspicions with Augusta and Jomana." Philip nodded, unmoving. She couldn't disagree with his statement about so much happening in Egypt, even before Napoleon's invasion. But Layla couldn't dismiss her aunts' suspicions, either. "She told them my father was acting strangely, and she suspected something was wrong."

"What proof do they have?" He still hadn't moved. He held himself so stationary, Layla thought he looked like a predator, coiled and motionless, waiting to pounce.

The thought sent a shiver down her spine, but not out of fear. Out of something else she couldn't name but desperately wanted to explore with him. She'd had that same feeling when he kissed her. She wanted more, wanted all.

Suddenly flushed, she tore her gaze from him. She extracted the packet of letters, still wrapped neatly in their bundle, and held them close.

"The other night, they showed me a list of names. Some are crossed out because of new evidence, or because they've died since."

He tilted his head, the barest movement. "Did you recognize anyone on that list?"

Layla licked her lips, clutching the papers tightly against her. How did she tell him she hadn't read anything in ten years? That the words she'd seen on that paper had sparked a vague memory but hadn't made any sense?

"I know no one anymore," she said quietly and truthfully. "I spent the last ten years locked away from the world."

"Ah." A flash of dark fury crossed Philip's face. She knew it wasn't directed at her but, rather, at Omar. The look only solidified her belief that he'd protect her no matter what. Then he cleared his throat and looked embarrassed. "Yes, I'm sorry." He offered a sheepish smile and held out a hand.

She handed him the papers and looked over his shoulder. The sun had moved, casting long shadows through the room, but there was still barely enough light to read by. Her heart pounded in anticipation, and she was both curious and dreading whatever evidence her aunts had gathered.

Argus nudged her leg, and Layla laid a hand on his head, relishing the warm press of his body.

"Let's move someplace with a little more room." Philip stood and waited while Layla rewrapped her hijab. He patiently held out his hand, which she gratefully took.

"Why do you do that?" She liked the feel of his hand wrapped around hers. It was a solid presence that kept her in the present moment.

"What?" He looked down at her, frowning.

She raised their joined hands. "Take my hand."

His grip tightened for a moment, then loosened. "Do you not like it?"

"I do," she said hurriedly, squeezing his hand in reassurance. "I'm merely curious."

He grinned as they entered the dining room, where Laska had already placed trays of rice and fish, as if he'd anticipated their arrival. Argus took up his usual place under the table between the two of them.

The windows were open, allowing the sea breeze through and lending an interesting scent: a mix of sea and wharves. At least there was light and fresh air. Layla sat, automatically scooping rice and tilapia onto her plate. She probably shouldn't indulge in this meal, not after the breakfast feast and the tea ceremony, but she couldn't resist.

"Now then." Philip piled his plate as well and untied the packet. He moved his plate to the side and spread the papers out over the table. "Let's see what they have."

Her shoulders sagged in relief as he read the names aloud. She wouldn't have to confess. He ran a finger down the list of names, glancing at her after every few, but she recognized none of them.

Once upon a time, she could read and write in two languages. That was a forgotten skill now. However, with every day, every conversation, she grew more confident in her English. Perhaps all those years of whispering in the language with her mother had truly worked.

"Why didn't your aunts continue their investigation?" he asked as he unfolded the rest of the papers.

"They were scared," she whispered, sneaking Argus a piece of fish. "Papa died, and they believed Mama and I had as well. Mostafa, Aunt Jomana's eldest, had also been poisoned." She looked up from Argus, holding Philip's gaze. "They didn't want any more of their family to die."

"I don't blame them." He shook his head and looked again at the papers. "Is this list in English because they were afraid of its discovery?"

"I don't know." She'd wondered that but hadn't thought to ask. "The papers were locked in a small box." She snuck another piece of tilapia to Argus, who took it just as gently as he had the first. "For secrecy, I presume. Afterward, after we disappeared, presumed dead, and Mostafa, no more deaths occurred."

"I'm sorry."

She nodded and stared blankly at the table, remembering the times Mostafa, Charlie, and she would look over the ledgers, studying them intently, as if they were in charge of the business and not their fathers.

Philip finished his meal, and Layla took the plates to the kitchens. She paused, annoyed with herself. *Galley*. It was called the galley, and she knew that. Shaking her head, she handed Laska the plates and smiled.

"The fish and rice were delicious. Just what I needed; thank you. You're most generous."

He offered the barest smile and nodded, silently taking the

plates. When she turned back, Kaz was already clearing off the rest of the table and offering hot cups of coffee. Layla shook her head. The cooks were far too efficient, and she marveled at the way they worked together.

Philip had spread the papers out on the table. His gaze pierced her, and she stumbled. She may not have been used to being seen, but the way he looked at her sparked a heat that had absolutely nothing to do with visibility. Pressing her lips together, she remembered their kiss, the taste of him. The need that had scraped along her nerves, urging her to take more. To take everything.

Once more, she felt like pacing the small area in hopes of expending her sudden nervous energy. Once more, there was very little room to do so.

"Anything that might show us where to look first?" She folded her hands tightly before her and looked blankly down at the papers. Her feet hurt from her new shoes, and she desperately wanted to take them off and stretch her toes. "A hint at who we might speak with first?"

"I don't know. There's a chronological list; let's start at the top."

* * *

THE LIST of names Philip read was long and extensive. Most had notes beside them—notes like "fish merchant" or "customs agent." A few did not. He wondered who they were and why there was nothing additional beside their names.

Neither Shadi nor al-Najjar were on this list.

He didn't know what that meant. Maybe her aunts didn't believe either man was involved, or maybe they simply hadn't explored that direction. Or maybe recent events colored his own perception of what happened ten years ago.

He glanced through the other papers. They didn't contain

more names, merely notes on what they'd gathered. He'd been right: the names were in chronological order, which made him wonder why the women had gathered so much evidence only to suddenly stop. Perhaps it was fear of their own safety, especially since Mostafa was also a victim.

"You were ten when this happened." He met her gaze. "Why do they think you're in danger now?"

"I think," she began slowly, "it has more to do with the lack of answers. They said they wanted me safe, that the entire town had heard of my reappearance." She looked at Argus on the floor, a soft smile curling the corners of her lips. "Aunt Augusta said perhaps fresh eyes might discover something new. Perhaps they simply want answers and hope you and I might find them."

"Which puts you in danger," he pointed out, a hint of annoyance ignited at that. They claimed they wanted her safe yet put her on the trail of a killer? It made no sense. "They think whoever it is will come after you."

She nodded, but he saw her own questions swirling behind her eyes. "I suppose that makes sense."

"In case your mother said something to you." He looked back at the lists. "Or you overheard a conversation."

"I never heard anything, but would I believe that if I killed three people to conceal what I'd done?" She sighed and moved her fingers in a small, concise wave. "Whatever it was."

"What do you remember of your mother?" He rubbed his eyes and sipped his coffee, flavored with just a hint of cardamom. Since making port, he hadn't had much sleep, and he desperately needed his wits about him, for both his trade meetings and to keep up with Layla's subtly sly cleverness.

To keep up with the mystery surrounding her, too, apparently.

"She was happy." Layla sounded surprised. She closed her eyes, a soft smile playing around her lips. "She was sick for so long. Sometimes I thought she might be better, but those days never lasted."

It sounded as if all her energy had been spent caring for her mother.

"After those first months, I don't know how long, Heba wanted repayment, or maybe Omar insisted. They asked for small things. Trips to the souk at first, since they knew I'd return for Mama. After those first months, when even I could see she wasn't getting better, I selfishly enjoyed the trips outside the house. That enjoyment didn't last, of course. I felt far too guilty afterward. Then Aunt Heba insisted I take on more chores, even when Mama felt better." Layla straightened, a look of horror on her face. "Do you think they poisoned her?"

"It's hard to say," he said slowly, sympathy coating his words. He didn't know how he'd react if their places had been switched. "How could they have poisoned your father? How would they have initially done so with your mother if she didn't live with them?"

"I don't know. I don't know a lot of things," she admitted quietly. "After she died, I tried to remember her as we were before, the three of us. The longer I remained in that house, the harder things became."

Argus had shifted until he bumped Philip's leg, and the sounds from the galley had quieted. Philip stacked the parchment together and set it aside. "What else do you remember?"

"Freedom." She shook her head, the word soft and wistful. "When I was in that house, cooking food I wasn't allowed to eat and cleaning rooms I'd never otherwise set foot in, I sometimes remembered how it used to be. When the three of us, Amirah, Evelyn, and I, would laugh as if no harm could ever befall any of us."

It'd been years ago, and Layla had suffered terribly since then. Philip wasn't surprised she didn't remember much else. He'd been defending himself in the schoolyard, where he hadn't let even the barest slight pass by. He took up every challenge, every dare.

Fingers pressed into the table, he pushed those memories away. They had no place here. No place in his life any longer. He wasn't that careless boy anymore, the one set on proving himself over and over.

"Whatever your mother and aunts suspected, they kept it well hidden." He had no idea how they were going to pick up on a trail that was a decade cold.

"I've lost years of my life living with people who were too scared to speak with me." Her voice rose slightly, her shoulders back, her gaze hard as she watched him. "After Mama died, it took my female cousins *years* before they spat more than the day's instructions at me."

He paused. "Do you miss them?"

"It's strange." She sighed, her shoulders sagging just slightly. "I've had some time to think on this, and I believe they were as scared of Omar as I was. With Nanet's betrothal, my cousin only a few years older, she had the opportunity to escape, and I think she wanted that for all of us."

"How many cousins lived with you?"

"Three. Four if you count the oldest, Amr." Her smile turned wistful. "He left in the middle of the night, snuck out of the house. We only learned he was alive months later, when he returned for a short visit. As far as I know, he hasn't returned since."

It sounded as if none of Omar's children liked him much. Once more, Philip considered himself lucky that his parents supported him. Even when he ignored their warnings about his father's problems. Especially when he fought every school bully. When he spiraled out of control.

"I want answers." She met his gaze, unflinching. "Answers about why Omar lied about me. About what really happened to my parents. I can't change the past, but I can figure out what happened that made Mama run from people who loved her into a house that didn't."

"Did she suspect them?" he asked, having wondered that since she started her story. "Do you believe that's why she left?"

Layla shuddered, as if a cold wind blew through the room. "Why would my aunts tell me then?"

"I don't know," he admitted. Unfortunately, sometimes answers weren't forthcoming. He'd wanted to ask more about her family, but something in her words stopped him. "What did you plan after leaving?" He gave a quick shake of his head. "I don't mean finding *The Clement* or seeking out el-Nebi and Bartley. What if you hadn't found them?"

She cleared her throat and offered a weak smile. "Would you believe I stole money and planned to purchase passage on the first ship leaving Damietta?"

He laughed. She looked so sheepish and yet so defiant that the laugh escaped before he even thought about stifling it. Too late now, and the sound filled the room. Even Argus woofed in response.

"I thought I'd been abandoned by everyone I loved and that was my only choice." Layla's lips tilted into a smile, and her eyes shone with mirth. He considered that a win. She offered smiles so rarely, and laughter even less. He treasured this moment.

"You planned to sail anywhere?"

Her fingers waved slightly in dismissal. Another small win— she didn't move in grand, extravagant ways. "I wasn't choosy. I wanted gone from here and thought that the first ship was my only chance." She sighed and offered him a small smile again. "Of course, I didn't realize that boarding the wrong ship would lead to quite a different life."

A life that still needed figuring out, he supposed, but that was another conversation. Still, he knew his family would love Layla, even with—despite?—the circumstances surrounding their marriage. After they teased him over it, of course.

"Aunt Heba…she didn't exactly give me money, but sometimes a coin or two made its way into my room. Nanet, after the betrothal, she, ah, *accidentally* dropped a few coins in my room. The rest I sometimes…lied about. Said the merchants charged a little more than they did. Not always, but I saved everything I could."

Layla looked uncomfortable as she folded her hands before her. Mindful of her wariness, Philip gently laid his fingers over hers. She didn't pull back. "I respect that, your…what would you call it? Resourcefulness," he decided with another grin.

"I appreciate that wording." She sounded surprised but pleased, if her smile was any indication.

Philip most certainly did not stare at her lips and remember their kiss. Control. He prided himself on that, and yet the moment he'd seen her he'd lost all control. Philip twined their fingers. He'd promised she could set the pace for their intimacy, and he intended to keep that promise.

"Let's talk about something else." She didn't move her hand or look away, which he considered another win. Three in one conversation.

"Such as?"

"You know much about me. Tell me something about you."

He grinned and stood, still holding her hand. "Perhaps we can finish our tour of the ship."

"As long as we spend time above deck; I quite enjoy the fresh air."

"As my lady commands." He gestured for her to precede him. The day was another beautifully sunny one, with a gorgeous sea breeze and not a cloud in the sky. He might never leave Damietta if every day was like this—endless blue skies, warmth that seeped into his cold English bones.

"I still never expect this view." She looked over the port, which offered a lovely vista of the wharves and not much else. "I keep thinking it should be more—" She tilted her head and frowned. "I'm not sure of the word."

"Expansive? Sprawling?" He waved toward the custom-houses and merchant buildings. Not exactly a view designed to entice, he'd give her that. "Appealing?"

"Hmm, perhaps." She turned slightly and nodded down the wharves. "Our offices were there. They still are, of course; they never moved." Her voice lowered and grew wistful. "You've been?" He nodded. "I haven't seen them in far too long."

He made a silent promise to take her there. He wasn't certain what they'd find regarding this new mystery, but escorting her someplace she'd spent much time in as a child might bring her a modicum of joy.

"I thought you went there after you left Shadi's house. No?" He couldn't remember the specifics of what she'd said that first day. So much had happened between then and now.

"I was lost," she whispered with a rueful smile. "I asked others, pretended I was a servant with a message. Eventually, someone pointed me toward *The Clement*. I asked after my uncles; I think they were there, overseeing either the loading or unloading. I never did learn what."

"Word must've spread," he agreed. "Then when Harry went out looking for them…"

"Yes." She shook her head, a small movement. "Ports are small communities in and of themselves. People talk."

"After the wars, we expanded. Conrad Shipping has offices in London and Lisbon. The ports all look the same. My eldest brother, Grayson, he oversees most of the business now. My parents pretend they've retired to their country house, but we all know they can't stay still."

Paul and Kaya Conrad spent much of their time traveling, checking in on their children, and spoiling their grandchildren. Still, they always knew which ship sailed where and with what crew.

"You speak much about your family." She turned, and the wind took the ends of her hijab, fluttering it behind her. "What about you?"

Philip stilled. He rarely talked about himself. Part of that reason was because he was an extension of his family, their businesses, their actions. But it was mostly because he didn't want a whiff of his boyhood to tarnish the man he'd become.

CHAPTER 11

"*I* like birds." Philip sighed and rolled his eyes. *Oh, very good, a surefire way to entice a woman, let alone seduce her.*

Layla giggled. "That's it? That's all there is to you? Philip Conrad, bird lover?"

He grinned back and led her along the deck. His crew gave them a respectful berth, tipping their hats at Layla and offering deferential nods and smiles. Argus had stayed below, in the captain's dining room, away from the midday sun. And no doubt because he wanted to be close to the galley and Kaz's free hand with a meal.

"Yes, that's me." That gave him pause—did he only enjoy bird-watching? Looking at the ship docked next to *The Lady Kaya*, he shrugged but waved it off with a laugh. "Captain of the seas, watcher of birds."

"All right." She nodded sagely as they crossed to the bow. "What else?"

"Ah…" He had nothing.

After that silent moment in which he scrambled for anything

more interesting than his love of birding, she sighed. "You're a difficult man to know, Philip."

"You think so?" He watched her, surprised, but she kept her gaze on the port spread out before them.

"You control your every move, keep yourself tightly under wraps." She glanced at him with a line between her brows, one he wanted to erase. He held back, that control she'd so shrewdly observed in full force. "What are you hiding?"

Glancing at her sharply, he frowned. "I'm not hiding anything."

The lie tasted sour on his tongue. Layla stepped back, pulling her hand from his. "We know very little about each other." She held up a hand, but he hadn't a retort anyway. "We've known each other for a short amount of time. Please do not lie."

He didn't move, too surprised by her observation. He'd promised he wouldn't lie. "I…" He floundered for a moment, then fell back on his usual excuse. He offered his most charming smile, and she narrowed her eyes. "I'm not fond of talking about myself."

She took another step back, taking the warmth and comfort of her closeness with her. "I see." The words were short, clipped, as if she didn't believe him but wouldn't call him out.

"I don't." He cleared his throat and watched her seriously. "I…I have very few friends; I don't make them easily. Those who offer me their friendship…well, they usually do so out of a need for something. Money or connections or investment opportunities."

Or because they still believed he was that out-of-control boy, only interested in drinking and gambling. Ready for a good time no matter who it hurt.

"You don't talk about yourself with your family?" She frowned again and remained where she stood, out of arm's reach but no more distant. "With those few you consider friends?"

"What's there for us to talk about?" His past he'd rather forget? The mistakes he'd made that affected not only his life but his parents and younger brother? No, he'd talked of those things far more than he'd ever wanted to. Those memories were always there; he couldn't ever escape them. "Business, animals, politics?" He shrugged that away.

"I do not know," she admitted with the slightest of smiles. "It's been a while since I spoke with a friend."

"If you could, what would you speak of?"

Her head tilted, that slight movement she made when she was seriously considering something. A movement he found endearing. "What do friends normally speak about? Their day? Plans for the future?"

"Yes. All of that." He and Tristan used to talk about their future plans all the time. "People they know, things that happened."

"In that case, what are your plans? Or what were they, before I stumbled on board," she amended with a slight smile and that brief wave of her fingers.

He closed off again, his iron control slamming shut around him. Layla noticed, because she frowned again and the small way she'd opened up caved in. He cursed and ran a hand down his face. He'd bullocked this all up, and he had no idea how he might climb out of the rather deep hole he'd dug.

"I—it's not that—" He sighed. When he opened his mouth to speak next, he wasn't entirely certain what might come out. "I have four siblings, two loving parents, a wide variety of aunts and uncles and cousins who were always in my life."

She waited, and when he smiled at that last part, she returned it. The iron grip tightened around his chest, constricting his lungs. He didn't know what he should share. They'd known each other for such a short time.

He'd promised his siblings he'd only share his parents' past with the woman he trusted most. The one he married. Well, he'd married a woman in desperate need of help and protection, and now he had no idea what came next and no one to discuss it with. When he'd vowed to sail alone with his second-chance crew, he hadn't realized he'd be quite so alone.

"For all that," he said in a rush, the words tumbling out, "I still managed to mess up."

"Mess up?" She repeated, confused. "I don't understand what that means."

Philip turned and leaned against the railing. Arms folded across his chest, he looked over his ship. Before he met Layla, *The Lady Kaya* was the most beautiful thing in his life. But she never stole his breath the way Layla did.

She also never asked uncomfortable questions.

"From the outside looking in," he said slowly, "I had the perfect life. Money, status, a family who loved and supported me." He pressed his fingers against his eyes. "This isn't how I envisioned my stay in Damietta." Her choked, disbelieving laugh made him smile down at her.

"This is not how I envisioned my life, either," she agreed softly. Clearing her throat, she asked in a steadier voice, "What did you expect?"

He grasped that segue with both hands. "Oh, something simple. To sail in, meet with our previous merchants, find new ones if need be." He tried to swallow the next words, but they came out anyway. Damn his tongue. "I planned on taking a trip down the Nile, to see Cairo."

"Oh?" She perked up, her face alight with the prospect. Shifting so that her back remained to the sun, she smiled up at him. "I always wanted to sail the Nile in a felucca." Philip didn't hear what she said next because the sun illuminated her from behind. Her beauty and enthusiasm for something so simple stole his breath. "Why Cairo?"

He blinked, but the spell didn't break. She drew him in, her vitality despite all she'd gone through. Her curiosity, her willingness to jump into this mystery of her parents' deaths.

"My parents met there," he reminded her. "Since I was in Egypt, I thought I should see the city."

Another partial truth, but Layla only regarded him curiously. She had an unerring ability to sense his lies and partial truths. It was disconcerting. The sun had shifted, taking away its perfect light around her. She was no less beautiful.

"I do not understand." She shook her head, frowning, but her dark eyes remained steady on his. "You say your parents loved and supported you. Does your family no longer love and support you?"

"I—no, that's not what I meant." He cleared his throat, uncertain how they'd stumbled onto this topic. "They do. Too much," he admitted and clamped his jaw tight. It didn't stop the words. They tumbled out.

In the middle of the afternoon, with the sun setting on a beautiful day and Layla watching him with a curious interest that focused entirely on him, Philip talked. He had never admitted his true reasons for what his family caringly called his "rebellion." Now, with his wife standing close, her attention only on him, he confessed.

Damn his tongue.

"My eldest sister sailed for Upper Canada on a mission to uncover thieves who were damaging our cargo. My older brother sailed for Portugal on orders from the highest echelon in government to find out if the information they'd been given about French troop movements was true. Yara, my other sister, she carried letters from London to Brighton for that same colonel, in hopes of ferreting out a spy."

"It sounds as if they had exciting adventures." Her tone suggested interest, not a burning desire to experience the same adventures.

"Exactly. When I was young, that's all I wanted, those same

adventures. But by the time I was old enough, the wars had ended and there was no place for any of that. Not in the way they'd experienced."

He spun from her, from the way she glowed in the setting sunlight. Her soft gaze was full of too much understanding. The railing bit into his hands, but he tightened his fingers around it until they ached.

"I craved those adventures so desperately that I sought out excitement wherever I could." He turned his head just enough to meet her gaze. "I even convinced my youngest brother that he should leave his fiancée and explore on his own." Bitterness coated his throat, but he forced an acidic laugh out anyway. "I wanted excitement and adventure so badly, I ruined both my life and his."

* * *

COMPASSION. That's what moved through her. Compassion and sorrow and the vaguest hint of understanding. Not at wanting adventure and excitement, but at wanting more. Layla tentatively reached for him. When he didn't pull back, she covered his hand with hers.

Beneath her touch, his rigid hold on the ship's railing flinched.

"Did your younger brother have a choice?"

"What?" The word came out harsh, hoarse.

"Did you force him?" she clarified. "Did he choose to leave, or did you force him at dagger point?"

He looked confused, his brow creased in such a vicious frown that she wondered he didn't give himself a headache. "He —it doesn't matter. He listened to me go on about glory and grandeur and what all." He made a movement, a strange half shrug that bent his elbows, but his hands hadn't loosened from the railing.

"He still made his own choice. Just as you did."

Philip snorted. His hands ripped from the railing and balled up at his sides. "You don't understand. I was wild. Took him down with me. He was so much smarter than I was. Than I am. He could've gone on to university. But no, he listened to me."

He only made partial sense, and she knew there was so much he didn't tell her. She let that float away in the current. For now. He knew so much about her life. But then, she'd dropped in on him, quite unexpectedly, all her troubles out in the open. She had needed his help. Still did; she had no idea where they might begin searching for answers.

If there was one thing that she remembered from her parents' marriage, it was that they were together. They'd stood together in the face of censure and gossip at the scandalous marriage between an Egyptian widow and an English merchant. Even, it seemed, through poisonous betrayal.

"Why don't we return to the cabin?" She wrapped his clenched fist in both of her hands. "I don't think you want your crew to overhear this."

He snorted, a harsh sound, and when he looked at her again, his eyes were wild and angry. "They know." He kept his voice low. "Everyone knows. They all know about my drunken, brawling past. Where I picked fights with anyone who'd fight me." He laughed bitterly. "My second-chance crew."

Surprised but undeterred, she tugged him away from the poop deck, down the short flight of steps, and toward the main staircase that took them belowdecks. The crew seemed to have scattered, either because they'd overheard or thought they were having a couple's argument. Either way, the path remained clear, with no eavesdroppers in sight.

Once they were in the day cabin, with Argus lying comfortably in his favorite corner, Layla poured a glass of carob juice and set it on the table. Neither of them touched it. The last of the afternoon's sunlight lit the room, and in the strained silence, she heard the call of the gulls Philip loved so much.

"I wasn't going to tell you all that," Philip admitted. He sounded exhausted but not angry. He tossed his hat onto the table, and the sunlight glinted off his hair, highlighting striking shades of red in the strands. "I hadn't planned on admitting any of it."

Ever, it seemed, though Layla supposed she'd have learned of it sooner or later. Whispers had a way of carrying on the wind. It wouldn't have changed her mind about marrying him, her desperation aside. His confession had eased some of her confusion over his earlier comments. How he knew the sort of man Omar was, how quickly he'd stepped into confrontation with both Omar and al-Najjar.

"Why did you?" The room was close, stuffy in the late afternoon heat. Layla didn't move but stood before him and held his gaze. This was her first step toward a marriage based on togetherness, and she wouldn't back down.

He collapsed into the chair, his elbows once more on his knees as he examined his hands so closely she wanted to ask if they offered any answers. "The words just came out. So much for my control," he added bitterly.

"That's why." It suddenly made sense, and she hesitantly reached for him. Beneath her touch, his shoulder remained rigid, but he didn't jerk back. "That's why you hold yourself so still."

"Still" wasn't the right word, but she didn't have the words to describe what she saw. The way he watched the world, as if standing on the outside looking in.

"I suppose, if I'm confessing..." He sighed and looked up at the ceiling before meeting her gaze. "I promised I'd never reveal this except to the person I trust the most."

She blinked. "You don't have to tell me." The words rushed

out. She wasn't sure she was ready to hear whatever momentous confession he planned.

"Oh, there's more, but this—it's important." His lips ticked up, and she thought he might smile, but instead he watched her seriously. "My father has problems with alcohol. We don't drink in our family because he can't control it. I knew this, knew it might be a problem, but I was so determined to find those adventures, that excitement, I didn't care."

Layla crouched before him, not sure what made her move. Compassion, perhaps. His understanding about his need for control. "All right." She doubted that was the right thing to say, but she didn't understand, and saying she did would be false.

"In school, I gambled and drank and found fights. It's why I have no friends." He paused and shook his head. "Well, Harry. I consider Harry my friend, my only one."

"He seems very nice," she ventured. "Loyal."

"I suspect it's because he understands. That he has things in his past he wishes would remain buried." Philip stood, bringing her up with him. His hands were gentle and warm on her shoulders. "The men I once considered friends were like me—drinking, gambling, finding fights wherever they could. When I cut them from my life, it wasn't any easier to find peace, but at least they weren't constantly there, badgering me to have fun."

"Is that fun? Fighting others, drinking, and wagering your money?"

His laugh, though small and nearly silent, was as real as the smile on his face. His hands slipped up her throat to cup her cheeks. "Not as much in hindsight as it was in the moment."

She wrapped her hands around his wrists and smiled. "Thank you for telling me. I won't share your confidence with anyone." She tilted her head, and her gaze slid to Argus. "Well, perhaps with Argus, though he seems to have slept through everything."

Philip's laugh was louder and fuller than it had been a moment ago. "Oh, he keeps all my secrets."

Argus raised his head and offered a soft woof, his tail thumping against the floor.

"I shall as well," she promised.

His lips were cool as they pressed against her forehead. "I appreciate that. More than I think you know. It's hard when everyone knows what you've done and judges you on only that. Not on the man you've become."

"It can't have been easy." Now probably wasn't the time, but Layla wanted his lips on hers, not on her forehead. Licking her lips, she pushed aside the remembered taste of his kiss. "If ports are their own communities, so are schools."

Not that she knew anything about school, but she knew about gossip. Knew how quickly it traveled, even in her insular life. The last ten days had proved that.

"And counties." Philip sighed and dropped his hands. She instantly missed his touch. "Word spreads fast; the world is not as large as people believe, I don't think."

"You said the crew knew about your past. Is that because of others' talk?"

"Partly. Those who didn't know soon learned—gossip never stays quiet." He scowled, offering her the glass of carob juice she'd poured. Then he paused and shook his head, a strange sort of smile on his lips. "They're my second-chance crew because this is my second chance. But it's also theirs. Everyone needs to eat. I worked hard to earn their trust, proved I knew what I was doing. Not only as captain, but that I knew all the workings of the ship."

"And that you could control yourself." She sipped the juice she didn't want as another curiosity about him slotted into place.

"Exactly." He poured his own glass and raised it in salute. His shoulders had lost some of their tension, and his smile wasn't so cynical. "No ridiculous bets on which ship would arrive in port first. No drunken sailing nor racing along the inlets."

"They clearly trust you." She closed her eyes, and though it was a little murky, given her exhaustion and the stress of that day, she remembered their first encounter. "When I boarded, the sailor who held me listened immediately when you ordered him not to touch me."

"Hutton should've known better; he's sailed this route for years." Philip scowled again, and she was sorry to have caused that. "He shouldn't touch any woman like that, let alone in a different country."

"True," she allowed. Hutton treated her with deference now. Was that only because of her marriage? "However, when you ordered him to release me, he did so without hesitation or question. I think that shows more about how he views you than what he thought of me."

He growled something she didn't understand. In one gulp, he finished his juice and set the cup back on the table. "I'm tired of talking about myself."

She finished her juice as well and set her cup beside his. "And I'm tired of talking about myself. What shall we speak of then?"

For a moment he looked lost for a topic, but then he grinned, a wide smile with just a hint of sinful wickedness. It sent shivers down her spine. Layla forcibly held herself back so as not to pull him against her and kiss him.

"Fancy a bit of bird-watching?"

Laughing, she slipped her hand through the crook of his elbow and allowed him to lead her once more above deck, Argus at her side. "Perhaps my first khanjar lesson?"

"We'll start slow," he promised.

CHAPTER 12

$\mathscr{L}$ayla washed slowly the next morning, even as her mind raced over the events of the previous day. Though Philip had left early, just after sunrise, Argus remained to keep her company. She appreciated the serene moment; she'd had so few of them.

"I'm not used to such a slow, quiet morning," she told her companion, who watched her patiently from beside the door—the locked door, for which she was also grateful, though she doubted any of the crew would force their way in. "By now there was breakfast and cleaning and mending. A visit to the souk for food."

She sighed and sat back on the bed. Argus padded over and laid his head on her lap, watching her with large, dark eyes. It might've only been a few days, but she felt more comfortable around him than she would've thought. When she ran a hand over his head and down his back, she found serenity in that touch.

She no longer wondered why Philip had brought Argus. The dog's companionship warmed her, made her feel a sense of safety she hadn't before.

"How do you spend your days? Pacing the ship?" He licked her wrist, startling her. "Is that a good sign?" She had no idea. "Come on, then. Want to pace the ship with me? We'll find breakfast, perhaps?"

Argus perked up at the mention of food, not that she blamed him. She liked to eat her fill as well.

Before he left, Philip had promised her she'd be safe. He and Harry wouldn't be long; they were only visiting one merchant today. Someone new who had reached out, he said. No one on their list of suspects, but she wondered nonetheless. Perhaps they needed to expand their list, though she'd no idea how.

Her suspicions weighed on her, but she straightened beneath their heaviness. She'd survived. She'd survived, and she wouldn't let anything take away her chance at happiness and freedom now. Still, she stared up at the opening that led above deck as if that faceless assassin might appear.

Laska and Kaz were there if she needed them. Laska seemed to have kept an eye out for her, because once she entered, he brought out a plate. "Coffee?"

"Please." She was slightly uncomfortable, but she pushed that aside. She had plans for her life that didn't include hiding away from the world. "You're very kind," she added.

Laska watched her for a moment, and she didn't think he was going to respond. "I know what it's like, running away."

Startled, she set down her glass of carob juice, her head tilted. "I'm sorry." She didn't wish to pry, and she knew only what Philip had told her, but she was curious. "It's not easy, starting over. I didn't have a plan when I left."

"Sometimes," he said slowly, his words carefully chosen, "fate has a way of working out."

Fate. Evelyn had also said something about that during her henna party. "Do you believe in fate?"

Laska looked over his shoulder. Kaz exited the galley with a single cup of coffee on a tray. "I didn't. I used to believe we made our own way." He turned back toward her. "Then I was forced to flee my homeland with only the clothes on my back and my loyalty to a man who promised us safety. We fought for everything."

She thanked Kaz, who watched Laska for a long, quiet moment before disappearing into the galley. Part of her dreaded the answer, but she asked anyway. "Did he deliver on that promise?"

"Oh, aye. Percy didn't lie. It took a bit, but we sailed from Riga to Amsterdam and back again, outrunning the Russians, outwitting the French, and taking everyone's gold." He flashed a smile, which lit his entire face and made him look years younger. "Percy retired with his new wife, but land doesn't suit me. So, I joined Captain Philip." He paused, then said carefully, "He also keeps his promises."

Questions burned her tongue, but Layla swallowed them down. Questions about Laska, Kaz, and, yes, of course Philip. However, she wouldn't betray Philip's trust. It had been less than a full day since he confided in her. And she wouldn't pry into Laska's life any more than what he'd already shared.

"I'm not sure we'll sail that far," she admitted, though she only had a vague notion of the places Laska spoke of. It was as if she'd once known where they were, but the memories had faded along with so many others. "But I do look forward to seeing what fate has laid out for me." She picked up her coffee cup. "I think so far, it's been very good to me."

"Things have a way of working out." He nodded and turned, then almost immediately turned back. "He's very lucky."

"He is?" she asked before she could stop herself. "I think I am."

That smile flashed over his face, and he shook his head. "He needed you."

With that, Laska left her alone, with only Argus and her whirling thoughts for company.

As she finished her breakfast, Layla planned out her day. When Philip returned, they planned to look over her aunts' notes and retrace their steps. She wanted to check in with Augusta and Jomana, let both women know how she was faring with this mystery—though perhaps she wouldn't divulge the entire truth. Perhaps none of the truth, given she'd gotten nowhere with the investigation.

She sighed. Perhaps she'd wait another day for that visit.

Her aunts thought she and Philip could solve this mystery within days when they couldn't in years. They had placed so much faith in Layla, it terrified her.

Plus, Layla didn't want them to learn she couldn't read. Shame burned through her. But if there'd been any books or newspapers in Omar's house, he certainly hadn't left them where she could see them.

Aunt Heba.

Layla closed her eyes and pushed the mostly empty plate away from her. She should call on her aunt, she knew that. But dread filled her at the idea of it. The very thought of returning, of seeing that house and stepping back into those memories, stole the air from her lungs.

Kaz's laughter rang from the galley, easing her worries. She wasn't alone.

Argus bumped her knee, and she looked down at his hopeful eyes. Snagging the last of her egg, she offered it to him as she breathed through the utterly terrifying thought of returning to the house where she'd known only loneliness and heartache.

Perhaps she'd ask Evelyn to join her. Perhaps she'd ask all her cousins in a reminder that she wasn't alone.

"Come on, Argus." She stood and called out a thanks into the galley. "Let's practice the movements Philip showed me last night."

Not on deck, no matter how she longed for the open skies and sunlight. Being up there with Philip was one thing, but being there alone wasn't something she felt comfortable with. Not yet. However, if this was to be her life, sailing with her husband to various ports around the world, she'd need to get comfortable.

One step at a time. And today's step was practicing the forms she'd learned last night.

* * *

PHILIP BOARDED his ship not expecting any of what greeted him. Argus bounded down from the poop deck, barking enthusiastically and wagging his tail. All right, that he expected. But Layla also walked down, albeit more slowly, from where she'd been overlooking the sea. That surprised him.

"Saied Harry." She nodded at Harry, who offered a small bow in return. "Philip." Her smile rivaled the sun.

"I'll see to the, ah…" Harry jerked his head and disappeared. Philip didn't watch him leave.

"Did you have a productive meeting with your merchant?" He nodded, scrambling for words. "Did this mysterious new merchant say anything about my father?" Her lips curled slightly, and any thought he'd managed to snag disappeared.

"Only that he knew of him," Philip admitted. "Abdel Saeed, we've worked with him before." There was someone else, too, but he couldn't remember the man's name right then; he'd been English. It didn't matter. Not when he faced a beaming, beautiful Layla. "I didn't expect you on deck."

She looked startled, and that wonderful smile dimmed. "Did you not wish me here? It was a lovely morning and—"

"No!" Philip cursed his carelessness. He wanted to smack himself. "I only meant—" He didn't know what he meant. "You being here surprised me." He stepped closer, one hand on Argus's head in greeting and the other reaching for her hand.

"In a good way. I'm...well, I'm not used to being greeted like this."

Her smile returned, and desire clawed through him. Philip clenched his jaw, fighting for that control he so prided himself on. His heart did a strange flip, beating harder in his chest. As if beating against that control.

"I'm glad." She raised his hand, turning it slightly so that her own could slip around his elbow. "Are you hungry? Laska promised a lavish luncheon, though I am waiting on word from Aunt Jomana."

"Oh?" He wasn't hungry. Laska had gone out of his way to provide generous meals all the time now that Layla lived on board. However, Philip wasn't going to turn down spending time with her. He'd missed her while he and Harry were making new contacts. "What about your aunt?"

"I should pay Aunt Heba a visit." Layla waited until he joined her at the base of the stairs, Argus faithfully following his own stomach toward the galley. "I'm not sure what might happen now, but I feel obligated to at least see her."

"You have no obligation whatsoever," he growled. She made a deliciously enticing squeak in the back of her throat. He grappled for control, so as not to push her against the wall and kiss her senseless. Making a mental note about that lovely little sound, he schooled his features and evened out his voice. "From what you've said, the only kind thing she ever did was leave you money so one day you might leave."

"That's true," Layla said slowly, a strange look on her face that quickly disappeared. She licked her lips, and Philip forgot why he wasn't kissing her. "The household was hard. Everything there was. The beds were hard, the food a day old because it was cheaper. Even the clothing was uncomfortable."

"All the more reason never to return." He stopped as Kaz brought out a tray of fish and rice. "On the other hand," he said slowly, meeting her gaze in the dim light of the dining room.

"Exactly." She nodded decisively. She did have a way of reading his mind, which should've disconcerted Philip more than it did. "I have questions."

"Are your aunts joining you?" He slipped a piece of fish to Argus, though Philip was confident the dog had already eaten. At least twice since he'd left hours earlier.

"I hope so, though there is—what's the saying? No lost love between them."

"No love lost." He chuckled, reaching across the table and taking her hand. "You've decided to pay your respects about her husband's death in order to interrogate her about your mother? I do enjoy the way your mind works."

She looked surprised, that bright smile returning. "I shall take that as a compliment." She hesitated, then added, "Though I'm uncertain what 'interrogate' means."

He'd forgotten that she'd lived in near isolation for ten years and probably hadn't any chance to expand her English. "Questioning her, *al-tahqiq*…maybe *estegwab*."

"Who taught you Egyptian?" She didn't look suspicious, as she had early in their relationship, merely curious. "You speak very well for a man who's only here to foster trade."

Once more he paused, and once more he offered a half truth. He'd already confessed so much about his youth; he didn't feel up to confessing the rest of his family's secrets. Those, he would keep close to his heart until he'd had more than a few days with Layla.

"My mother. When she lived here, she learned the language." Which was completely true. In a way.

"My mother also taught me the language." She gave him a soft smile. Not the bright grin of earlier, but one that bespoke of shared intimacies. "Though she could speak English well, it wasn't until she married my father that she could read and write it." Layla sighed, a wistful sound that wound around him and tugged at something deep inside. "My father taught me English. Some French, too, though I'm afraid I've lost all that."

"I'm sorry." He squeezed her hand. He'd taken to touching her often, which he couldn't say he minded. But neither could he say where the impulse came from. He normally didn't touch others. "I know some French, though I studied Portuguese more and am fluent in that."

She turned her hand over, twining her fingers with his. Philip wondered how so simple a touch could make him want to toss all control to the winds, pull her onto his lap, and kiss her senseless. "Why Portuguese? Oh, you have offices in Portugal, yes?"

"Grayson." The word came out strangled. He finished his carob juice, but it didn't clear his throat. "His wife is Portuguese." The entire port's worth of carob wouldn't be enough to quench his thirst. Not with the way Layla watched him. "That's why we have offices in Lisbon. After the war, they returned." He sighed, frowning. "There isn't much left, I'm afraid. The war destroyed so much of the country."

"I'm sorry for her," she whispered. "War is terrible for everyone but those who want it."

"Yes," he agreed, remembering all those times he'd wanted to be a part of war, if only to prove himself. The thrill of chasing spies, of defeating the French. How naïve he'd been. "We'll start slow," he said instead. "Perhaps you remember more French than you think."

"I'd like that." She tilted her head but didn't remove her hand from his. "I—" She hesitated, shaking her head. "I practiced the movements you showed me."

"Good." He most definitely did not envision how she'd moved last night. Not at all. The way her arms stretched outward, long and elegant—no, that image was definitely not burned into his brain. "We'll stretch those muscles again." He looked around for more juice, anything to ease his dry throat.

As if that would erase the images of her body moving in slow, smooth stretches. He doubted anything would.

"Mrs. Layla," Hutton called from the doorway, bowing respectfully. "I'm sorry to disturb you, but your aunt is here."

"Oh, thank you." Layla stood, taking his hand with her. She laughed, a far lighter sound than Philip expected, but she didn't immediately release him. "Are you joining us? Or have you more business?" Another pause, and he wondered what she really wanted to ask. "Additional meetings?"

"You meet with your aunt." He stood as well, kissing the backs of her fingers. "I'll be here when you finish."

Layla paused, her eyes widening slightly. Her fingers tightened around his, and her lips parted. He leaned over, helpless in the midst of such temptation. So much for his control.

Her lips were warm and soft beneath his. The kiss was quick, no more than a press against hers. When he pulled back, her breath caught.

"Philip."

A growl caught in his throat. He didn't want to let her go, but now was hardly the time. No matter how his arousal heated his blood and stirred his cock.

"I'll—" He cleared his throat, but once again it was a hopeless endeavor. "I'll escort you to your aunt's house if that's what you want."

She nodded, her lips still parted. "All right. If you have no more meetings, we'll look over the papers then?"

"Yes, see what they found and where might be best to begin."

He rounded the table, ignoring Hutton, who had taken up guard outside the door, where Sayedah el-Nebi waited patiently. Her lips lifted in a knowing smile, and for the first time in years Philip felt a blush heat his cheeks.

"Sayedah." He nodded respectfully at Layla's aunt, though he had a feeling she saw his blush—and knew the reason for it.

"Captain." Jomana glanced at Hutton, who took the hint and returned to his duties. "Have you learned anything new?"

"That's what I wanted to speak with you about, Auntie." Layla gestured back toward the room, where the sunlight shone so brightly through the glass, Philip felt nothing could hide there. "I feel I should call on Aunt Heba."

Philip stayed at the doorway, giving them additional privacy. Layla met his gaze and smiled. She looked relaxed, at ease. Nothing at all like the woman who first climbed on board his ship. Who'd sat at that very table at stiff attention, as if a drill sergeant were making his way down the row, whip in hand.

"I have some questions for her, about Mama and why we lived there."

He turned, leaving them to their discussion. Argus stayed, though Philip couldn't say if he planned to guard Layla or wished to remain close to the food. Though he no longer gambled, Philip bet it was both.

"Harry!" He grinned at his friend, who turned from the railing overlooking the sea. "Any word from our friendly wool merchant?" His voice darkened, and he felt his control slip again. Not in the way it did around Layla. In the dangerous way it did before he'd tamped it into obedience years ago.

"No, nor his sons." Harry shook his head, his blue eyes gleaming like gemstones. "I don't like that."

"Keep an ear open," Philip said. "He doesn't strike me as the sort to allow a slight to pass by." Unless al-Najjar was behind Shadi's death. Or was that what connected Harry Braithwaite to Mariam Braithwaite to Omar? A direct link, but was it the right one?

"I'll have a couple of the men who know the port wander around. They know the people, the language, the customs." He gestured, and two men hurried over immediately.

Harry frowned. "Where's Watkins?"

"Starboard."

Harry nodded, a short, curt gesture, and went to find Watkins. Philip met both the sailors' gazes. He knew them; they'd been with Conrad Shipping since he cleaned himself up, took a true interest in the business, and stopped visiting London's gambling hells. They were two of the first on board *The Lady Kaya* to welcome him.

"I want to know of anything anyone says about my wife," he told them. The words came out clipped and angry, but there was nothing he could do about that.

"Someone's talking about her?" Lange asked, his face darkening.

"I want to know if anyone does," he corrected. "And if anyone follows her as she visits her family in Damietta."

"Aye, Cap." Pitt said, rolling his impressive shoulders. "We'll find out. You want us to act as guards when she's out and about?"

"I'll be with her," Philip said before he'd thought it through. Layla did have a way of making him forget years of training. He found he jumped in with both feet whenever danger closed in around her. "I want you two scattered behind. Just in case someone does follow us."

The men nodded, and when Watkins joined them, the three went off, talking quietly between themselves.

With the mystery about her parents' deaths now following her, Philip didn't want any more danger looming over her. Whoever poisoned her parents might also be after her. The years between the two incidents aside, the person responsible might tie up loose ends. If it were him, he would. He'd make everything—and everyone—neatly disappear.

Philip had promised he'd keep her safe. He intended to see that promise through, no matter what.

CHAPTER 13

*L*ayla followed the slow, smooth movements Philip showed her. Unfortunately, his graceful transfer between each position had not transferred to her.

"No, sweeping."

Layla stopped, contemplating her sloppy movements. In all fairness, this was only her second lesson. And her body ached. Oh, did she ache. She could barely lift her arms, and keeping her hips straight moved them in a way she was wholly unused to.

"Try again; move only your hips."

"They hurt," she grumbled. "As do my arms."

He nodded. She might have noted a hint of sympathy, but that control he wrapped tight around himself hadn't cracked. "Here."

Then he stepped behind her, his hands on her hips. Layla forgot about her aching muscles, why they were practicing to begin with, and the reason they'd migrated from his cabin to the larger storage hold.

Philip's hard body pressed close. All the breath rushed out of her, and Layla found herself leaning backward into the hard expanse of his chest. Into the warmth that surrounded her. The comfort in his embrace.

"Your hips control your movements." His hands turned her hips one way, then the other and back again. She jerked, stiffening away from his hard, warm chest. "Layla," he sighed, his warm breath fluttering over her cheek. "You have to loosen your hips. They're too rigid."

With his body against hers, his chest pressed tight against her back, his hand slipping around her belly, she had no idea what his words meant. Blood rushed through her ears. She turned her head, just slightly, and met his gaze.

His dark eyes held hers, and in the dancing shadows of the storage hold, she swore they sparked with heat. A heat that threatened to burn her. Something within Layla snapped. She wanted that. With everything in her, she wanted it. Wanted the flames to consume her, wanted his control broken into shards at her feet.

"Philip." Her voice sounded foreign as it echoed around them. Low and husky and enticing.

"You tempt me like nothing else." The words ripped from him, low and harsh. "I want—"

He broke off and pulled back. Not physically—his hand actually tightened around her—but she felt the walls of his control close in around him.

"What do you want?" She surprised herself with her boldness, but the heat in his gaze had scattered her own control into the winds.

His jaw actually tightened, and she feared he'd crack a bone. Layla turned in his arms, placing her hands on his chest. Her heart raced, and beneath her touch she felt his own heart beat wildly. A small part of her liked that it wasn't only she who felt so wild and untamed, wanted to take what she wanted without fully understanding herself.

"I want you to kiss me." Her words echoed loudly in the hold, though she had only just managed to push them out.

Philip made a strangled sound and pulled her closer against him, his eyes so focused on her she felt both beautiful and unrestrained. He was her husband, after all. And she desperately wanted his kiss. His beautiful mouth on hers.

"You are a temptation, Layla." His fingers brushed over her cheek, the roughness of his calloused fingertips sending shivers down her spine.

She almost laughed and called *him* the temptation. The admission danced on her tongue, her hunger heating her blood and clawing low in her belly. She didn't have the words, or perhaps the courage. Instead, she slid her hand up his chest, her fingers brushing the side of his throat.

Philip shuddered at her touch, that low growl once more breaking free. That sound moved deep inside her. Lips parted, fingers gliding along the back of his neck, Layla leaped.

His mouth was hard on hers, taking everything and demanding more. She willingly gave it all, everything in her. He tasted of coffee and that elusive bit of him she so craved. In one quick move, he lifted her, walking backward until he hit a barrel.

She shifted, cupping the back of his head. A faint voice inside her cheered with joy—his hair truly was as soft as it looked, and she could touch it as much as she wanted. Tangling her fingers in his curls, she pulled him closer as he sat on the barrel and lifted her onto his lap.

"Layla." He panted the word against her throat, his hands sliding over her hips. "What do you want?"

She hadn't the words. Honestly, her only coherent thought was that she never wanted the kiss to end. "You. All of you. All of this," she breathed. "I don't want it to ever stop."

His hand tangled in her hair, twisting through her braids and holding her motionless against him. His mouth devoured her, and still she wanted more. Her hips moved over his, seeking to fulfill that indefinable need. She knew what happened between a man and woman, but she'd never felt any such need herself. Until Philip entered her life.

He hummed against her skin, tugging her head back as he tasted down her throat. He nipped gently at the spot between her neck and shoulder, and she gasped as a bolt of lightning shot through her.

In the next breath, he pulled back. Just as suddenly as he'd lifted her, he set her on her feet and stood out of arm's reach.

Layla blinked at him, confused. "What—?" Breathing hard, she tried to steady herself, but her knees wobbled, and she wasn't certain they'd hold her upright.

"Temptation," he repeated, stepping toward the ladder. "A beautiful, vibrant temptation." He shook his head, and she wondered if he needed to shake some sense into himself, as she felt that same need. "I'll send one of the men down with a hay bale."

With that he climbed upward, never once looking back. Hay bale? Whatever for? Before Layla could decide whether to follow him above deck or stay here and sort through what had happened, Hutton tossed down said hay bale, as if he'd been waiting for word to do just that.

"Mrs. Layla." He nodded in greeting from the top of the cargo hold right before he climbed down.

"What's that for?" she managed, not sure what had happened in the last few moments.

"For practice," he grunted, shifting it into a corner. "Cap said you wanted to practice throwing your dagger."

Layla stared at him and slowly nodded. "Yes." She cleared her throat and prayed he hadn't heard the still-breathless quality of the sound. "Thank you."

He nodded, offered a quick bow, and disappeared back

topside. She turned, stared at the hay bale, reached for the khanjar Philip had gifted her two nights prior, and threw it. She hadn't the form nor the strength, and it clattered onto the floor. Undeterred, Layla crossed the hold, picked the dagger up, and tried again.

This wasn't how she'd envisioned expending the turbulent energy still sparking through her veins. However, given she had no alternative, it'd do.

That was how Evelyn found her sometime later. Sweaty, sore, and aggravated at herself, Philip, and the khanjar, she sat on the bale as her cousin climbed down the ladder.

"What are you doing here?" Evelyn asked, peering curiously at Layla in the faint light from the sun overhead. "And why is there a stack of hay?"

Layla managed to lift her weak right arm, her fingers still gripped tightly around the khanjar's hilt. "Practicing."

Evelyn's eyebrows shot upward, and Layla's arm dropped. She might never move her arms again. "Practicing for what?"

"Philip's mother taught his sisters how to defend themselves." She sighed. She desperately wanted a drink but had no energy for the climb upward. "I wanted to learn."

That perked Evelyn right up, and she crossed to the hay bale. "Can you show me?"

"I cannot, at present, lift my arms." Layla sighed but smiled at Evelyn's laugh. She'd expended most of her anger at Philip, though she still didn't understand the man. "I did, however, manage several hits on the hay where the khanjar embedded itself."

"I'm impressed." Evelyn laughed but studied her seriously. "Mama told me you wish to visit Heba." Layla offered a single nod. "Are you certain that's wise?"

"I have questions," she said cautiously. She didn't know how much Evelyn knew of her parents, if she knew anything.

"About why Aunt Mariam stayed there for years and not

with us?" Evelyn stood and offered her a hand. "I'd have questions, too."

Layla kept her agreement tight against her heart. Part of her knew she could trust Evelyn, that she could trust all her family. However, years of fending for herself had made her wary. She trusted Philip more than she thought wise, though it felt right.

Still, it lingered. The fear of her family betraying her parents. But why would they? And why had her aunts shared with her the mystery surrounding her parents' deaths?

"What brings you here?" Layla sighed and eyed the ladder, still uncertain that her arms had the strength to climb up. "Not that I'm unhappy you visited."

"I brought your jewelry. I know it's unorthodox, doing it this way, but..." Layla waved away Evelyn's apology. Everything about her marriage was unorthodox. "I have a favor," Evelyn admitted, eyeing her critically. "Can you climb up?"

She didn't have much of a choice if she wanted a drink. Or to ever see the light of day again. That hay bale did not look comfortable to sleep on. Slipping the khanjar in her pocket, Layla lifted her arms. Only the vaguest whimper escaped her. "If I fall, don't tell anyone."

"I promise," Evelyn said seriously. "But I'm not sure I can catch you."

"Leave me in a puddle on the floor, I'll be fine." Layla hauled herself up the first rung and seriously debated staying in the cargo hold forever. She didn't need anything to drink. Or fresh air. Or sunlight. And the hay was probably more comfortable than her bed at Heba's house.

No, no. Definitely not. She didn't want anyone to know of her pain. Or that she'd probably overdone her practicing because she was so angry with Philip.

"What's your favor?" Another rung, then another, and the afternoon sky grew closer.

"When you and Saied Conrad leave, I'd like to join you."

* * *

"WHAT'S WRONG, ARGUS, HMM?" Philip crouched by the dog, who waited outside the cabin door.

Argus's tail thumped excitedly, and he jumped up, licking Philip's face in greeting. At least someone was happy to see him.

"What are you doing out here?" Philip eyed the closed door, behind which his crew assured him that Layla had entertained her cousin for most of the day. Argus whined and bumped against the door, which of course didn't budge.

"Layla?" He unlocked the door and stepped in. Argus didn't follow. "What is that smell?"

He stopped dead and looked on in confusion as Evelyn changed out bandages on Layla's arms, the pungent scent of... *something* heavy in the air.

"What happened?" He glared at Evelyn, who ignored him. Crossing the room in quick strides, he crouched beside the bed, where Layla lay on her stomach, naked from the waist up, long strips of cloth covering her arms. Terror squeezed his heart. "What happened?" he demanded in a harsh voice.

"It's nothing," Layla assured him, head turned so she met his gaze. "I overused my arms, and Evelyn is merely covering the muscles with a cold cloth."

He nodded dumbly and stared at her. She didn't seem otherwise harmed, but it took a moment before his heart resumed its normal beat. It was just some sore muscles. Philip sank back, leaning on his heels and reordering his thoughts. He turned and stared at Argus, who sat just outside the door.

"Overused your muscles," he repeated, feeling foolish for doing so.

He vaguely heard Evelyn leave, closing the door behind her. Argus decided to stay outside.

Reaching for Layla's hand, Philip brushed his thumb over her knuckles. She didn't move but stayed still under the cold cloths steeped in that god-awful scent. She didn't pull away from his touch.

Considering Philip had thought she'd lay into him, he thought that a very good sign.

"What happened?" he asked for the third time. At least his voice wasn't quite so loud and demanding now. "How did you hurt yourself?"

"I didn't hurt myself," she said stiffly. "I'm simply not used to throwing a dagger at a bale of hay."

His eyebrows shot up. How many times had she done so? If she'd thrown her dagger as many times as he'd gone round-for-round against the local pugilist this afternoon, he understood.

"I see."

"I'm certain you do not," she retorted.

Unfortunately, he did understand. All too well. They had many things in common. Overextending themselves was yet another one. "What's that smell?" he asked.

"Local herbs known to ease muscle aches." She held his gaze, cool and defiant. "If you don't mind, please call Evelyn. I'd like to dress."

"Yes, of course," he said. It wasn't what he planned. *I'll help you dress* lay on the tip of his tongue, and Philip thought he might not hold back. For one moment, he envisioned it all too easily.

The beautiful expanse of her back lay bare, tempting him. He sat close enough he could reach out and touch her, trace his fingers down her spine, kiss along her shoulder.

Philip abruptly stood. "I'll call her in."

He opened the door and nearly tripped over Argus. Scratching the poor dog behind the ears, he nodded at Evelyn, who waited patiently just outside the room. She didn't speak to him as she entered. Not that Philip had any idea what they might converse about.

He rubbed his eyes and hoped it would ease his headache. It

did not. Maybe Layla had local herbs for that, though, given their exchange, he doubted she'd willingly share. He didn't blame her.

"I thought you were apologizing." Harry ambled down the corridor, a bowl of fruit in his hand.

Philip narrowed his eyes. "What makes you say that?"

Snorting, Harry stopped and offered Argus a piece of mango. "You've been in a fine temper all day, snarling at Darwish and Bingham, even snapping at me." He looked up, unperturbed. "Spending all afternoon in the boxing club." Harry returned his attention to Argus. "One more, boy. Mrs. Layla said you can't have too much."

What was this about Layla and Argus?

"And that requires an apology?"

Philip had planned to apologize, but, like so much of his life, his apology hadn't gone as planned. When he'd walked into their cabin, he hadn't expected a half-naked Layla lying on their bed. Not that they shared the bed. No, he slept in the chair, which he didn't mind. Except when he woke in the middle of the night, his cock hard, listening to Layla's soft breathing.

"Whatever you did or said seems to." Harry looked up with another frown. He'd frowned a lot today.

Philip was absolutely not going to tell his friend that he'd lost control and kissed Layla to within an inch of her life. That he'd been so tempted by her he'd forgotten himself in the cargo hold of his ship.

Instead, he growled, "Mind your business," and stalked off.

"It's your marriage," he heard Harry call behind him.

Philip ignored that. He didn't know where he was headed, but his pace ate the distance down the hallway. Annoyed, he climbed lower into the cargo hold—a mistake, that. The hay bale Hutton had found for Layla's practice still sat there, looking far worse for wear than he'd expected.

"How many times did she throw the khanjar?" he wondered aloud. Of course, the echo offered no answer.

Sitting on the bale, he practiced the breathing techniques that had helped him work through the anger and arrogance of his younger years. It'd been a while since he needed to breathe like this. Eyes closed, he stood and worked through the movements his father had taught him as a boy, sweeping actions that mimicked the way he fought with his dagger.

"What are you doing?" Layla's voice broke his concentration.

"I didn't hear you," he admitted. Philip looked around, annoyed with himself. "How did you get down here so quietly?"

The serene look on her face darkened. "I climbed," she snapped. "I'm sorry I did." She turned, grasped the ladder's rung, and hauled herself up.

"No, wait." He stepped forward, placing one hand on her arm. "I'm sorry."

She watched him for a long, drawn-out moment, then nodded. "What were you doing?" She asked again, softer as she stepped back into the empty cargo hold.

"Oh." He pulled back and knew she saw it. Once more she closed herself off, and he cursed his carelessness. "This isn't the place for such a conversation."

Head tilted, she watched him. After a moment, she looked around the hold, then upward at the open hatches, and nodded. "Will you join me for an early supper? Evelyn and I ate only a light meal this afternoon."

"Gladly." He gestured for her to precede him, which she did at a slow, measured pace but with no complaints. No one else was in the dining room, but then, this room was used only for special gatherings, not for the crew's everyday meals.

"When I was young and, well, in my troubled times," he began as Laska nodded at him from the galley, "one of the tricks, I guess you could say, that helped me control my temper was to count my breaths."

"*Shukran.*" Layla smiled at Kaz as he delivered their meal. "*Dziękuję,*" she said slowly. "Is that right?"

Kaz grinned back, clearly pleased. "*Proszę bardzo,* Mrs. Layla."

Envy slammed through Philip. Jaw clenched, he counted his breaths, but that did absolutely nothing. He missed that smile, bestowed so rarely on him. Annoyed with himself, he accepted a glass of carob juice and drained half of it. Kaz disappeared, and Layla watched Philip with that silent, assessing look she often wore.

"If you no longer wish to be married, I understand."

The words slammed into him as if she'd punched him. He opened his mouth, but all that came out was, "What?"

"Our marriage was rather…unusual," she said, the words so low he might've thought he imagined them. They echoed in his ears, racing round his brain. "And we have yet to consummate it."

His mouth snapped shut, his jaw clenched.

"All I ask is that first you help me discover who murdered my parents." Her hands folded primly in front of her plate, and she held his gaze. He tried to interrupt, to say of course he'd help, but she continued, "Although, my understanding is that many women stay in Damietta while their husbands are on voyage. I doubt I'll stand out as unusual."

Breathe in and hold, breathe out and hold. It did nothing for his temper—nor his shock—this time. "I didn't marry you on a lark," he growled. All right, he'd proposed on a whim, because she needed his help, but that wasn't the same thing. He could just imagine his mother's disappointment when she found out her second son was still an impulsive failure. Then again, this had nothing to do with his mother, but everything to do with him and Layla. He pushed the question out: "Do you wish to separate?"

"I wish," she began slowly, "that you talk to me." She held up a hand. "Honestly."

CHAPTER 14

"I am more honest with you than with anyone else in my life." The words came out harsh, a near snarl. Probably not a tone that would inspire faith in his words.

Layla's face betrayed nothing. No surprise, no fear, not even a condescending look at the way his words and tone clearly did not connect.

The dining room remained quiet. Even the galley was silent, as if the entire crew congregated elsewhere. Philip didn't think the privacy was so much for him, but for Mrs. Layla. Either way, he begrudgingly appreciated the lack of eavesdroppers.

Philip ran a hand down his face. Idiot. "Is this about the kiss?"

"No." The word was flat, final. "It's about your disappearance after it."

He wasn't proud of that. Nor was he proud that he knew what she'd gone through and had still kissed her like that. And then left. Philip wondered if Shadi's ill treatment of Layla was because her mother had married an Englishman, or if it had to do with the fact that Harry Braithwaite was far more successful than Shadi could ever be. Then there was her belief that her family had simply abandoned her.

In the weeks they'd known each other, Philip had seen Layla transform from a strong but scared woman into a confident, powerful woman. One just as beautiful as when he'd first met her, but with a vivaciousness she'd buried deep inside.

"I've never been married before," he finally said. "I'm not sure of the rules."

Her head tilted, and he swore her fingers loosened from around each other. "Rules? I don't understand. Do the English have rules about marriage? I don't recall this."

He laughed, a quick, low sound, and shook his head. She constantly surprised him, kept him on his toes. He liked that about her…liked it far more than he thought he should, given they'd known each other for so short a time.

"You keep me on my toes," he admitted.

Layla looked at the table as if she could see through it. She tore off a piece of aish baladi bread and scooped up a bit of the ful medames that Laska had provided. "For dancing? Do you wish to dance? What does this have to do with marriage?" She sighed and scooped up another bit. "I don't understand you."

"We can dance later, if you'd like." He swallowed a grin and ate a little of the meal, too. Sparring at the boxing ring had taken a lot out of him. "I mean that you keep me alert. I never know what you might do or say next." He looked around for more carob juice. Even some of that hibiscus tea, though it wasn't his favorite. He didn't stand, determined to prove he didn't always run from awkward conversations with his wife.

That wasn't who he was any more.

"I disagree." But her lips curved slightly. "I find myself… hmm, what's the word. Staying straight?" She lifted her hands and moved them parallel before her, as if describing a path. "Straight on the road, never veering." She exhaled a long, silent breath, but her smile never wavered. "For so long I was afraid that if I stepped off that road I'd lose my way. Lost in the desert."

"And now?" With every conversation they shared, he learned more about her, relaxed into her presence as if they'd always shared space.

"Now I remember what it's like to hold choices in my hands." She cupped them, holding them before her as if she held a piece of sunlight. "I meant what I said, Philip."

He might never tire of hearing her say his name. Nor the feel of her hand resting on his, as it did now.

"About a separation?" The words hurt. She'd said it so simply that he had a feeling she didn't just mean it in the scandalous, complicated English way.

"About choices," she corrected. "What do you want? From us, I mean. From me."

He had no answer. Not immediately. "Would you believe that no one's ever asked me that?"

She jerked upright. "Never?" She grinned, though it held a sad tinge. "I understand."

"I know, and I hate that." Rage burned through him over the way she'd been treated, the lies Shadi told, even how her family had believed them for years. He wrapped that up tightly and kept focused. "Perhaps that's why fate brought us together."

"I thought you didn't believe in fate."

"Layla, since meeting you, I have no idea what I believe in anymore."

Her. It struck him like a blow. He believed in her. She'd shown him a resilience he hadn't realized existed, not because she had a supportive family and chance after chance to redeem himself.

Because she didn't. She hadn't much of anything, and yet she kept on. Even when she thought everyone had deserted her, she kept going, head high, believing in herself.

"I believe in you," he heard himself admit.

* * *

"Oh." Her breath left her in a rush. "I—no one's ever told me that before."

It surged through her, warm and comforting. His belief in her brought up other feelings she didn't remember ever experiencing before she met Philip. Like safety and acceptance. When she met his gaze, he looked as surprised as she, but he nodded as if agreeing with his own statement.

"I don't believe I've ever believed in someone else before," Philip said slowly. He took a moment, breaking off a piece of aish baladi and scooping up the ful medames. "Myself," he said eventually. "Far too much, but nothing like this."

He trailed off, and Layla thought she should say something. Something profound and moving and honest and open. But her mind completely blanked. What did one say when faced with such a poignant statement? "Does this mean you don't want a separation or divorce?"

Oh, not that. She closed her eyes even as the shocked look on Philip's face embedded in her mind. His laughter filled the room, echoing loudly and joyously across the empty space.

"That's not what I meant to say," she mumbled, her face in her hands.

"What did you mean, then?" The laughter was still clear in his tone.

"I don't know," she admitted, looking up at him. "You surprised me."

How could she explain the way his confession had settled in her? Were there words for that? Phrases everyone else knew but she did not? Ways to tell her husband that she held his confession close against her heart and would never betray it?

"No." He lifted her hand and kissed the back of it, his lips warm and smooth over her knuckles. Her fingers tightened around his, and she wanted more of his lips on her skin. "No, I don't want any of that. Two weeks probably isn't long enough to figure anything out," he added. "We have more time. And if, after everything, you decide you'd rather stay here in Damietta, I won't stop you."

She didn't think she would. She enjoyed the time with her family after so long. Though that lingering fear remained. That nagging question. What if they were responsible for everything? She loved Damietta now that she was slowly exploring it outside such strict confines. But she didn't think she'd prefer to stay. Not if seeing the world was her alternative.

"All right," she said anyway. She didn't necessarily want a separation or divorce, either. But then, she hadn't wanted marriage at all. Not to al-Najjar, and not even to Philip, though that was certainly the better choice.

He hadn't released her hand, and his thumb ran over her knuckles as if embedding his kiss into her skin. Now she was being ridiculously fanciful. But that splash of reality did not stop her heart from fluttering. Nor did it stop that pull of arousal.

"Then why did you stop kissing me?" Her cheeks heated again, but she pushed on, determined. She wanted answers—for many questions, but only he could answer this one. "I appreciate you waiting. Everything was so rushed. Our acquaintance lasted only a few hours before our betrothal. However, we are married now."

"Is that—was that—" He stopped, looking perplexed. Whatever thoughts raced through his mind, he took only a moment before his face cleared, his control firmly locked in place. "You're right." His smile slid sinfully across his face, sending shivers over her arms.

Oh. Suddenly Layla wasn't so certain she was ready. But

then he leaned over, his lips brushing her cheek, and yes, she definitely wanted his mouth on her skin. Wanted that so desperately it tore through her, an ache she wanted sated.

"We should consummate the marriage." His low voice brushed her skin like a feather, a darkness there that drew her in. "So there is no doubt between us."

Layla turned, to see him or kiss him or—his teeth nipped below her ear, at the spot just behind her jaw. The sound that escaped her would've been embarrassing, except she didn't care. Was it too bold of her to ask that he do it again? Probably. She couldn't find her voice anyway. Only that low, needy whimper.

"Yes." The word slipped from her, a want, a promise. All that and more.

"Tonight, then." Philip pulled back, his eyes dark and hungry as they watched her.

Tonight? She wanted him right now. Clearing her throat and stretching her cramped toes from where they pressed tightly into the floorboards, she nodded.

Tonight, then.

Even with the ache low in her belly and the clawing want heating her veins.

"What happens next?" She remembered being so much better at keeping her voice calm and even. No one in Omar's household had ever heard anything from her but soft-spoken agreements. Even when she was worried or angry, she'd remained calm and reasonable. But Philip had shattered her control with a simple kiss. "You contact your merchants, and I search through the evidence for who poisoned my parents?"

"No." The word shot between them. "I don't want you going out alone."

She tilted her head in exasperation. He had a way of making her want him in one breath and frustrating her in the next. "I've spent most of the last years alone." Unfortunately, she found herself very comfortable with that. "I've navigated the souk perfectly fine on my own."

"Layla," he said gently, and she braced. The way he said her name made her feel far more than comfort. It made her envision how he might say it while they were in bed together, his hands on her bare skin, his lips on hers. Tonight. "When you visited the souk, it was as a servant."

She stiffened but didn't pull away.

"Now you'll walk the stalls as my wife." He shook his head, but his hand was still gentle around hers, his eyes serious. Once more, he lifted her fingers to his mouth, this time kissing her palm.

Flutter? Her heart skidded to a halt.

"I'll be with you no matter where this investigation takes us." That promise sank into her bones. She completely believed him. Believed in him.

"And what about your own reasons for being in Damietta?" She licked her lips and tried to push away the memory of their kiss. It tempted her, drawing her toward Philip, an irresistible pull of wanting more. "Your business contracts?"

He shrugged, an easy, quick movement. "You can join me for those, too. Unless you want to stay on the ship?"

"No." Maybe. Being here reassured her. No one boarded without the crew's knowledge, and no one, not al-Najjar, not his sons, not even the mysterious assailants who killed her father, could reach her. "That's not how I'll solve this mystery."

"All right then." He stood, pulling her up with him. "Let's get started."

He was the most confusing man. Layla still wasn't certain they'd settled anything about their kiss, though she supposed he'd been quite clear about wanting to explore their relationship. Tonight seemed a very long way off.

"Philip." She pulled on her hand, stopping him before they

reached the door. "I—" The words stopped, forming a lump in her throat. "About the letters," she began again.

He waited patiently, nonjudgmental. Nonetheless, Layla felt her cheeks heat, and the shame of her ignorance weighed on her shoulders like a boulder.

"Do you wish to read through them yourself?"

"No." The word barely made it past her lips. "No, I mean…" Lips pressed tight together, she raised her gaze and met his. This wasn't the hardest thing she'd ever done. That was escaping Omar's house and sneaking through Damietta. That was risking everything in hopes that Muhammad and Josiah might pity her enough to grant her passage on board one of their ships.

Life was strange, she supposed. So much of her life had been a lie. That straight road she thought she walked was full of more turns than she'd imagined.

"I can't read English." The words escaped in a rush. "I've forgotten how."

He didn't look disgusted, though she had no idea what reaction she'd expected. Instead, he merely nodded. "I suppose, after ten years of being exposed only to Arabic, that makes sense."

"I'm not sure I remember how to read that, either," she whispered, though some of that weight had lifted. "Omar didn't exactly allow me reading material after my chores."

He grunted, his face darkening. He opened his mouth, then snapped it closed. Layla had a feeling that if Omar weren't already dead, Philip might have paid him a visit. She couldn't be sorry about that.

"Then I suppose we ought to get started." His fingers brushed over her cheek, tilting her chin. Pressing a kiss against her forehead, he pulled her into his arms. "I don't judge you for that, Layla."

She wrapped her arms around his waist and wondered if she judged herself, or if she had just expected that others would.

"Thank you," she said instead of the jumble of gratitude she didn't have the right words for.

"Is that why you haven't looked at the papers yet?" She felt him nod in answer to his own question.

"I thought about asking Evelyn for help, but I don't think she knows what happened. I was afraid that if I told her, when neither Aunt Augusta nor Jomana seemed to have, that it would only endanger her." She pulled back, but only enough to see his face. "I don't want her in danger; she's had enough heartache."

She'd forgotten about Evelyn's request to sail with them back to England. She'd ask Philip later; this didn't feel like the right time for that.

"We'll find out who did this." He stepped back and took her hand again. She quite enjoyed that touch. "No one else should be involved, I agree." The corridor lay empty as they headed for their quarters.

Theirs.

It hadn't truly struck her before; Philip slept in the chair and was never there in the morning when she woke. He'd enter the room long after she'd fallen asleep. Layla had worried it was because he didn't want her, but today's kiss, and the promise of tonight, told her otherwise.

She had no idea how to set about seducing her husband, but that's exactly what she planned to do. He gave her space, gave her options. Consummation aside, she wanted him. Now all she had to do was figure out how to show him that.

"All right."

Argus bumped her leg, and she cooed at him. "Were you in here the whole time? I didn't bring you anything, I'm sorry."

He whimpered but nuzzled her hand, so she hoped all was forgiven.

"Let's start at the top." Philip looked at her from his desk and gestured for the chair beside him. She sat, not sure how she might be of any help. "Egypt is full of surprises."

She grinned. "I agree, but how so?"

"I didn't expect this marriage." He shook his head and angled the lantern so they could both see the first page. "And I certainly didn't expect to find a partner in crime."

Her laughter echoed through the day cabin. "Partners in crime?" She grinned again, feeling much lighter than she had all day. "I like it."

CHAPTER 15

The sun had shifted so it brightened the room, making a lantern unnecessary. Layla sat in one of the chairs facing the windows that overlooked the sea, and Philip sat beside her. He held on to his control so tightly he thought it might snap.

Of all the conversations he thought they'd share after this morning, what they'd actually spoken of was not even in the realm of his thoughts. Nothing that had happened since they'd docked had been in the realm of what he expected.

Fate truly had a way of toying with him.

Layla shifted, and the faint scent of the herbs wafted over him. She frowned at the paper, one finger holding the corner, as if she feared touching it.

Not now. He would not seduce her in the day cabin in the middle of the afternoon. No matter how temptingly her lips moved as she mouthed the opening lines of the written sheet.

"This is almost a diary entry." Philip tore his gaze from her mouth and ran a finger down each line. "Or pieces taken from one. Do you remember, is this your mother's handwriting? It's different from the handwriting on the list of names." He shifted the parchment and watched her. Eventually, she nodded, a long, slow movement.

"I believe so. It's neither of my aunts'; I've seen their writing recently." She met his gaze. "And I doubt Mama would've sought Aunt Heba's help."

"That still puzzles me. Why would Mariam Braithwaite go to her estranged sister's household rather than the women she considered family?

"It follows me like a phantom," she admitted. "The fear they're involved. But then I remember they didn't have to share their fears with me. They could've said nothing, and we would've left port." She swallowed hard and shuddered. "Or they could've killed me as well, and no one would've ever known anything was connected."

"That is a possibility," he admitted, still trying to piece everything together. "However, I agree. If it were one of them, why tell you anything at all?"

If it'd been one of her uncles, however, and neither of her aunts realized it, perhaps they'd unwittingly brought the danger to her.

"What..." She licked her lips. "What does she say?"

"*15 April 1806, Harry feeling ill but refuses to see a physician. Third night in a row he hasn't eaten supper, claims stomach pains. 16 April 1806, Harry vomiting this morning but still refuses help.*"

"I remember him being ill." Layla blinked at him, her eyes wide. "Mama was sick for so long, I'd forgotten. But I remember his sickness." Her lips curled into a sad half smile. "Evelyn, Amirah, and I were playing on the roof."

His mouth opened then closed again. "The roof?" He choked out a laugh. "You never cease to surprise me, Layla."

"We wanted to see the ships putting to port." She moved her hand in that small wave of her fingers. "We were planning how to sail our own ships, with an all-female crew." Her eyes closed, and a breath of laughter escaped her. "Evelyn and Amirah had brothers who would inherit, but I was an only child. I didn't care what anyone thought; I was going to take over the Braithwaite third of the business."

"I have every confidence you can succeed." He tore his attention from her, the softness of her lips, the wistfulness of her dreams. "It goes on. There's more about your father's illness. Do you remember how long he was ill? This skips from mid-April to the end of May."

"I—no. He seemed better, I think." She frowned again. "My mother might've been sick; I can't remember when that began."

"You think it's related?" He held her gaze and watched as she sorted through her memories. "Makes sense, if whoever poisoned your father thought he might've told your mother what happened."

"I think that's probably true." She frowned again, and Philip wanted nothing more than to ease it. Take away the knowledge that her parents were murdered and whoever did it might be after her.

They'd be safe in England, but not knowing would haunt her forever. And she'd want to return, visit family—assuming they weren't involved.

"What else does it say?"

"Goes on a bit with these entries. Hmm, her handwriting is shakier at the end." The effects of her own illness no doubt taking over. "It stops in early June 1806."

"That's when he died. The third of June 1806." Her fingers curled into tight fists on the tabletop, but her voice didn't shake.

Philip reached out but paused before he took her hand. He understood this, too. The restraint she used so as not to break down. He hated that she understood that, the need for such constraints. Easing his fingers over hers, he waited for her to wrestle her control. When she met his gaze, her eyes were clear but angry.

"A little less than two months, then." Her fingers twitched

beneath his. "I'm no expert on poisons, but it must've been something slow-acting."

"Aunt Augusta and Jomana aren't experts either, but—" Her voice wavered, and she pressed her lips together. "Perhaps whoever poisoned him stopped? I don't know how any of that works. Maybe they were afraid they'd be caught?" She shook her head, seeming to be at a complete loss about how any of it could've happened. "What do the other papers say?"

His hand tightened around hers in a gesture he hoped conveyed understanding. She squeezed back and gave a small nod. Picking up the next page, he started at the top.

"This isn't your mother's writing."

She glanced at it. "Aunt Augusta's. Both Uncle Muhammad and Aunt Jomana are fluent in English, but that's Augusta's handwriting."

"It's another short list." He frowned at it. "*5 June 1806, Mariam and Layla left after the funeral.*"

"It was an English funeral, I think." Layla nodded and looked around the table. "If that matters."

He stood and crossed to the door, intending to call for Laska or Kaz. Naturally, there was a tray with two glasses and a carafe of carob juice waiting by the door. Philip rolled his eyes and picked up the tray. Of course Laska had seen to Layla's unspoken needs. Beside it lay another tray, with several bowls of fruit and one full of cut-up tilapia. For Argus, no doubt.

"Thank you," she whispered as he set the trays on the table. "Laska is very thoughtful."

"He likes you more than he does me," Philip grumbled as he set the bowl of fish on the floor for Argus. "He likes Argus more than he likes me, too."

Her laughter rang softly over the table, and they shared a smile. Settling back before the papers, he ran his eyes over them.

"Your aunts asked around. The clerks at the offices, the

customs agents, anyone it seemed." He pointed out a line. "In late June, they heard from Shadi."

Her breath stopped, and she set the glass aside. Laska had left the good glasses, of course. "What does it say?"

"*Omar contacted Muhammad.*" This was in a different handwriting, a looser script than Augusta's. "*Mariam and Layla are dead. He claimed the plague took them, but, given Harry's suspicious death, it was possibly the same assailant.*"

"He wasted no time, did he?" Layla growled. "Not a month after Papa's death and he claimed we died, too. Why?"

She didn't bang on the table but pressed her fingers onto its surface. Her voice rose, unusual for her, but Philip didn't blame her for her anger. He couldn't imagine what she felt, nor how she might reconcile what she'd believed all these years with what truly happened.

"They suspect him in the next line." Philip rotated the page and followed the words with his finger. The sun had shifted again, taking its light with it, but he didn't move from her side. Not yet. "*What reason could Omar have? Money? Bribery?*" He snorted. "I wouldn't put it past him."

"He never had the comfortable lifestyle we did." She turned in the chair, leaning one arm on the back, resting her head there, and closing her eyes. "I think Mama gave Aunt Heba money; maybe that's why she'd sometimes leave a coin or two for me."

"What did he do for work? Shadi. How did he feed his family?" Philip couldn't see the man working, not with his hands. Not with his mind, either, not with a temper like that. Though he supposed having a temper didn't necessarily make one a bad worker. Merely a bad family man.

She blinked and sat up. "I don't know. Shipbuilding, I'd presume. Or maybe a dockworker, given we live in Damietta." She tilted her head. "Why?"

"He owed al-Najjar money. But when I paid al-Najjar a visit, he seemed satisfied with the outcome." "Satisfied" might've been too strong a word, but it was the best he had in the moment.

"Do you believe al-Najjar killed Omar, or had him killed?" She frowned, her fingers tapping on the chair spindle.

He tilted his head from side to side, but he still didn't see a clear answer. "I don't know," he admitted. "If Omar didn't repay whatever he owed from what your uncles negotiated, perhaps. But that wasn't the sense I got after my visit."

"If his entire reason for agreeing to marry me to al-Najjar, or one of his sons, was repayment, then why wouldn't he have paid off that debt?"

"I don't know that, either." Gathering the papers, he stood and offered his hand.

The sun had set behind the rest of the ships in port, darkening the day cabin. Slivers of light bounced off the water, making it look like a sparkling sapphire gem. Beautiful and vast and laid out endlessly before them.

"We should visit some of the locations," she said, gathering their empty bowls and glasses.

The intimacy of the domestic moment struck him, and he set a bowl on the tray a little too hard. It clattered against the others. Layla tutted and took the last one before he could shatter anything. It didn't matter; the moment weaved itself through him.

She looked up, eyes bright in the darkened cabin, a smile tugging at her lips despite the topic of their conversation.

"Aunt Jomana and Augusta are accompanying me to visit Aunt Heba." She paused, staring at an empty glass. "It will be strange, returning."

"Are men allowed to visit during mourning?" He shook his head, but that didn't clear it. "Husbands?"

"Yes," she said slowly. "Do you wish to accompany us?"

Slipping a hand around her waist, he pulled her to him. "I told you, Layla." He dipped his head and met her gaze, which was still sparkling in the rapidly darkening night. "You aren't going anywhere without me."

"Not even the galley?" she asked, breathless.

"No." He pressed his lips against her cheek.

"The cargo hold?"

Another kiss along her jaw. "No."

"Bed?"

"Definitely no." The kiss was slow, a testament to his hold over this wild, uncontrollable need for her. If he drowned in her, it'd be glorious. "How else could I seduce you?"

* * *

HIS MOUTH GENTLED ON HERS, and she relaxed against him. Only he mattered, only his touch, the way he held her so close and gentle. His kisses made her knees weaken even as her blood raced, and her breath came short. Philip didn't simply consummate this marriage; he made her feel a part of it. He made her forget her past and her fears and the uncertainty of tomorrow.

With each touch, every caress over her bare shoulders, she craved more. His touch, his kiss, ignited her senses until she knew only him. Needed him more than she needed her next breath.

He nipped at the side of her throat, and Layla gasped, arching into him, winding her arms around his neck. He lifted her and sat on the bed, her most intimate parts pressed tight against him. His pulsed hard and thick against her.

"Oh." She pulled back, aching for more, craving the feel of his hands on her skin. Blinking rapidly, she fought for breath. "You do control yourself well, don't you?"

Tentatively, she reached between them, unsure where this boldness came from but not shying away from it, either. From him. She knew she whimpered, a small, needy sound that only spurred him on. He grabbed her hand and held her fingers immobile against his cock.

"I won't lose control around you," he promised. It was a dark, low vow that curled through her.

She wasn't so certain she wanted his control. Stroking her fingers against him, that need tightening through her, Layla was quite convinced she wanted him as out of control as she felt.

"I won't break," she whispered, kissing him again.

He growled, and the sound pierced through her. Her fingers clenched around him, making him growl again, and Layla knew she teetered on the edge of her own control. What might it be like to spiral wildly in his arms?

"I want to find out," she said aloud, though she doubted she'd voice her other thoughts. "Make love to me, Philip."

She tasted down his neck, breathing in the scent of him, tugging his shirt up and out of her way. Her nails scraped down his back, drawing him closer. His fingers clenched on her hips, bunching her skirts upward and out of his way. *Yes. Yes, please.* Rolling her hips against his, she felt him against her entrance. She wanted him inside her with a desperation that clawed through her.

She might never have enough of him. Of the way his fingers slid up her legs over her stockings. How they teased the inside of her thighs until she broke the kiss on a gasp.

"Stand up," he said, the words strangled. "Turn around. Our first time shouldn't be like this."

Knees shaking, she obeyed, though she wanted nothing more than to feel him spread her open as she sank onto him. Shocked by her thoughts, she waited as Philip worked the ties on her gown.

"I think," she managed around a dry throat, "I should like that."

"Layla." Her name sounded raw, as if it had been ripped from his very soul. "Next time."

She turned as the gown pooled onto the floor, leaving her in a chemise and stockings. "Good."

"This isn't the ideal bed," he said against the side of her throat. "I'd like something larger, much larger, where I can explore every inch of you." His lips were soft on hers, his kiss gentle as he guided her onto the bed. "But I'll make do."

Layla sighed and opened to him, letting the passion burn between them and engulf her. She leaned closer and wound her arms around him, pulling him against her. Slowly kissing down her neck, he nipped at her skin. Her hips jerked upward, and she inhaled sharply, arching against him. He bunched up her chemise, urging her upright so he could toss it onto the floor.

Open, bare, aroused, she lay before his hungry gaze. In one long, slow movement, his fingers ran down her body, over her breasts, her belly, her hips, to the very spot she needed him most. His mouth trailed down as well, kissing the side of her breast, down lower, and her breath stopped. Philip nipped the inside of her thigh then kissed it, moving upward so slowly.

His fingers slipped into her wetness, and she jerked.

"Oh. Yes." Her hands bunched the bedding as she looked down her body, watching. "More like that."

His breath was warm as he chuckled. "I'll give you everything."

His fingers moved as he pressed his tongue over her sensitive bud. Then his thumb replaced his tongue, moving in short, hard circles as her pleasure built. Without warning, it crashed over her, like a wave, and Layla cried out, her hips jerking.

"I'm not finished." The promise wafted over her sensitive nub as his words tempted her. He sat up, one arm braced beside her head, the fingers of his other hand capturing hers. "Still curious?"

More than she had words to express. Breathing hard, she nodded, and when he wrapped her hand around him, that small, needy sound broke free. His jaw clenched, and he helped her guide him into her.

"Bend your knees." The words were short, clipped. "It'll help."

She did as instructed, shifting until he was fully seated within her. "I want to fly again." Her fingers dug into his shoulders as she moved her hips, not certain what she was doing. "I want that wonderful feeling—oh!"

He moved. Short, jerky strokes that stole her breath and every thought in her head except for him. His fingers found her center again, and she had the fleeting thought that she'd like to touch herself for this wonderful pleasure.

Before she could uncurl her hands from his shoulders, that blindingly beautiful pleasure broke over her. Winding her legs about his hips, she held on as he moved, letting the pleasure fizzle through her veins as he found his own release.

Mumbling something she didn't catch, he shattered and rolled onto his side. It took a moment, longer probably, for her to regain her wits enough to look at him.

"I very much enjoyed that."

"Good." He tugged her against him. "I want to explore much more of your body," he said, even as his breathing remained ragged.

Body still tingling, blood still buzzing, Layla snuggled deeper into Philip's arms and decided she might never leave. His fingers ran over her arm, a movement that was both comforting and arousing.

She'd been right. Having his mouth on her skin was divine. A simmering pleasure that stole her breath and made her crave more. It was second only to his hands. The memory of his calloused fingers gliding over her skin shuddered through her. She might never get enough of that.

"What's England like?"

"Cold. Rainy." He kissed her shoulder. "Why? Eager to leave already?"

"Eager, no." Not entirely. "Curious. My father left there years before I was born, and as far as I know never returned."

"Your mother never wanted to visit?"

"Not that I'm aware." She shifted only enough to meet his gaze. "She seemed happy here. My father, too. Is England so terrible no one wants to return?"

He laughed, but it was a quiet sound. Not the boisterous, joyful one she preferred. "I suppose that depends on your experience. If I didn't have family I loved, I might not return." He took her hand, twining their fingers together. "Not after everything. But when I was young, I preferred to run from my problems."

"I'm glad you have a family you love. I should like to meet them." She lifted their hands and turned them over in the light from the single lantern. "Are you still interested in visiting Cairo?" He stiffened. It surprised her so much, Layla dropped their hands and turned in his arms. "Philip?"

"Yes." He offered a smile, but in the uncertain light it looked strained. "After we solve your parents' murder."

She felt herself nod, but she was still frowning. "What's wrong? Do you prefer to sail to Cairo alone?"

"No, it's not that." He urged her head back against his chest. His heart beat steadily beneath her ear, and his fingers resumed their leisurely travel down her spine. "I'd...well, I had forgotten that plan."

That was her fault. She'd found her way on board, with her troubles and her desperation, and uprooted all his plans. "I'm sorry. My being here changed everything for you."

"No, not exactly." She felt his lips brush the top of her head, and he held her closer. "Granted, I didn't expect to marry." She heard his smile now and relaxed slightly. "However, discovering the root of this secret is more important."

"Where did they meet?" She lifted her head and rested her chin on her folded hands. "Your parents. Though I suppose, they being English, it was the English Quarter."

An odd look crossed his face, but she chalked it up to the swaying lantern light. His hand hadn't stopped its caress, and she felt her eyelids grow heavy.

"Get some sleep, Layla." Another kiss brushed against her head. "We'll figure out where to start in the morning."

CHAPTER 16

Layla shifted, and Philip's eyes snapped open. The cabin remained dark, and a quick look around showed not even the barest hint of sunlight. Argus huffed in the corner, but even he didn't move.

"Do me a favor?" He heard her shuffle toward the table and the rustle of parchment. "Read over the names again?"

Rubbing his eyes and wondering if he'd ever get more than a few hours' sleep while in Egypt, Philip swung his legs over the bed and stretched. "Are you always an early bird?"

"It's lovely, sleeping in." She handed him the papers and pressed a kiss against his cheek. "And I very much enjoy sleeping against you. However, we've much to do."

He snorted, pulled her onto his lap, and kissed her good morning properly. It tugged his heart, the way she sank against him, sighing his name and winding her arms around him. More than just the sex, this closeness they shared was worth it. Worth everything. "I can think of much better ways to wake up."

"Hmm, I'm open to suggestions." She pulled back and pecked him on the lips. "Tomorrow."

Laughing, he found the lantern and lit the room. She kept

him on his toes, all right. Layla sat on the bed, playing with the ties of her chemise. Her hair fell over her shoulders, giving her a shy, innocent look. She stole his breath.

The memory of those gentle hands at odds with the memory of her bold, curious touch last night… She met his gaze, and the heat behind her eyes ignited an equal one in him. She did more than steal his breath. His cock hardened, and he shifted, suddenly uncomfortable and aching.

"Do you mind?" she sighed. Mind that she looked like a goddess? That she tasted like heaven? That he'd never get enough of the way she sighed his name? Philip cleared his throat. "I suppose I should've asked before."

"Mind?" He met her gaze. "Ask what?"

"That my mother was Egyptian and my father English." Her voice trailed off, as if her lineage were a point of embarrassment for her.

"Do I mind?" It had never occurred to him. "Who said something?" he demanded, suddenly furious at the thought of her being hurt. "One of the crew? Your family?" He'd hunt them all down and—

"No," she said quickly. "I didn't realize anything was wrong when I was young. No one said anything or brought it up. Everyone worked together, and we all lived in the same house, and—" She waved it off. "Omar brought it up." She frowned, a dark angry scowl. "Repeatedly."

Now, he thought. Now was the time to tell her. He waited, unwilling to leap into something so very important.

"It never even occurred to me," he admitted slowly, his thoughts scattered. "I spent a lot of my life trusting the wrong people for the wrong reasons." He carefully set the papers onto the table so as not to crush them. "I thought adventure and taking chances and, I don't know…leaping. I thought that leaping before I looked was what life was meant to be. Full of danger and action and excitement."

She watched him, and he wondered what she thought. If she realized he hadn't lied about believing in her. She was the only thing he believed in. Other than Argus. A smile tugged at his lips, but he didn't move or look away from her.

"You're the first person, outside of my family, who I've trusted. Truly, sincerely trusted. I'm sure there are reasons why I shouldn't so quickly trust an acquaintance, but nothing about our situation is normal." He paused, but only for a moment. "I don't care who your parents were. Your heritage makes you who you are, and I happen to respect you very much."

"Respect" wasn't entirely accurate, but he shied from that larger, deeper word.

He paused again. The words weren't there. Hoping he didn't muck this all up, he sorted through his thoughts. But, much like the way he felt for Layla, that was hopeless. "I also don't care because I, too, am Egyptian and English."

Layla sat up, her back ramrod straight. In the flickering lantern light, she nodded slowly. "Your parents met in Cairo because your mother was born here."

"Yes. But it's a bit more complicated than that. My great-grandfather contracted her to an English soldier he'd met years prior in Bombay. My father helped him, and my great-grandfather never forgot that."

"That's an awful lot of trust for something that happened once, years prior." Her head tilted, and her fingers played with the ends of her hair, twirling a lock round and round. Philip wanted to feel her hair sliding between his own fingers. "I see why you wanted adventure. Your family has had a lot of it, haven't they?"

"Yes." Clearing his throat, he folded his hands on the table. Now wasn't the time to talk about adventure. "So you see why it doesn't matter to me. That sort of thing doesn't. Without my own heritage, would it matter? I don't know. But I do know that the one thing that has stayed with me, even as I was destroying myself with gambling and drink, is that a person's birth doesn't matter. Only who they are when I need them."

Another hard-learned lesson. His so-called friends hadn't been there for anything other than the drinking and the gambling.

Layla hummed, as if thinking through everything. He cared for her no matter her heritage. Her smile lit his day; her laugh made him answer with his own.

"That's why you speak such excellent Egyptian."

"I speak many languages. Some French and Polish. My schoolteachers tried to drill Greek and Latin into me." He'd been far too busy pursuing other pleasures to care about that. "English, Egyptian, and Portuguese."

"No one knows your secret." She looked at her hands, clasped together now before her. "Everyone knows mine."

He opened his mouth to refute, but of course she was correct. He snapped it closed. "True. We've kept all our secrets close. I didn't lie or exaggerate when I said I don't like talking about myself."

"People would judge you for your heritage."

"Yes," he agreed. "I swore the only person I'd ever tell was the one I was closest to, the one I intended to marry." She made a surprised squeak, and he smiled. "The Conrads cause enough scandal with our bucking society's conventions. Which," he admitted with a small movement of his head, "is often. No need to lose all our business contacts because of it. Everyone has to eat."

She did laugh then, and once more he smiled in return. He might've never wanted her to know his past, but he found he didn't mind her knowing such an intimate part of him. He'd never much thought about the secrets he kept, even if he always kept them, even in his drunken state. Telling Layla, sharing that part of himself and his family with her, eased the stranglehold he'd carried around his chest since disavowing the drink.

"I promise I shall keep your secrets. About your father, your mother, even yours. Even if you claim everyone already knows of those."

The sincerity in her voice settled deep within him. In one move, he crouched in front of her and took her hands. "Thank you." That wasn't enough. It didn't convey at all what he wanted to tell her. "I, well…I hadn't ever planned to reveal any of that."

Her hand cupped his cheek, her thumb brushing softly over it. "I'm grateful you've placed such trust in me."

He lifted her hands to his lips and kissed each one. "I'm grateful to have found someone I could."

Her kiss was soft and soothing. *A balm*, he thought as he leaned into her. Bracing one hand on the bed, he gently urged her backward. The papers could wait.

"*Woof!*"

"Argus." Layla laughed and leaned around him, petting the dog's head and cooing good mornings at him.

Philip blinked. His own dog. "See if I take you anywhere ever again."

"Oh, hush. He's sweet." She returned her attention back to Argus. "Aren't you?"

Frowning, Philip sat back in the chair with a grumbled humph. Definitely not how he'd planned his morning. "What did you want with the papers?"

When Layla looked up from Argus's exuberant greeting, her smile made his heart skip. She looked so happy and settled and vibrant. Stole his breath? She *was* his breath.

"I want the names." Her smile didn't dim but changed, more determined now. "I want the names of the still-living merchants for when I visit Aunt Heba."

His eyebrows shot up. "So you can see if she recognizes anyone? Would she know? Would Omar have told her?"

"Most likely not," she admitted. "I'm not even certain Omar

was involved. If so, he'd be a runner, not the main person behind this."

"Given he died so soon after the city knew you were still alive, I'd wager you're correct."

Her lips curved slightly. "I thought you weren't a gambling man."

Philip snorted. "If I were. His sudden death is suspicious." He held up a hand. "I know I said it wasn't at first, but things have changed." He tilted his head at the papers. "Perhaps after paying our respects to your aunt, we should pay a visit to al-Najjar. He seems to know many things. Too many."

"You think he's involved?"

"Even if he isn't, he'll have heard a hint about it, I'm certain."

* * *

LAYLA WATCHED Philip and Saied Harry talk by the ship's wheel. Another beautiful day had dawned, and she closed her eyes against the warm sun. Dressed in her hijab and a long-sleeved gown Evelyn had chosen, she basked in this moment. Life outside felt different now. Not only because of her marriage, but because of the feeling that sat within her.

Wandering freely wherever she might wish made every day feel different than it had when she was confined in the house. She enjoyed this freedom, embraced it. She didn't wander, but she could, should she wish. Every day, she grew more confident in herself and this new life spread before her. The wind picked up, and she watched the birds gliding along, tilting their wings as they stayed the course.

"Ready?" Philip appeared by her side, hat pulled low over his brow.

"Everything all right?" She took his hand, surprised when it twitched in her grip. "What's wrong?"

"Nothing." He snorted. "I thought I was the suspicious one."

"You are," she allowed as they stepped onto the wharves. "However, life has taught me to be suspicious as well."

And fear, perhaps, but she thought she'd done well in putting the last ten years behind her. Once she escaped, it was as if everything opened up. She thought she didn't hold herself as still as before, that she moved more freely now, breathed easier. She didn't jump at every sound.

"It seems you have every reason to be suspicious." He held out his arm, and she happily took it. It wasn't the same as holding hands—this was far more proper. However, she liked walking beside him. Liked having someone to walk beside.

"If there were others involved, it's no wonder my aunts couldn't discover the culprit." She worked through her logic but still felt as if she'd missed an important clue.

"I may be biased," Philip said. She made a sound in the back of her throat, one he ignored with a grin. "However, I'm convinced Omar was involved."

"You are biased," she agreed as they walked slowly down the main street. "Is someone following us?"

"A few of my men who speak the language. Why?" He looked down at her sharply. "Do you see someone?"

"No, just a feeling. You're walking much...easier? More confident, perhaps, than the last time we walked these streets. As if you have others with you." Perhaps that's what he and Saied Harry had been speaking about on deck. Philip took her safety very seriously.

She loved him for that.

Layla tripped on the stones, her eyes wide, her heart racing.

"Layla?" Philip held her by the shoulders, his voice frantic. "Are you all right?"

No. No, she was not. It seemed impossible that she had fallen in love with her husband after just over two weeks. She couldn't even say what love was, though of course she remembered watching her parents and aunts and uncles together.

Being around family again reminded her of that feeling, but it paled in comparison to the fierceness of emotion that burned within her for Philip. A consuming feeling that both warmed her and made her feel as if she could do anything. That she could and would do anything to keep him from harm.

"Are you injured, Mrs. Layla?" Lange appeared beside them, watching her back, but Layla couldn't focus.

"I'm perfectly well," she lied, breathless. "Thank you, Lange. I wasn't watching where I was walking." The man looked dubious but accepted her small falsehood and disappeared back into the scenery. Philip looked less accepting but once more offered his arm. "It's of no matter. What were you saying? About some of the men?"

"I have reinforcements," he said. He didn't look convinced by her small lie. "And the men seem very keen on keeping you safe."

"They're all very nice." She didn't look around, no matter how badly she wanted to. Neither did she meet his gaze. "I feel quite safe on the ship with them around."

They walked in silence for a while, and she found she enjoyed it far more than she had in the house. There, silence weighed heavy in the air. A living, breathing malevolence. Part of Layla wanted to break the silence between her and Philip, but a newer, stronger part of her basked in the companionship.

Was that love? She couldn't say. However, she enjoyed the closeness she and Philip shared in something so simple as walking quietly together.

"I won't say Omar wasn't involved," she said slowly as they neared the house she'd spent her childhood in. They would meet her aunts here and travel by litter to Heba's. "However, he couldn't have been the one to conceive of such a thing. He was a…what do you call it. Bully?"

"Aye, he was that." His hand covered hers, strong and warm.

"He hurt people, especially those who relied on him. It's why

Amr returned only once. And why Nanet agreed to marry the first man who offered."

"You think he was capable of murder?"

"Oh, yes." There were times Layla thought he'd kill her himself. When his rage beat strongly inside him as he screamed and hit her. "However, even if he was involved, I still don't believe it was his idea."

"Hmm. No, I think you're right. Which means either al-Najjar conceived of it or someone else."

"Why al-Najjar?" She looked up at Philip as they waited for a servant to open the door.

"Because he reached out to your uncle to contract you in marriage."

"Good point," she conceded. "The question remains, why."

"You know my theory."

Money. "Apparently, I am worth quite a bit."

He snorted, then raised her hand to his lips and kissed her knuckles softly. "More precious than rubies, and nothing you desire can compare."

Startled, Layla's heart skipped as she looked up at him. What did that mean? Of course, that was when the door opened, and Jomana beckoned them inside.

"Are you ready, my dear?" She took Layla's hand, her eyes intense in the cool, dim interior. "Are you certain about this?"

"It's admirable you wish to visit," Augusta added, equally sincere as she joined them. "However, Jomana is correct. You needn't return."

"I know." Layla also knew she'd only feel guilty if she didn't see Heba after what happened. Though she wasn't sure why. "I have some questions for her that I hope this visit will answer."

Jomana tutted, but Augusta merely nodded at Philip. "Captain. You're joining us, yes?"

"As a silent escort only," he promised.

Layla did not roll her eyes, tempted as she might have been.

He might be a silent escort, but he'd be observing everything. Philip had quizzed her on the layout of the house—fairly typical from the outside, from what she knew, though she'd recited the path through the rooms from memory. Other servants—none unless they suddenly discovered enough money to feed them, which was doubtful. The activities of her two remaining cousins still living there—helping Heba with the mending she took in to keep food on the table and avoiding Omar at night.

Layla did wonder how the three of them spent their evenings now, after Omar's death, but she doubted much had changed. Heba brought in most of the money for food and clothing.

"I will be right there," Philip promised as they exited the house. "I promise."

"I know." It eased the pressure in her chest, knowing she only needed to call his name. She didn't think she would have to, but knowing he'd come running if she did made this trip far less difficult.

The three of them entered their litters, the tiny enclosed carriage an extravagance she never imagined before. She had a vague memory of traveling like this with her mother, but she couldn't pinpoint where they were headed or why. Philip winked at her as he latched the door. It made her heart skip and that warm, fluttery feeling returned as the four paid men lifted the litter and stepped forward.

She worried about an attack while in the litter, or an attack on Philip, and she was grateful he accompanied her on foot. The journey took longer this way than it would've if she'd walked, but Layla kept quiet and enjoyed the gentle sway as the litter moved with every step. She'd have to ask Philip if they had these in England, or if they traveled by other means.

Bringing her mind back to al-Najjar and Omar, Layla wondered if creeping in at night and searching his papers might offer answers. She doubted he kept details of such a nature there, but one never knew.

Suddenly, all too soon, they arrived, and Philip was there as she stepped out. They stood before Heba's house, and Layla wanted to vomit. Dread pooled in her belly and spread through her veins, but she refused to let that stop her. Still, her hand latched tightly around Philip's arm, and she knew he noticed.

"Are you ready?"

"No," she told him honestly as Augusta and Jomana exited their litters. "I never wished to return here."

"We can leave."

She wanted that very much. So much that her mind whirled with excuses. Argus needed her company. Evelyn required her assistance. Amirah required help now that she was with child. But Layla shook her head.

"No," she said again. "Even if Aunt Heba has no answers about what happened to Mama, it's right I pay my respects now."

"All right. Let's see what she has to say."

CHAPTER 17

Layla keenly felt Philip's presence in the house, though he wasn't in the same room as she. He'd silently nodded at Aunt Heba when she answered the door, then left her, Jomana, and Augusta as they followed Heba into the small room. She didn't know where her younger cousins had disappeared to.

Now, as they sat awkwardly in a room devoid of nearly all decoration, she realized her earlier panic was misplaced. The house was merely a house, one that still held her darkest memories, but also one that no longer held anything over her. It was smaller than she remembered, though she thought that might have more to do with her own sense of freedom, with the knowledge she could leave here at any time and never worry.

Jomana and Augusta sat beside her, more for silent support than anything. Heba had eyed them suspiciously when they entered, but after their initial greetings, none of them spoke to each other. Studying her aunt, Layla saw the fading mark of a bruise on her cheek.

No, she wasn't the only person Omar had ever hit.

"I appreciate your visit, Layla, but it was quite unnecessary,"

Heba said stiffly into the stuffy afternoon heat and even stuffier silence.

Layla had expected that and nodded slightly. "Do you require anything, Aunt?"

Heba's dull, dark eyes met hers. Omar had beat any life from her years ago. "No."

A lie, but Layla let it slide. The house felt off, but she couldn't understand why. Unless it was because Omar's presence no longer tainted it. The stoop remained well swept and Heba's clothing neatly mended. Worn, of course, but Heba's way with a stitch was second to none.

"I won't keep you," Layla said. She didn't move. Her hands were folded tightly on her lap, and though she knew no one could harm her, her toes pressed hard against the soles of her shoes. "I only have a question about my mother."

Heba stiffened, and her lips twitched. "What about her?"

"I found some of her old diaries," she lied, but she did wonder what happened to them. When Philip had read the opening pages of the investigation, she had a nearly perfect memory of her mother writing diligently in her diaries. "They mention several business acquaintances of my father's." Heba stiffened even more; Layla had no idea how her body didn't break apart, shatter at her feet. "Do you know any of them?"

"Bah! No, of course not. We never spoke of such things." Heba's eyes shifted for the barest moment, and her face tensed as if she held something back.

"I only ask because Captain Conrad is interested in fostering trade relations here in Damietta." Heba met her gaze again but said nothing. Whatever she didn't say itched beneath Layla's skin. Heart thundering, she licked her lips and leaped.

"She also mentioned, in her entries, that she wasn't well. Do you know why?" Still nothing. It beat between them, the answer, the truth. Steady and loud and so close Layla thought she could reach out and touch the words. "Is that why we came here? Why we lived with you after Papa's death?"

"Be careful, Layla," Heba hissed, her eyes darting to Augusta and Jomana. Her hands shook around her teacup, and her voice thinned, rising in obvious fear. "Your father's business killed them both."

Cold slithered down her spine. She scooted to the edge of her chair, her heart thundering in her ears. Afraid to look away from Heba lest the answers slip through her fingers, Layla tried to contain her interest. It was no use; it brimmed over in her eagerness. "What do you mean?"

"Layla—"

"Aunt Heba, please." She reached across the space and, for the first time in memory, took her aunt's hands. They both stilled in shock, but Layla didn't let go, as if their connection might bring out the truth. "I need to know what happened. If Mama's illness is in any way connected to Uncle's death, I have to keep myself, and my husband, protected."

Heba jerked her hands from her grip. "You spend too much time with the English," she spat. But her voice trembled. "Making up fanciful stories."

"They aren't stories, though, are they?" Layla sat straight in the chair. She knew any cooperation Heba might have offered had already vanished. She'd closed herself off, whether from fear or because her other aunts sat in the room. If Layla were a betting woman, she'd say it was fear. It trembled through her aunt from her lips to her hands and even her legs, which shook only the slightest against the chair.

Heba sat before them utterly terrified.

"What happened? What happened to my parents?" Heba closed up, and Layla knew they were going to be asked to leave. Layla stood before her aunt could speak. "Think on it. Send a messenger round to *The Lady Kaya* if you change your mind. Whatever happened to Uncle might very well happen to you, and to my cousins. Even after everything, I'd rather see no harm come to any of you."

Something in Heba changed, but she merely pressed her lips together and looked away. Jomana's hand brushed Layla's arm and urged her toward the door. The house remained unnaturally silent, as if only ghosts walked the rooms.

Philip waited beside the front door, as if he hadn't moved since their arrival. Silent, he nodded and held out his arm, escorting Layla out and into the brightly hot afternoon sun. She looked back, worried about who would lock the door, even if it shouldn't matter. It did. Thankfully, her younger cousin, Malik, hovered around the corner.

He raised a hand in timid greeting just before the door swung closed and locked.

"We'll meet you at the house," Augusta said with a quick nod at Philip.

"Did you discover anything?" Layla asked Philip as her aunts climbed back into their litters.

"No," he whispered, walking her toward her own litter. "The house is mostly empty; only your two younger cousins were there. They didn't speak at all, even when I passed them in the halls. Either Omar sold everything before his death or your aunt did so after, to keep the creditors at bay."

"It was a hard house," she reminded him, though probably needlessly. "No one spoke much, even when Omar wasn't there. I doubt his death would change that."

"I gave some money to your cousins. For food," he admitted.

Her head jerked up. "Thank you. What happened isn't their fault."

She closed her eyes but only saw the dim hallways, the closed-off rooms, the floor, where she looked most often. In her memory, she saw very little of value in that house, even in those early days. She found it hard to remember now, after leaving and finding a life she hadn't expected, one full of love and laughter and light. And material possessions.

Drat. She forgot to ask Heba about why Omar had lied about her and Mama's deaths. Her emotions had been so jumbled; it'd been hard, returning. Yet her brief visit had also shed light, improbable though it might've been, on the years she'd spent there. Layla hesitated but didn't turn back. She couldn't bring herself to set foot in there again. Never again.

"If your mother brought any papers or journals with her, they're long gone."

Layla glanced toward the house again, feeling as if it looked darker than its neighbors. Her imagination, she knew, but a pall hung over that dwelling, and everyone in the neighborhood recognized it.

"Aunt Heba is scared, but I don't know if she's scared enough to help, or if she'll merely hide and hope no one finds her."

"I can protect her," Philip promised, handing her up the steps and into the litter. "Your cousins, too, though I'm certain they know nothing about what happened ten years ago."

"Why?"

He frowned at her, his hand on the door. "Because they're so young. Even if they remember when you and your mother arrived, I doubt they'd remember any serious conversations."

"No." Her lips quirked upward just a tick. "I mean why would you offer?"

"Oh." He shook his head. "Because they're your family, and after Omar's death it'll be harder to keep food on the table. It's always hard to keep food on the table. I come from a family who believes in helping." He opened his mouth but shrugged away whatever he was going to say. "Because they're your family," he repeated. "As much as I don't care what happens, given the way they treated you, *you* care."

She nodded slowly. "I didn't think I would. I didn't think I'd bother to care once I escaped. I have a new...what's the word.

Outlook? A new clarity on them now. Not Omar." Never him, and no matter how she tried, Layla couldn't find it in her to mourn him. Or forgive him. "They're as trapped in that house as I was."

"And that's why." Philip nodded once, that hard, controlled look returning. "I'll see you back at the ship. Enjoy your time with your family, I have meetings. And don't worry. The men will protect you, I swear it." He raised her hand and kissed her palm. As always, his lips on her skin sent hot flutters of arousal skittering along her nerves. "We'll dine together."

"All right." Her agreement came out breathless, and the wicked smile he gave her heated her blood.

Before she knew it, she'd half leaned out of the chair and toward him, intent on kissing him no matter their public location.

"Until tonight," he promised in that low growl. Then he swung the door closed and tapped the side.

Sitting back as the litter lifted, swaying with each step of the footmen, she tried to control her breath. It was no use, and her thoughts bounced between the scorching feel of Philip's touch on her bare skin and what Heba hadn't said.

* * *

"Captain." Lange, who'd clearly been waiting for him, nodded respectfully, but there was tension in his shoulders. Pitt must've heard him, because he immediately appeared also.

Philip's muscles tensed. He clenched his jaw, though he had a dozen questions he wanted to fire off. Restraint wasn't going to work today. "Where's my wife?"

"She's below," Lange said quickly. "She's safe."

That knife in his heart eased, and he nodded, breathing easier. "What happened?"

"Thieves," Pitt said, and only then did Philip see the gash

across his face, gleaming with some sort of salve in the bright sunlight. "They attacked all three litters, but we fought them off. The hired guards fought, too; they didn't seem involved."

"And Watkins?"

"Took on five at a time." Lange shook his head in awe. "Never saw anything like it. Took two knives to the back and still fought."

Admiration, gratitude, indebtedness moved through Philip at Watkins's actions. He knew he ought to see him first, but his feet were already taking him toward Layla.

"He's with Laska. I believe Mrs. Layla is there as well."

He stilled. "She is?" He didn't quite know what to make of that.

"Aye." Pitt gestured along his cheek. "She knows a might about healing. Fine hand with a needle, too."

His mouth hung open, he realized. Snapping it closed, Philip nodded, as if this were an everyday conversation. "Did you question them?"

That anger burned through him, a fire that licked at his control and threatened everything he'd worked for. It didn't matter. They'd threatened his wife, wished harm on her and her aunts.

No, this wasn't a mere robbery.

"Oh, aye." Lange snorted in derision. "Hired nobodies."

"Aye, they were hired for a couple coins and their way with a knife." Pitt sneered at that. "They won't be using their knives anymore."

Hands tightly fisted, angry with himself for leaving Layla, Philip nodded. "Take whatever time you need and heal. This isn't over."

"Where Mrs. Layla goes, we go," Lange said. "She was truly amazing, Captain."

"Aye, never saw anything like it. Once we made it here, she moved like the wind, shouting orders, calling for herbs." Pitt shook his head. "We won't let you down, Captain. We'll protect her."

Philip couldn't say their promise surprised him. In the short time she'd been on board, Layla had charmed his entire crew. Or maybe they understood that she, too, needed a second chance. He nodded again and disappeared belowdecks.

Layla stood in the captain's day room, looking tired but whole. Throat closed, he crossed the room in two long strides and barely registered the happiness in her smile before he kissed her.

Her hands pressed against his back, and she held tight, sighing deeply into their kiss. She leaned into him as he held her tightly. He couldn't let her go, afraid if he did she'd disappear. Argus woofed from beside her, and Philip looked down. Apparently, his dog had claimed Layla as his own also.

"You're unharmed?"

"None of us were injured." She brushed cool, calloused fingers over his forehead, her smile soft now. "One of Aunt Augusta's footmen was initially attacked, but he escaped mostly unscathed. Otherwise, we're all well."

"How is Watkins?"

She looked tired, and he ran a finger over her cheek. Leaning into his touch, she closed her eyes. "Sleeping. He didn't want opium, so Laska brewed chamomile."

He nodded again, his throat tight, that fury over not having been with her beating against his temples. "I'm never leaving you again."

Opening her eyes, she offered a small, gentle laugh. "Your men are very, what's the word…attentive. Quick. I didn't know what was happening until the litter rocked."

His hands tightened on her shoulders. "You were harmed."

"No, merely startled. They never touched me."

"I should've been there," he growled, his control in tatters, his fear for her drowning him.

Layla's lips pressed against his. "I am unharmed and unafraid. That's what they wanted, was it not? To frighten me?"

"No doubt." The words came out in a growl, but he couldn't control that. He could either contain his need to burn the port and everyone who wished Layla harm to the ground, or he could control his voice. He wasn't strong enough for both.

"I refuse." Her chin raised, and her eyes met his, clear and harder than he'd ever seen them. And strong. So strong. "They, whoever they are, will not win." She stepped back and toward the door, calling out to Kaz. Within a moment, Kaz appeared with a tray holding a small meal.

Yes, his crew was as enamored with her as he. Drowning? He'd already drowned. In her strength, her kindness and determination and courage.

"Did you meet with anyone on the list?" Layla asked.

The sun had slipped beyond the windows, and as he stood there, stunned at this turn, grappling with his own fear, she lit a single lantern. Then she sat at the table and smiled softly up at him. The starlight slipped between ships and illuminated her. Her beauty stole his breath and drew him like a moth to a flame.

"No, these were people your uncles recommended." He swallowed hard at this sudden switch in subject. Then he reached over and took her hand, quite uncertain where the impulse came from. He didn't have to justify himself. Layla was his wife, and he enjoyed touching her. "They have many contacts; it makes introductions easier. One, an Englishman named Bingham, remembered your grandfather."

Layla paused in surprise, then turned her hand over and folded her fingers against his. "My grandfather? I never met him, or if I did I don't remember. He died when I was very young."

"He seemed pleased you were still alive; he'd heard the story Shadi spread about your death."

She narrowed her eyes. "You sound suspicious."

He laughed, a coarse, rough sound. But it moved through him and made it easier to breathe. Raising her hand, he pressed his lips against it harder than he should've, but his fear hadn't dissipated. "Layla, I think everyone is suspicious."

She smiled, a soft, sincere one that punched him in the gut. Philip didn't realize how much she'd changed since accidentally setting foot on *The Lady Kaya*—until today, where she'd stood up to the ghosts from her past and come out stronger. He admired that about her.

His feelings ran deeper than admiration, but he didn't wish to name that emotion.

It terrified him.

"I was thinking on the way back from Aunt Heba's."

She met his gaze, her own far more heated than talk of her aunt should've caused. A lump formed in his throat, but he knew no amount of coffee could dislodge it. Tempted to push aside their meal and take her on the table, he forced himself to focus. He had no idea what she was talking about.

"Yes?" That sounded neutral enough.

"I think Aunt Jomana and Aunt Augusta didn't suspect Omar because they believed Mama and I had died. Perhaps not from the plague, as he claimed, but since they couldn't find any hint of us, they believed him."

Right. That. Not ravishing her on the table. Which sounded far more pleasurable.

"Heba didn't say why your mother returned there?"

"No." Layla frowned, and he pushed aside his thoughts of ravishing her. His body ignored his rational mind. "She didn't say much, closed herself off. Why would Mama have gone there if she suspected Omar? It makes no sense. Therefore, my aunts didn't believe it was him. They thought the poisoning came from a business contact. Hence their extensive list."

"Agreed." He drained his carob juice, but it did absolutely nothing to quench his thirst.

"If there is that connection we discussed, it didn't begin with him but with someone else. Which also might be why they couldn't connect anything." Layla paused and frowned. "How?"

"What?" But as soon as he said the word, Philip knew what she meant. "How did he, or anyone, poison them?"

"Exactly. A servant? Someone at the souk?" She shook her head. "That would be dangerous. How would they know they'd poisoned the right person?"

"Unless they didn't, and Mostafa was an accident." Philip's mind raced. How had someone poisoned both her parents and Mostafa, given the entire family ate from one bowl? Even now, he and Layla shared the bowl, scooping up the ful medames. "We're missing something important. A key, the entire reason."

"We should retrace their steps," she said, her eyes bright. "I don't know how, and I don't want anyone else involved." She looked at the table and pushed her plate away. "Just in case."

"All right." He couldn't fault her logic, even if it wasn't at all what he'd discuss here and now. "Who do you think it started with? Al-Najjar?"

"No," she said slowly, a small frown between her brows. If he could, he'd ensure she never frowned again. "I thought so, at first. I even thought of entering his offices when he wasn't there."

Philip paused. "You wanted to break in?" He nodded in amazement at how closely her thoughts aligned with his. He'd take Harry, of course. Hutton and Lange, too. Leave Pitt here with Layla. "I approve."

She grinned, a quick, wide smile. "As much as I'd like to think he was somehow involved, other than, well"—she waved a hand—"marriage, why would he poison my parents?"

Philip offered a small grin. "Why would anyone, that's the question. Even if he did poison them, why wait a decade before demanding your hand in marriage? That's what I can't follow. We're missing something in the middle." He tapped his fingers on the table, and Argus took it as a signal that he was getting a second dinner.

"What do you mean?" She slipped her hand from his and broke off a piece of tilapia. Argus took it gently, looking adoringly up at her. "Such a good Argus; yes, you are."

Philip rolled his eyes, but that fond smile returned. There was something about the quiet of supper, just the two of them—with Argus, of course. It was as if they'd done this a hundred times and planned on a hundred more. It tugged at him and settled around him.

This was what he wanted. He might not have ever realized it, but he loved this intimacy. Sharing the day together. It's what his parents had. He hadn't realized he'd wanted that too until he sat here with Layla.

"If al-Najjar poisoned Harry and Mariam, why not demand your hand the moment Omar took you in? And why would Omar take you in if he had a hand in the poisonings?"

She sighed and rubbed her forehead. "There are still so many questions."

"I know." He took her hand again, squeezing in what he hoped was sympathy. "As I said, there's something—and someone—we're missing." He didn't like it; the thought settled like ice in his stomach, but Layla wanted answers.

For his part, Philip wouldn't care if they left Damietta and never returned. That'd keep her safe, at least. However, her family was another story, and he meant what he said earlier. He'd take care of them because they were her family.

"I think I need to have a conversation with al-Najjar."

Her gaze shot from Argus up to his. "Yes," she breathed in obvious excitement. He'd rather hear her say that while beneath him, half naked. "When do we leave?"

Damn it, he knew, just knew, she'd include herself. Stupid slip of his tongue. The ice block in his stomach didn't thaw; it stabbed his heart instead. "Layla," he began, "I don't want you involved."

She snorted, an excellent imitation of himself. Philip stilled at that realization. "I'm already involved. I always have been, just didn't realize it until recently."

Damn it, she had a point, one he'd hoped she wouldn't point out. "You absolutely cannot accompany me to al-Najjar's offices."

She straightened, back stiff, chin raised. "Then I shall visit myself."

His jaw slammed shut, his teeth clacking together. He'd protect her with his life, no matter what he had to do. Calling himself all sorts of a stupid, stupid fool, Philip resorted to pointing at her angrily. "No."

It had no effect.

"Philip," she said, a hint of iron threaded through her soft tone. "I need to be there."

Damn it, damn it, damn it! Stupid fool a dozen times over. If he didn't accompany her, he knew, like a knife to the heart, that she'd sneak out on her own and confront the man herself. The thought terrified him to the depths of his soul.

Blowing out a breath, he nodded. "All right. But you don't leave my side, and you do as I say."

He'd need extra men to accompany them. He'd need all the men to ensure her safety, especially after this afternoon.

"Shall we retire to bed now?"

Confused, he looked up at her as she stood next to him. "What?"

"Oh." She looked abashed now. "I'm sorry, I should have said that in a smoother, uh, manner." Her fingers made that small waving gesture she so favored. "There is an art to changing topics, isn't there? I missed something; I shouldn't have been so abrupt."

Philip stood and took her hands. "No." He kissed the backs

of her hands in turn, and they relaxed in his. "You didn't miss anything. What do you think you might have missed?"

"I don't know." She sighed and shook her head. "I feel so very out of place. I can't remember all the polite manners I'm certain Mama once taught me. What to say and how to say it." She offered a rueful smile. "Such as how to move the conversation from one topic onto a more pleasurable one."

Leaning over, he pressed his lips against hers. "I think what you said was perfectly fine."

"You were confused," she pointed out.

"Startled," he amended. He skimmed his lips along her jaw, pressing them lightly against the corner of her mouth. "Not because I don't want you."

He kissed the other corner of her mouth, and her breath shuddered in her chest. Moving lower, he nipped her shoulder, where the neckline of her English-style dress stopped. Backing her toward the door that separated the day room from their private cabin, he found her mouth again. She sighed into the kiss, tangling her hands in his hair.

He pushed open the door and guided her toward the bed, kicking the door closed behind him. He pressed his tongue over the spot he'd just nipped and felt her shudder against him.

"I don't think you realize how much I want you," he whispered along her skin.

"You sound surprised," she breathed, tugging his shirt over his head and tossing it aside.

Spinning her around, Philip kissed her neck while untying the ribbons of her gown. He enjoyed undressing her as much as he did dressing her—though he supposed she ought to have a lady's maid. A problem for another day.

"Surprised?" He trailed kisses down her exposed back, and she shivered, gasping his name. He'd fallen in love with everything about her—her taste, her scent, her laugh. The way she fought for her freedom as much as she fought to avenge her parents. Though they'd only spoken briefly of business, he had a feeling she'd be excellent at running a shipping company.

"Not surprised." He laid her on the bed, and she pulled him against her. Insatiable. Ravenous. "Greedy for everything."

Beneath him, her breath caught, but he didn't relent. He took one hard nipple into his mouth, teasing it with his tongue until her soft moans ended on a sharp hiss of need. He bit down, and she cried out, rocking against him.

Running his tongue over the hard peak once more, Philip took her other nipple between his fingers and tugged it, pinching it until she cried out in a breathless sob of need. His mouth found hers again, and he wondered if she knew how much he needed her. How much he loved her.

That fear teased him. He was afraid to grab what he wanted, afraid of them. But then Layla breathed his name, her nails scraping down his back, her hips rocking against his.

"Philip." Her voice hitched, and her legs wound tight around his hips.

"God, you're beautiful," he whispered.

Layla opened her eyes. They were dark with passion, and he was lost. A wildfire burned through him, promise and seduction wrapped together.

Philip's control snapped.

He tugged off his boots and pushed off his trousers. Layla's husky laugh rolled through him. The laugh that drew him in, made him want to lose himself in her passion and love. Her fingers brushed his cock, teasing him with strokes that were entirely too light. Her nails scraped over his hips and sank into his back; her teeth scraped over his shoulder and neck.

He grabbed Layla's hips and pulled her onto his lap, settling her just over his cock.

She looked down at him, her expression tender and loving. Her fingers brushed lightly over his cheek and jaw, through his hair. Her eyes had gone soft, and the fierce love that burned through him reflected in her gaze.

"Layla," he began.

She shook her head and kissed him again. In that kiss he tasted worry, concern. Trust. Holding her against him, one hand tangled in her long dark hair, Philip slipped the other hand between her legs and teased her core.

She moaned his name and a breathless "Yes." Then she arched against him, her hips grinding against his hand.

He thrust a finger into her wetness, his cock pulsing against her thigh. Jaw clenched, he grappled for that last shred of the control he so treasured. But then she opened her eyes and looked down at him. Her breaths grew short, her cheeks flushed, and her hair fell wildly about her shoulders.

She was the most beautiful woman he'd ever met, and Philip honestly didn't know what he'd do without her. He believed in her. She'd become his world in a few short weeks. He grasped her hips and lifted her over him. With one hard thrust, he entered her.

Layla cried out, her fingers digging into him as she rocked against him. She rose over him and slammed down, taking him deeper every time. Philip felt his own climax tighten through him, the lightning feel of release. He wanted to postpone it, to enjoy Layla's heat as it surrounded him.

He found and circled her sensitive nub. Tightening around his cock, she climaxed hard, her legs and arms wrapped around him as she rode out her orgasm. Still he moved over her nub, watching her pleasure climb again. Laying her on her back, Philip moved hard within her, his own climax coiling through him.

Layla shouted his name just as he felt his control snap.

CHAPTER 18

ozing with Layla in his arms, Philip let his mind wander. She fit so perfectly in his arms, and he could never get enough of her smiles and laughter, her sighs and kisses. His fingers tingled—well, maybe she didn't fit *so* perfectly. The bed was cramped, bolted against the wall, and as much as he loved the warm weight of her in his arms, his hand had fallen asleep.

"Did you really mean you'd continue to help Aunt Heba?" Layla shifted slightly, turning awkwardly on the bed.

"I won't lie, I thought about letting them all rot." He sighed, sitting upright and stretching his arm. "That was my first instinct." And his second, but he'd talked himself out of such pettiness. It hadn't been easy. "My parents. They were very fortunate in life, and they believe in helping those who are less so."

Philip watched her stand and stretch, his heart thudding in his chest. She pulled on her chemise, and sat back on the bed, leaning against the wall and stretching out her legs.

"I like that," she said quietly. "I've been both. I've known safety and security. And I've seen firsthand how difficult it is to keep food on the table and a roof over one's head." In the darkness, he saw her eyes had closed, but she turned her head to face him. "Life is hard enough without worrying about where your next meal might come from."

He lifted her fingers to his lips and kissed them. "My father wasn't always wealthy." He snorted at the memory of the story he'd been told. "The emerald?"

Her eyes opened, and she sat upright. Her gaze darted toward the trunk she'd claimed as hers. "Yes?"

"It was from my great-grandfather, part of a dozen or so jewels he gave my parents as they left Cairo."

"Is that why you carried it? Because it was a gift to your parents? No," she said in the next breath. "It's more than that. Sentiment?" She frowned. "Something so valuable would be, I suppose."

"It was my introduction." Saying it aloud sounded foolish now. "I hadn't planned it out, I admit. I'm not sure how an emerald could have proved my identity, but it was all I had." He ran a hand down his face and shook his head. "I'm not the planner of the family; that's Yara. I chose Egypt as my first solo voyage because I wanted to try and find my great-grandfather. No one even knows if he's still alive. It's been over thirty years since my parents left."

"That's why you wanted to sail to Cairo." She nodded decisively. "I understand. It's entirely possible he's still alive; my family survived the last twenty years."

His lips quirked upward. Conversations with her moved from one topic to another with a rapidity he hadn't experienced before.

"What's his name? Perhaps we can send a messenger, one of the company's trusted ones. Charlie is in Cairo with Amirah's husband. They can search until we can sail there ourselves."

Again he smiled, feeling that tug between them. Together. That's the word he was looking for. Whatever happened from now on, they would see to it together. He rather liked that. Pulling her back into his arms, he kissed her hard and fast.

"One day," he promised. He'd made her quite a few promises, and yet he couldn't regret any of them. "And we still might." He hoped. "However, if a messenger can't find my great-grandfather…"

He hadn't actually considered that until now. More grand plans from his childhood. Philip shook his head, but Layla offered a slight smile and took his hand.

"We might still find him," she said.

"Let's not discuss my great-grandfather in bed."

She smiled, settling over him, straddling his hips and bracing her hands on his chest. "There are more pleasurable activities we can engage in, I agree."

* * *

THE NEXT MORNING, Layla stood on the deck as Philip spoke with Saied Harry. He looked tired—Philip, not Harry—and she wondered if he'd slept last night. She had, quite soundly, but Layla remembered hearing him move about long after they'd made love and she'd fallen asleep, warm and sated and happy.

"Mrs. Layla." Hutton nodded and held out a small tray with a glass of carob juice. "From Laska."

"Oh, thank you, Hutton. I would've gone down for it."

"No trouble, missus." He smiled and tugged briefly at his hat. "'Tis another fine day here. It's why I love this route." He grinned and gestured broadly at the cloudless sky. "The weather is a mite finer than England."

"Is it so bad there that everyone wishes to escape?" She frowned into her glass. "Ph—ah, Captain Conrad said the same, or something similar."

"It's not the northern countries," he admitted, "where it snows well into summer and in the winter the seas freeze." She stared at him in shock, utterly unable to comprehend such a thing. He nodded toward the ship's railing. "Benedito's returned from your aunts' house."

"Thank you," she said instinctively, still stunned by the concept of a frozen sea in winter. She looked at the Mediterranean and couldn't imagine it freezing. Stepping for the gangway, she stopped after a single step. "Hutton, do you speak Egyptian?"

"More than a bit of Arabic, yes, but not like the captain." He walked a half step behind her as she crossed the ship. "Been sailing this route for twenty years. Escaped Barbary pirates, the French, the Turkish, the French again—or their allies, at least." He grinned, revealing a missing tooth. "Even the English."

That sounded like enough experience for the vague plan she'd been hatching since she woke. She and Philip hadn't set a time for their meeting with al-Najjar, but she had a feeling they'd need someone listening in at all entryways.

"What made you become a sailor?" she asked as Benedito checked in with Philip.

"The Conrads; they gave me a second chance."

She stilled and met his gaze in understanding. Philip had said something about that, his second-chance crew. She'd thought he meant they'd given him a second chance. Perhaps he meant they'd all received one.

She certainly had, once she boarded this ship.

"Mrs. Layla." Benedito crossed the deck and nodded at Hutton, who disappeared to his own duties. "Your response." He reached into an inner pocket and produced a neatly folded letter. "Your cousin has accepted your invitation and promised to be here within the hour. No one watched the house except our men and those your uncle hired."

"Thank you, Benedito. I'm grateful." She took the letter and offered a small smile. "I appreciate you seeing to my errand. I wasn't sure who to ask."

Nor how else she might get in touch with her aunts and Evelyn without leaving the ship. She'd rather not be carried in a litter. That took entirely too long, though she understood the status of arriving in one. But fear nagged at the back of her mind. She knew from experience that even with enough men, even expensive litters could be attacked. She also hadn't wished to ask Philip, who had already dropped everything to help her.

"It was my pleasure, ma'am." Benedito nodded and turned back to his duties.

Layla opened the missive, several short lines from Aunt Augusta in neat rows. Philip came to stand beside her, one hand on her elbow as he steered her toward the poop deck. She glanced up and saw his slight frown.

"What's wrong? Is everything all right with Saied Harry?"

"There are a few questions on the wharves he's concerned about." Philip looked over the bow but shook his head. "I've been remiss, should've paid better attention."

"Merchants? Or something else?"

"Questions about you. About the ship as well. Harry's looking into it." He tried to smile, but that control he wrapped around himself had returned. She didn't push. Something was wrong, and he was only telling her half of it. "He's a master of disguise; he'll figure it out."

"That's my fault," she whispered. "You were busy with my problems when you should've been seeing to what's happening here."

"No, not at all." He took her hand, and his smile was more sincere now. "There are always rumors in any port. Pirates, corrupt customs agents." He shook his head. "Smuggling."

"Which would have been your only problems if I hadn't boarded the wrong ship," she pointed out. "I've brought so much trouble, and now you must also deal with a new bride whose family has been murdered by unknown persons for unknown reasons."

"True, but I'm still glad I met you." He grinned down at her, that spark of warmth in his smile that never failed to make her heart jump. "I wouldn't trade these last weeks for anything. What did your aunts have to say?" He looked over his shoulder. "And when did you become so friendly with my crew?"

"They're all so lovely," she said in a rush, defending the crew that had embraced her welcomingly. "And very kind. I see why they accept you, despite what you might think."

Philip looked at her oddly, as if sorting through that observation. "Everyone deserves a second chance," he said quietly. "Sometimes even a third."

In the case of him, he meant. Layla nodded and stepped closer, not sure what she planned but wanting him to know she understood. In the open, with so many eyes on them, she couldn't hold him close or kiss him. Rather, she brushed her fingertips over his hand and silently vowed she'd do everything in her power to see he never doubted himself.

"Thank you for my second chance."

He grinned, that quick, lopsided smile, and gestured to the letter. "Did she answer your questions?"

She handed him the letter and stepped closer, so it looked as if they were both reading the missive. Only he knew she couldn't read more than a handful of words.

"It's Aunt Augusta's handwriting." Her stomach swooped, but she couldn't tell if it was fear or anticipation or both.

"I agree that your uncle would never have conceived such a plan himself. Could he have worked with another? After some discussion, Jomana and I believe so. We were wrong not to have looked deeper into his connections." There was a blotch of ink, as if Augusta's hand had shaken as she wrote. *"Please be careful, Layla. If you need to return here for your own safety, you are always welcome."*

"I'm safe here," she said before Philip could speak. "The crew takes very good care of me." She swallowed and paused. The words lay on her tongue, but she couldn't utter them. Not yet. "You take very good care of me."

He looked down at her sharply. "I promised I'd protect you, and I shall. Always." He huffed out a breath. "We still keep watch in port. I'll double the guard."

Perhaps that was where he went while she slept. Checking the guard. Something deep inside her heart thought it otherwise; however, she didn't ask. Not now, in broad daylight, the weight of her aunts' warnings lying heavily upon her.

"I have meetings today." He carefully folded the letter and handed it back. "Please don't leave the ship."

"Meetings" sounded entirely too vague, and Layla watched him carefully. "A meeting with al-Najjar?" she asked with enough innocence he might not suspect anything.

That sharp look returned. He suspected. "No." She believed him. "It's with Darwish, the coffee grower."

"Are negotiations not working in your favor?" She frowned. "You've met with him quite often."

"He has other exports. Since his father died and communication was cut off, apparently, he has expanded." Philip rubbed his eyes, and once again Layla wondered why he got so little sleep. Perhaps there was more trouble here than she realized. "Sugar among them, but I'm not sure if he uses slave labor."

Suddenly cold in the warm morning sun, Layla shivered. "I've heard of the slave markets. Even Aunt Heba warned me about them. Did Darwish's father use slaves?"

"Not that I know of. If he did, and we knew or even suspected, my family never would've signed that initial contract." He took her hand again, rubbing it between his. As much as she appreciated the gesture, it did little to warm her. "We don't deal with growers who use slaves. We don't have any contracts with farmers who use them."

She nodded numbly. She believed him. Any family who used their wealth and power to help rather than to grow wealthier and more powerful wouldn't rely on slave labor. Her gaze flicked around the deck, briefly landing on the men she'd gotten to know over the last weeks.

Men who needed a second chance. She didn't believe they'd condone slave labor, but then, she knew so very little about people in general.

"I promise you, Layla. If I discover that Darwish is using slaves, we won't conduct any business with him."

"Thank you," she said through numb lips. Then she felt very foolish, thanking him for something like that when she had no real say in the matter and he'd planned on it anyway.

"What are your plans for today?" He raised her hand and kissed her knuckles. She very much enjoyed that touch, and she hoped he never stopped.

"Evelyn is coming round. Benedito kindly delivered a message to her while delivering my letter." Their letter, as he had written the missive, and then she copied the wording so as not to expose her secret.

"All right." He kept hold of her hand as he looked round the deck, nodding at Reeves, the helmsman. "I don't know how long I'll be."

"Do what you need." She swallowed against the cold fear the talk of the slave markets had instilled. She'd seen one only once, purely by accident, when she'd gotten lost on the way back from the souk during those first few weeks at Omar's house. It'd terrified her so deeply she ran all the way back to the house. It was the only time she'd been glad to arrive there.

"Don't leave the ship," he warned.

"I promised I would not," she reminded him in what might've been an unnecessarily snappish tone.

"I know." He sighed and shook his head, his fingers once more pressed against his eyes. "When I return, we'll plan how best to approach al-Najjar." His lips twitched. "His offices, at least."

She nodded, but before she could ask what that plan might entail or confide in him about her own schemes, a call from the wharves echoed upward. She didn't understand the word, but the ship itself seemed to. The men leaped into action, and before Layla realized it, Evelyn was on deck.

"What was all that?" she asked, meeting Philip's smug gaze.

"Code words. For the men watching your family's house." She nodded wordlessly. "It's to let the ship know that one of them has escorted someone—in this case, Evelyn—and that all is well."

She opened her mouth again, then snapped it closed. "I'm impressed." Offering a small laugh, she held his gaze. "Thank you for keeping my family safe."

He didn't have to, of course. Betting woman or not, she knew it never occurred to him not to keep them safe. They were important to her; therefore, he'd used his resources in whatever way possible to ensure their safety.

That warm wave of love washed over her again, and, uncaring about their location, she leaned up and kissed him. Layla supposed she ought to be embarrassed, but all she felt was gratitude and love.

Just as Evelyn climbed the stairs, she said, "We sent the message to Cairo, yes?"

His gaze held hers. "Yes, with one of your uncle's trusted messengers."

"Good," she said as Evelyn climbed onto the poop deck.

"I'll leave you to your visit." He grinned, but heat shone darkly in his gaze. A promise for later.

"Captain Conrad." Evelyn nodded at him as he stepped away. "Layla, dear, thank you for the invitation. I'm grateful to be away from the house."

"Is there a problem?" Layla gestured for the stairs that led belowdecks. She debated asking the crew to set up a table and chairs in the fresh air, but she also enjoyed the privacy of the captain's dining room.

"No," Evelyn hedged. "Not a problem. I simply wished for a change in scenery."

As she gestured for Evelyn to precede her, Layla wondered if that had anything to do with Evelyn's wishing to leave Damietta.

Layla nodded at Kaz, who stood at attention by the galley, then crossed the room and took the tray from him. "We'll be fine, Kaz," she promised. "You see to your own work."

He looked dubious, as if he didn't believe she wouldn't need something he would happily provide, but he nodded. "*Tak, pani Layla.*"

Considering that a win, to hear him speak, she returned to the table, where Evelyn watched the exchange with interest.

"They like you." Her smile was small, soft, wistful. "I'm glad, Layla. It seems you found your place."

"My place?" She set the tray on the table. "I suppose I have," she agreed slowly. "I hadn't realized how...settled I'd become in such a short time." Staring at the bowls of melons she'd set on the table, Layla smiled, letting the feeling of safety and contentment wash through her. "And you? What about you?"

"I still wish to leave." Evelyn sighed and stared into her coffee, holding the cup in two hands and breathing in the cardamom.

Drat. Layla had forgotten to ask Philip. She would tonight, as they planned their meeting with al-Najjar. Until then, she thought perhaps Evelyn needed someone to talk with as much as she did.

"After our coffee, perhaps we should practice more in the cargo hold."

Evelyn perked up. "I'd like that very much."

CHAPTER 19

*P*hilip stood on the deck of *The Lady Kaya* and didn't feel quite as clever as he had when he'd named the vessel. The sun had slipped behind the other ships, making him wish for the openness of the sea and the unending expanse of the setting sun over deceptively calm waters.

"Philip?" Harry asked. Probably not for the first time.

"Plans, Harry." He shook his head and turned away from the sun. Harry's clear blue gaze steadily held his. "The best laid plans of mice and men oft go awry."

"Burns?"

Philip nodded, trying to remember the next line, but he came up blank. It didn't matter; that one line summed up his life with near perfection. When planning for this voyage, he'd had so many ideas about proving his worth. Proving that he was more than the drunken, gambling Conrad, that he was a worthy part of the family.

He'd wanted to surprise his mother with news of her grandfather. He'd wanted to surprise both his parents with the vastness of his contacts and the contracts he'd negotiated. Oh, he'd surprise them, all right. With a new wife—though he wasn't worried about their reaction to Layla. They'd love her.

It was their reaction to his own impetuousness he worried about. Then again, he supposed he fit right in with his siblings and their wild adventures that led to matrimony.

Cairo beckoned, yet he couldn't leave Damietta now. Not when there were so many reasons to stay. It'd been barely a day since the messenger headed south, and while he was grateful for Layla's suggestion, he still wished to see Cairo for himself. They would, just perhaps later than planned.

"And leave us naught but grief and pain, for promised joy!"

"You're full of surprises, Harry." Philip grinned at his friend.

"I'm a man of many things." Harry bowed extravagantly with a wide grin and a wink. "Doesn't pay to stay in a rut, after all."

"No word on al-Najjar?" he asked rather than delve into Harry's many surprises. He scanned the deck for Layla, but she'd retired to their cabin after Evelyn's visit. He missed her, though they'd been apart for a scant hour.

"He doesn't hide," Harry huffed as the men continued their daily routine. The ship required maintenance before they put it back out to sea. Whenever that might be. "He's well-known in the city, though most of the more, ah, respectable merchants and ship's captains steer clear of him."

"He's really a wool merchant?" Philip shook his head. "I'd have guessed that was a ploy. What about his outside interests?"

"I know we spoke of gambling dens, but I can't say with any certainty. Either you're wrong"—Harry held up a hand—"and I don't think you are, or he's very discreet."

"Hmm." Philip tapped his leg, his fingers beating out one of the war songs from his youth.

When he realized the tune, he stopped. He'd been obsessed with those songs, memorizing every single one, imagining his life as a great spy. He'd created his own codes and learned those that Colonel Marcus Hilton used. Oh, yes, Philip had grand plans: working for Hilton as his older siblings had, finding out all of Napoleon's secrets—on his own, of course—and winning the war for Britain.

He snorted. Harry watched him with more than a hint of concern but said nothing. What he needed was a good walk. "Who isn't needed, either on guard duty or for their much-deserved rest?" Philip looked around. He knew if he asked, every one of his crew would jump at the chance to help. Especially after the attack.

That nagging feeling of foreboding cautioned him that he'd need them, and soon. No sense having everyone on board as exhausted as he.

"We can spare Hodgkins, Reinholt, and Oliveira. Unless you want Egyptian speakers?" Harry peered at him. "What are you planning?"

"Nothing so grand," Philip promised with a wry smile. "A simple visit to the *al-tajir*. I need the walk, and, given that she hasn't left the ship yet today, I thought I'd ask my wife along."

Layla had promised she wouldn't leave the ship without him.

"I'll tell the men their new orders."

Philip nodded and disappeared belowdecks. In their cabin, he found his wife sitting at the desk, her aunt's letter open before her. Argus sat at her feet. He opened one eye when Philip entered but didn't move.

Man's best friend, indeed.

"Did you enjoy your visit with Evelyn?" He crossed the room and kissed the top of her head. The gesture was warm and natural, as if he'd done it a thousand times before.

"Very." She smiled at him, her smile dazzling in its happiness. His heart turned over in his chest. "We practiced more with the khanjar you gave me." She grinned wider, clearly thrilled with her progress. "Can you show me more of the moves from before?"

His cock hardened at the mere thought of her in his arms as

they moved smoothly through the routines that he knew better than any dance move.

"Tomorrow," he promised, his voice strangled. "I've decided to stretch my legs. Would you care to accompany me?"

She stilled, but not in fear. Curiosity, perhaps. "Is it about—have you discovered something?"

"No, no." He took her hand. He hesitated, but she needed answers, and Philip wasn't entirely certain al-Najjar would tell him anything about the Braithwaites. He was even less certain the man would tell Layla anything, given that she and her aunts had been attacked in such a public place.

"Something feels off," he finally confessed. "The men see nothing, no one follows us, the house is secure, and yet...it's strange." He paced the tight cabin and tried to explain what bothered him. "I suppose it's possible that whoever poisoned your parents is long dead, but that offers us no answers."

"I've thought of that," she admitted softly. "We might never know, and I think I'm all right not knowing. It certainly might be safer." She tilted her head slightly and reached for his hand. "It sits here." She lifted their joined hands and placed them over her heart. "And I wonder about my family. Did they abandon me because of my heritage?" His hand tightened around hers, but he didn't interrupt. "Did they do so because they poisoned my parents?"

She lowered their hands and looked at them, breathing soft in the quiet cabin. Even Argus's breath barely dented the silence. Philip didn't speak, completely at a loss as to what he might say that would erase the devastated look on her face.

"I will never abandon you," he blurted out. "I'll protect you with my life."

She lifted her gaze and smiled softly at him. "I know. Let's hope it doesn't come to that. I quite like you alive."

He returned her small smile. One problem at a time. Except the problems seemed to pile up higher and higher.

He looked at her letter on the table. "What are you doing?"

"Practicing," she said decisively. "I know what the letter says, so I'm memorizing the words. It's been so long since I've seen English words; however, some look familiar." Her finger traced her aunt's signature. "I thought I might practice those, too."

They'd practice anything she wanted. Though he probably wasn't the best person to help her. "School wasn't my strength. It was too…regimented, I suppose." He snorted. "Given that, it's a wonder I thought the army was the life for me."

Her soft chuckle wrapped around him. "We have time." She waved her fingers. "Now then, a walk, yes?"

He held out his arm. "It's not far." He glanced at Argus, who woofed excitedly. "No, sorry, boy. You'll have to stay."

"We'll bring you back a treat," Layla promised.

Philip rolled his eyes and suppressed a groan. "You spoil him."

"He deserves it," she countered as she wrapped her hijab around her. "I'd like to talk to you about Evelyn." She looked over her shoulder as he followed her above deck. "She'd like to return with us to Britain."

* * *

THE *AL-TAJIR* HADN'T CHANGED as much as Layla had. She looked around the offices, with their high shelves covered in ledgers and papers, the desks that hadn't moved in ten years. Adeem, the new secretary, watched curiously as Layla and Philip walked the office. Muhammad and Josiah walked behind, allowing them this moment.

"Is it like you remembered?" Philip asked as he escorted her outside.

"Yes, surprisingly." She hadn't remembered much about the rooms, but once she stepped inside, as with so many of her memories, it all came back. "Haamid, he used to be the secretary, but otherwise nothing has changed."

"I asked Muhammad about him." Philip took her hand again as they stepped from the offices. "Apparently, he died in the invasion."

Many had, and Haamid's loss saddened Layla. Too many losses over the years.

"I'm still working through all the pieces," Layla said as they walked down the main thoroughfare in the opposite direction of her uncles' business. One-third hers now. The paperwork would be finalized by week's end.

"What have you worked out so far?" He kept his gait shorter, so she didn't have to rush to keep up. She noticed that about Philip, the way he'd adjust so she'd feel more at ease.

It welled through her, catching her off guard each time. The love she felt more surely every day. She hadn't admitted it aloud, not yet. Layla didn't know how to, and she certainly couldn't ask anyone. This afternoon, she'd been tempted to ask Evelyn when she visited but had let the moment pass.

"I still think that third man you mentioned is key."

"Or woman." He grinned down at her, the last rays of the setting sun highlighting the ends of his curling hair in magnificent shades of brown.

"I had not considered that, but you're correct." She curled her free hand into her skirts, the fine material wrinkling under her death grip. She would not embarrass herself, or him, in public by touching his hair. No matter how beautiful it looked or how much she adored running her fingers through it.

"You think this person is the reason someone—we're supposing it's Omar—poisoned your parents?" He nodded, but they didn't slow. Their pace remained steady, their conversation low enough so as not to look suspicious nor be overheard.

"I think Saied al-Najjar knows more about this," she said. The words came out harder than she'd anticipated. "I have too many questions about his involvement. I suppose," she added on a sigh. "Though maybe he's not involved, and we suspect him because of, well, the marriage contract."

"Could be," he agreed. "But I don't believe that, either."

"I'll speak with Aunt Heba again. Even if Omar kept things from her, that house was far too small for that many secrets."

And she still had questions about her mother's reasons for going there in the first place. She would not let another opportunity pass her by.

"Why does your cousin wish to return with us to Britain?" he asked as they passed from the nicer offices toward the less reputable ones. "I have no problem with her passage, but I thought she was happy here."

"She didn't say," Layla admitted. "I've lost so much time with them all, I barely know her anymore."

She knew Amirah even less, who had her own household to take care of. It was as if, even though she'd rediscovered her family, she'd lost them again due to time and distance. It saddened her, though Layla supposed she'd be leaving, too, once Philip completed his business.

Suddenly, Philip stilled.

A shiver worked its way down her spine, and despite the warm afternoon, cold settled in her bones. As casually as she could, Layla looked up at him. He didn't meet her gaze, which was unusual but expected given the sudden change in atmosphere.

"Is someone following us?" she whispered around a dry mouth.

"Watching." He met her gaze quickly, there and gone in a blink.

She wanted to ask how he'd done that but didn't wish to distract him. Too many jumbled questions raced through her mind. This was what she'd expected every time she left the ship.

Now that it happened, she wondered how it had. Philip and

his crew swore they weren't followed, and she believed him. So someone had waited for them. Or this was entirely happenstance, though Layla didn't believe anything that had happened since she left Omar's house almost a month ago was happenstance.

"Layla," he said casually, looking over her head and behind her. "When I say so, I want you to duck into that doorway to your left and not move." He paused. "You wouldn't happen to carry your khanjar, would you?"

"No." The word left her in a gasp of surprise. Bringing her dagger had honestly never occurred to her, though she realized now how foolish that had been. Not that she could do more than throw the dagger at a hay bale, but its weight might comfort her.

And scare off anyone who threatened her.

"That's fine." He held her gaze. "If anyone comes after you—"

"Don't worry about me," she interrupted. "I didn't cross Damietta in the middle of the night just so someone could harm me here."

His lips ticked into a slight smile that didn't reach his hard, dark eyes. "Don't move from that doorway until I say."

Layla nodded and waited for his signal. She had no desire to hide, despite all of three lessons using a dagger. Still, she wasn't foolish enough to believe she could be more than a hindrance during whatever was about to happen here on the street.

"Now."

He gave her a quick shove toward the door, and she hurried over, turning immediately once she was inside the frame. Philip moved, drawing his khanjar and sweeping it in a wide, smooth arc. Fascinated, she watched him even as several men circled around him.

The crew who'd followed them jumped into the fray almost immediately, and she lost track of what happened after that.

Not of Philip, who stood slightly taller than everyone else. Or maybe she only thought so because she knew him best.

Leaning back, Layla found a broom. Not exactly a weapon of choice, unless one was attacked by sand. Nonetheless, she gripped it as she would her dagger. At least it'd keep any of those men away.

She needn't bother. As quickly as the fight began, it was over. No one else entered the fight, and the street cleared out as soon as Philip stood still, as if that were some sort of indication. Like everyone knew what might happen and wanted no part of it. Even as the dust literally settled, no one ventured from wherever they'd disappeared to.

Looking like a wild beast, Philip scanned the street. The sun hadn't yet fully set, but it seemed dimmer. More foreboding. She shivered and gripped the broom tighter. For one long, eerily silent moment, nothing moved. No dogs barked. Even the sand hovered in the air as if suspended.

The moment snapped, and she breathed again. Philip stood over several men, each sporting superficial cuts over their arms, bellies, and faces. From her angle, she didn't think he'd seriously wounded anyone, which impressed her all the more. Even she realized it took far more skill to hold back than it did to cut deep. From the tick in his cheek, Philip had held everything back.

She watched him, ignoring the rest of the crew, who circled their captain in a loose formation, each man ready for another attack. None came. Finally, he met her gaze, his own as tightly controlled as ever, and nodded. Crossing the distance, she reached up and brushed her fingers over his lip, where someone had apparently hit him with a lucky punch.

"A broom?" He frowned down at it, wincing at the movement.

"Oh." She tossed it back toward the door. "It was all I could find." Dismissing the poor broom, she brushed his lips again. "Are you hurt anywhere else?"

"This?" He caught her fingers against his lips. "This isn't anything, I promise." His eyes, dark and hard already, narrowed. "When I find out who sent these men, that will be another story."

Layla didn't say anything; she didn't know what to say. What with her heart pounding so loudly she'd swear everyone could hear it and her entire focus solely on Philip. Eventually, she looked over her shoulder. "Anyone else harmed?"

"They're fine." He nodded at the five men gathered behind them, looking as furiously angry as she'd ever seen any of them. "Send word back to the ship," he ordered. "Be prepared."

Lange nodded, then offered a slight bow in her direction before disappearing. The fight had lasted such a short time, and yet Layla felt as if an eternity had passed.

"Who sent them?" she managed, swallowing hard. "Did you recognize anyone?"

He looked at her sharply. "No. Not even al-Najjar's son."

"Someone else, then?"

"I mean to find out. And when I do, they'll pay for putting you in harm's way."

"They attacked you," she pointed out as he picked up his hat and dusted it off. "Not me." She frowned. "They didn't even look at me."

"Hmm." He paused. "That means they wanted all of us out of the way first. No witnesses, no one following them." He looked ahead, toward al-Najjar's offices. "Or they wanted something else."

"A robbery?" Even as she said it, she dismissed that idea. "A lot of men for a simple robbery."

"I don't believe that." He took her hand and started back down the street.

"No," she agreed. "I don't, either.

CHAPTER 20

Philip didn't slam open the door to al-Najjar's offices, though he wanted to. Beside him, Layla stood tall and proud, her chin raised and her eyes hard. No, he wouldn't show his hand to the wool merchant, but inside he seethed with fury over the possibility that the man had endangered his wife, a molten wave of anger he barely clamped down on.

Ushering Layla inside, Philip didn't wait for the man to look up from his ledgers. "We met your welcoming committee. Thank you, but I know the way."

The old man snorted, his gaze steady on Philip's. "If I'd sent a welcoming committee, you'd know."

"Oh?" Philip feigned surprise, but he knew al-Najjar wasn't fooled. The man was far too canny for that. "And here I thought the group who met us as we turned onto your street worked for you. I suppose someone else is working your territory."

As expected, al-Najjar's eyes narrowed. He flicked his gaze toward Layla, but only for a moment. "Perhaps you shouldn't have brought your pretty wife here."

The implication that they'd been after Layla punched him in

the gut, but Philip had already suspected that. A quick glance around the room showed no one else, which surprised him. A man like al-Najjar usually had lackeys around, men waiting to do his bidding. The first time Philip had arrived, he'd been alone as well.

It sent a cold shiver up his spine.

"Seyda Conrad, a pleasure to see you again."

Philip stepped between al-Najjar and Layla, blocking the man's view of her. The violence that had followed him throughout his boyhood boiled so close to the surface, Philip had trouble finding words. Slamming al-Najjar's head onto the table? That seemed the quicker means to his end, but he held back. Barely.

"We seek information," Layla said, her voice cool and steady. She stepped beside Philip, her fingers brushing his hand. "We were given to understand you know much about what happens in Damietta."

Al-Najjar's dark eyes glittered, but he merely inclined his head. "Finally. A deal."

Layla's fingers twitched against his, but she otherwise showed no emotion. "What did you hold over my uncle?"

Philip waited, straining to hear any other sound. Another ambush. A musket shot to the back. The distinctive sound of a dagger cutting through the air. Nothing. Only the three of them. Not even a squeak from outside.

"A trade, perhaps," he offered into the silence. He knew this game, all too well, and he felt foolish that he hadn't recognized it earlier. "Information for—what?"

"This one is free." Al-Najjar held up his hand. His gaze flicked from Layla to Philip. "Because you already settled the debt." He laughed, a slight wheeze to the sound. "Shadi gambled. It was why your grandfather agreed to the marriage between your mother and father, even if he was English."

Layla stilled. Philip didn't think she so much as drew breath.

Al-Najjar shook his head. "Your father took over the *tjare*, merging it with his and making it far more profitable with his partners. It's not a secret. Though I suppose with your resurrection, no one bothered to explain that." Another shake of his head, and he set aside his reed pen. "Shadi gambled everything, more than he possessed."

"And for his debt you wanted my hand?" Hers found Philip's, and he held tight. "Am I worth so much?"

Al-Najjar snorted. "It was all he had left to offer."

With those words, Philip realized what happened. "Oh, but that's very clever." He nodded at al-Najjar, then met Layla's gaze. "He'd marry you, claim your third of the business, which also included your grandfather's part. Oh, he'd promise you safety and luxury, of course."

"A very lucrative transaction," al-Najjar admitted with a wave around the room. "He left everything to Braithwaite, who had only one child. I believe you might have been promised to one of your father's business partner's sons, but with your supposed death that all changed."

Al-Najjar waved it away and leaned forward, as if imparting a secret. A free piece of information. But that terrified Philip. Men like al-Najjar didn't offer anything for free.

"Until Shadi offered your hand for his debts, even I had no idea you still lived."

"It really was only about money, then." Her hand gripped his in defeat, but Philip wasn't finished. Before he could say anything, her head tilted, and he knew she was puzzling out more of her past.

If even al-Najjar had no idea she still lived until Shadi offered her in exchange for his gambling debts, then why would Shadi hide her all these years?

"Who did Shadi work for?" he asked, squeezing Layla's hand in warning. "Where did he find the money to gamble in your dens?"

The hoarse laugh filled the room, a strange echoing sound that reverberated along the walls. "And what do you have to offer for that piece of information?"

"I have a great many things." Philip shrugged as if it didn't matter, which it didn't. "Let's start with something small." His mind raced but settled on the lanterns in his day cabin. "A small item for a small piece of information."

Though he didn't look convinced, al-Najjar inclined his head.

"A pair of seventeenth-century lanterns, inlaid with gold." He'd won them in one of his first games. He'd liked them; the other man hadn't wished to part with them, and that made the win all the sweeter. Of course, it was only later that Philip realized slave labor in the Americas had contributed to the gold inlay. They seemed a good trade in this instance.

"They're Venetian," he added, and al-Najjar's eyes lit up. "Murano glass."

"Done." Al-Najjar nodded decisively. "Shadi worked for Bingham. I believe you know the man?"

That cold spike worked its way down his back again, and Philip inclined his head. "Indeed."

"Did odd jobs for him, is my understanding." Al-Najjar paused and shot Philip an assessing look. "The pair of lanterns? That's no small item for such information. Either you don't care about wealth, or you know more than you let on." He laughed again. "I like you, Conrad."

"One lantern." Layla's voice broke through al-Najjar's laughter. She said something derogatory in Arabic about his lack of bartering skills, to which she and al-Najjar laughed. Philip resisted rolling his eyes as he pretended not to understand them. "I've seen them. They're exquisitely wrought, with dancing copper figurines atop."

Al-Najjar sat straighter. "Your wife drives a hard bargain. All right." He nodded and leaned forward. "What information for the second lantern?"

"How did someone like Shadi fool the entire town into thinking my wife had died?" Philip asked casually. Beside him, Layla stiffened, but he didn't think al-Najjar realized it, astute as he was. "I met him only the once, but even that meeting proved he didn't have the temper to keep such a secret."

"Hmm, yes." Al-Najjar leaned back in his chair, a highbacked piece in dark wood that gleamed in the few rays of sunlight that slanted through the windows. "That is the question, is it not?"

Information al-Najjar did not possess? Philip straightened.

"Which begs my own. What do you suspect him of? Other than keeping the lovely seyda a secret all these years. Why offer two-hundred-year-old exquisite Venetian lanterns for this information?" He shook his head. "You drive a hard bargain, Captain. The entire port is abuzz with word of you and your men. How each one drives a harder bargain than the last."

"Yet here I am, offering off my prized possessions for information about my wife's past." He shrugged negligently and held the other man's gaze. "Doesn't seem like much in comparison."

"Hmm," al-Najjar said again.

"I've lost ten years of my life," Layla injected, that thread of iron back in her voice. "I want to know why and for whom." She lifted her chin. "And I think you know more than you're saying."

Al-Najjar's laugh was softer now. "That, I'm afraid I can't help you with, seyda. It is intriguing, however, is it not? How Shadi, who was no better than a day laborer for Bingham and who lived in abject poverty, managed that. Where did he find the extra money? He rarely won at Tarneeb, and even then only enough to satisfy his immediate creditors."

Bingham again. Philip hadn't looked into the man much. He'd seemed honest, hadn't set off any alarm bells when they spoke, and he had, if not a blessing, then at least an understanding from el-Nebi and Bartley.

Then again, Philip didn't know if he was seeing villains in every corner, or if the whirlwind that had been his first days in Damietta had obscured what he might've suspected about Bingham.

"Why lend him money?" Layla asked. "Or continue to?"

"Information," Philip supplied to al-Najjar's wide grin. "Shadi offered information about Bingham, his business, his contacts." Probably his personal life as well, anything that might give al-Najjar a leg up on the man.

"If you didn't send those men," Layla said slowly, looking up at al-Najjar, "then who did?"

"I think, seyda, that is a question you must ask Bingham."

Philip suddenly had many questions for Bingham. He nodded at al-Najjar. "I'll send round the lanterns."

Philip ignored al-Najjar's speculative look and ushered Layla out the door. His men waited, watching the silent street. Nodding, he held Layla's hand as they started back to the ship.

"I have many questions," she admitted softly. "However, I think al-Najjar is telling the truth."

"I'm afraid so, too," he said, scanning the darkening street. The men walked closer, keeping a tight formation. "I still don't understand how Shadi was able to keep you and Mariam a secret."

"Aunt Heba."

"What?" He looked down at her, diverting his attention from his surroundings.

"My grandfather must have arranged the marriage. He wouldn't have if he'd known Omar was a gambler, but by then it might've been too late."

"You think Heba is the reason there's food on the table?"

"She took in sewing. She's very good, but there must have been more." She nodded and moved closer. "I think we should visit her."

Now? Of course she meant now. That tingle of unease slithered over his shoulders, but he agreed. "The sooner we solve this hidden mystery, the better," he said.

"What do you know of Bingham?" she asked as they changed directions, walking toward Heba's. "I've heard you and Saied Harry speak of him."

"Not much," Philip admitted, scanning the area. "No one had anything to say about him, good or bad. I had the feeling he was fairly decent at his trade, but nothing so spectacular."

Certainly not anything like al-Najjar, whom everyone knew whether they wanted to or not. Or her uncles, whom people respected. He'd looked into that during the week between agreeing to marry her and the actual wedding. Those he—and Harry—had met with all spoke highly about the *al-tajir* and the men running it.

"Perhaps that is his...what do you call it?" She glanced up at him, her eyes sparkling in the fading light. "When someone shows one face while doing secretive things behind everyone's backs."

He snorted but had to agree. "I think he might be savvier than either of us give him credit for." They slowed as they entered Heba's street. "Are you sure about this?"

"Oh, yes."

* * *

LAYLA HAD LIED. She thought she was ready, thought she could handle stepping into the house again. Her reasons for doing so hadn't changed since the last time; indeed, those reasons had grown more certain. She needed answers, and all she'd found so far were more questions.

That, and because Philip was willing to part with truly gorgeous items in the name of helping her. It swelled through her, the love she felt for him.

As they waited for someone to open the door, the words

danced on her tongue. *I love you* was simple, easy. And they were the three hardest words she'd ever felt the need to utter.

"*Tahiat*," Malik said in surprise. "Layla."

"Malik." She bowed in formal greeting, at a complete loss as to how she ought to greet her cousin. "We're here to see Aunt Heba. I have questions."

Malik glanced at Philip, then peered between them at the men surrounding her. Layla had no idea what he might think about that, but then he merely stepped back.

She had no plan for this conversation, but as she walked into the kitchens, where Heba stood in shock, she thought perhaps that was for the best.

"What are—how dare—"

"We have questions, *ima*." Layla didn't wait for more spluttering. "I should have asked before. Long ago, when we first came." Or even later, after Mama had died, but she'd been so heartbroken, so very lost. "Why? Why did Mama come here. Why did we stay? How did you protect her?"

Heba's hard, closed-off look didn't crack, but her shoulders dropped. "I don't know," she admitted. "Mariam was sick; she required near constant attention and medicine we couldn't afford. I thought Jomana and Augusta kicked you out after Harry's death." Her gaze flicked to Philip, and she dusted her hands on her skirts.

"He knows," Layla admitted in a clear, strong voice. "He knows about my heritage."

Heba shrugged. "Mariam never said why. Only that she needed to protect you." She met Layla's gaze, hard and brittle. "That was all she cared about. Made me swear I'd hide you no matter what."

Layla hadn't expected this confession. Licking dry lips, she grasped for a coherent question, but all she had was, "How?"

"Omar, may his soul rot, spread lies. Ensured that even family knew you were dead." She dismissed that with an angry flick of her wrist. "I'm surprised he kept the secret all these years, but as long as the money came in, it didn't matter."

"Money?" Philip asked. Layla wanted to know about that, too, but she was far too surprised to do more than stare at her aunt. "You brought the money in...no," he said slowly. "You were the entire reason this household had any money at all. Sewing? Investments?"

"Not as stupid as you look," Heba muttered in Arabic. Layla's lips twitched, but she couldn't do more than stare at her aunt. Hopefully she could find the humor in that statement later. "Father realized Omar could never keep the business, so Mariam promised to invest a quarter of the profits for me and the children."

"You oversaw those investments," Layla breathed. "Did Omar know?"

"Bah, no." Heba scoffed and waved that away.

"That's how you had the money for Mama and me." Layla swallowed. "Is that why she came here?"

"I told Omar that Mariam brought money, and for a while he believed that. He kept the secret. Until he promised you to al-Najjar."

Layla nodded. This was far more complicated than she'd originally thought. Beside her, Philip shifted. His hand, large and warm and comforting, rested on the small of her back.

"It wasn't al-Najjar who killed him, though, was it?"

Heba met his gaze, the barest hint of a smile showing on her set face. "That, I don't know. He worked for Bingham; he worked for al-Najjar. He worked for many of the merchants, running errands, taking home what little they'd offer."

All those coins she'd taken, hidden away, lied about. They belonged to her mother anyway. Perhaps that was why Heba never spoke of it. She knew. Knew and couldn't say anything for fear that Omar might discover her ruse.

When Heba spoke again, her voice shook, as if whoever

killed Mariam and Harry Braithwaite were standing in the room with them. "Mariam was so sick," she whispered. "And so very scared. She worried that whoever poisoned Harry thought she knew, though of course she didn't. She never discovered that."

Layla nodded dumbly, mind racing, heart aching. "Why did she come here?"

"It was for you," Heba whispered. "I don't know, but everything she did was for you."

Tears blurred Layla's vision, and she quickly blinked them away. It was the best and only answer she'd get, but it was enough. She loved her mother, even after the long years of caring for her, of living in this terrible place.

"Why didn't you contact Aunt Jomana or Aunt Augusta?" But the moment she asked, Layla knew.

"Bah," Heba said. "Whoever killed your mother worked in that circle. Used them, or they were involved. How else could someone poison Harry and Mariam but no one else?"

"Mostafa." Philip paused and shook his head. "Mostafa also died under mysterious circumstances. Either someone was careless—doubtful, given the meticulousness of their previous poisons—or he discovered something on his own."

Heba waved that away, and all Layla could do was stare. All these years. Everything she knew about her life upended once more. Who could she trust? Heba? Jomana and Augusta? No one?

Philip's hand moved up her spine, jolting her back to the here and now. Philip. She trusted him. With her life, her heart, her soul.

CHAPTER 21

"**I** don't know what to believe." The words barely made it past Layla's lips as she and Philip left Heba's house once more.

The sun had set, and the street was dark. Shadowed and sinister, as if a threatening hand covered the sky. Layla stared down the street, where shadows moved like omens. Her fingers curled into her skirts, but nothing warmed them despite the lingering heat of the day.

"I don't know," Philip admitted on a sigh. "There are a lot of pieces here I didn't expect."

"Who do I trust?" She looked up at him, feeling alone and lost. "I don't know who to trust."

He gathered her close, tucking her head beneath his chin. The warmth of his body seeped through her, easing her chill and wrapping around her so tightly she felt safe. Warm and safe in his arms.

"I trust you," she heard herself say. Pulling back, she met his gaze. "I trust you with my life." She paused, but only for a breath before she leaped. "With my heart."

He stilled, and even in the darkness she saw his eyes widen. "Layla." The word sounded like it had been pulled from him.

"I love you. Not just because you keep me safe." She flattened her hands against his chest and swore she felt his heart pound against them. Or perhaps it was her own heart pounding so hard. "You listen. You hear me. You understand what I mean and what I need. You're the first person to ever do so, and I know I don't have a lot of experience—"

His lips crashed against hers, hard and demanding, and she gave him everything. She had no idea if this kiss was a means of silencing her confession or accepting it. Was he hoping she'd stop speaking or telling her without words that he felt the same? Either way, his kiss sparked deep within her, and she returned it with everything she had.

"This is not the place," he growled against her mouth.

"Oh." She swallowed and stepped back. She'd quite forgotten they stood on the street outside her aunt's house, in the early evening, with his men surrounding them. Flushing hot in embarrassment, she took another step back, but Philip held her close.

He pressed his lips against hers again and whispered, "I love you, too. More than words can convey. With everything in me, I love you."

"Oh," she said again, breathless this time. She thought she ought to say more, or have more to say. Something about how this love surprised her and warmed her and showed her a future she'd never imagined. Instead, she found she could only grin up at him. "I'm glad."

He laughed, the sound echoing over the darkening street. "Let's return to the ship. I fear we have too much to discuss, and this certainly isn't the place."

Winding her hand through the crook of his elbow, she walked beside him. She did not— absolutely not—make eye contact with any of his men. Not after that rather impassioned display of affection.

They walked quickly and silently down the darkened streets toward the wharves. It wasn't until they grew closer that she realized something stirred in the night.

"What is it?"

"We're being followed." Philip sighed in obvious frustration. "Again."

"If it's not al-Najjar, could it be Bingham?" She swallowed hard and frowned. "Or a purse thief, I suppose?"

He snorted. "It's the person who wants you dead, whether that be Bingham or someone else. He's the only other name we have." Philip didn't slow but hurried her toward the ship. "There's one thing I don't understand."

She snorted, a sound she'd picked up from him and discovered she enjoyed. The sound was robust, showing her feelings without the need for words. "One thing?"

He grunted, and in the twilight she swore he grinned. "Why attack you now? We've traveled to Damietta several times. Before our marriage, you were guarded by only a single man. Why not attack you then?"

"Because I didn't know how much she knew." The voice drifted from the shadows, freezing Layla in place.

"Ah, Bingham. It was you." Philip nodded casually, as if they were enjoying a cup of coffee in the day cabin. She admired that about him, envied him his cool reserve. "You overplayed your hand."

Her hand tightened on his arm, tense beneath her touch. She thought she should release him, allow him this fight, but the fact that she stood face-to-face with the man who murdered her parents froze her in place. She couldn't move, as if she'd forgotten how.

"Have I?" Bingham didn't sound worried. But then, she could

barely hear anything over the thundering of her heart in her ears. "It seems I have the distinct advantage."

Behind her, the crew shifted, spreading out as they prepared for an attack. She had no idea how many men Bingham had with him. For all she knew, he had half the wharf in his pay. If that were the case, there'd be no stopping them with only five men, Philip, and her very amateur dagger skills. The dagger she hadn't brought along. She hadn't even the broom with her.

Swallowing hard, Layla forced her fingers from Philip's arm. He'd need the mobility. She couldn't control her breathing; it came too fast and shallow, but she wouldn't let that stop her. Stepping slightly from his side, just enough so he could move, she raised her chin and willed her voice to remain even.

"Why?" Her hands bunched in her skirts, and her toes dug painfully into the soles of her shoes. "Why any of this? What was so—so important that you killed both my parents?"

Bingham laughed, and the sound sent a chill down her spine. "Is this the part where I confess all my secrets while you wait for reinforcements?" He laughed again, a strong, confident sound.

Ice settled in her stomach, but she didn't back down. "This is the part where you tell me why you poisoned my father and destroyed my mother—did you also kill my cousin, Mostafa?"

"Cousin, bah." Bingham snarled a very derogatory term that surprised her so much she stepped backward. Philip growled, said something in a language she didn't understand, and stood beside her. Grateful for his presence—more than grateful—she grappled for words.

"Your father was easy prey," Bingham said conversationally. "And no reinforcements are coming."

Layla didn't know what that meant, but in the midst of all this she had a vague memory of Philip telling one of the men to warn the ship.

Bingham had done something to Lange. Fury heated her spine.

"Mostafa wanted to bring in business, but he didn't have the patience or skill of his father. When he failed, he went to Braithwaite. Told the man everything." Bingham sneered down at her. Even in the uncertain light of the street, it churned her stomach.

"You killed them because of a bad business deal?" Philip laughed, a low, hard sound she'd never heard from him before. "How very...pathetic. No—there's more. It wasn't a bad business deal. How much money did you lose?"

They didn't do business with him, Layla remembered now. Bingham had come to Philip. Neither Muhammad nor Josiah worked with him, though neither had said why, not to her. They hadn't stopped Philip from speaking with him, however. If they'd known Bingham was involved, Layla knew for certain they'd never have allowed any contact.

"Mostafa was your target," Layla breathed, as that ice in her tone turned to fire. "You killed him for what? Revenge? Why? *How*? Why kill my parents?"

"Braithwaite knew too much," Bingham growled. He withdrew a pistol from somewhere and aimed it at Philip. "Your whore of a mother suspected," he said to Layla.

Fury colored her vision, and she stalked forward. "Never speak of her like that," she hissed. "She was a pure and honorable woman, not a poisonous snake like yourself."

"You have one shot, Bingham." Philip stepped beside her. "I don't care how many men you think you have with you." He nodded at the pistol. "Make it count if you want to live beyond this meeting."

"I have many men in my employ. Shadi was one."

Layla had forgotten about him. "You killed him." She forced out a mocking laugh despite the danger before her and the revelations that tangled inside her. "You killed him when you realized, no matter how much you paid, you didn't control him. You don't control anyone."

Bingham swung the pistol in her direction, and Layla braced.

She heard a sound, familiar yet foreign, and waited for the shot. The pistol never fired. Philip threw his khanjar at Bingham, and the curved blade imbedded in the man's belly.

"No one threatens my wife."

Layla didn't know what happened next. She stared at the man who had poisoned her parents, Mostafa, even Omar. Then a sound erupted, spreading over the street. Philip's crew. Barking—Argus.

Dropping to her knees, she blinked but couldn't stand up again. Argus sat before her, licking her hands, her face. Layla focused on him and tried to make sense of the last few minutes. Was it over? Looking past the dog, who whined and whimpered until she wrapped her arms around him, she spotted Bingham's body.

"Argus, come." Philip crouched down and lifted her as if she weighed no more than the birds he so loved. "Let's go home, love."

She thought she should protest, say she could walk. Instead, she rested her head on his chest and let him carry her back to the ship.

* * *

PHILIP CARRIED his quiet wife through the streets, the majority of his crew and the guards her uncles hired following them. People lined the street as if they paraded across a square, watching them with a silent fascination that seeped into his bones. How many men did Bingham employ? He'd have to find out, root out those in Layla's family's household. He had a strange feeling that al-Najjar would know more about those men. Odd that he'd suspected him only hours ago.

Life certainly had a way of changing on him.

"Is she unharmed?" Harry asked, falling into step beside him.

"Yes." Philip thought so at least, though she hadn't uttered a word since he'd killed Bingham.

The pistol hadn't fired, he knew that. When she'd collapsed onto the ground, his heart stopped. Argus, who was nipping at his hands, whining insistently, sounded as worried as Philip.

"She's—Bingham's revelations surprised her."

"I sent Hutton round to her family."

"Lange?" Philip didn't slow but glanced at his friend. "I sent him back to the ship; Bingham made it seem—"

"He's in bad shape. Several men worked him over well, but not completely." Harry made a harsh sound in the back of his throat. "According to him, he took down more than a few."

"I can walk." Layla pushed against Philip's chest and met his gaze. Her dark eyes met his, clear and calm, with that hint of fire he so adored. "I refuse to let Bingham take anything more from me."

Philip wanted to protest that there was no shame in him carrying her, but he didn't. Careful of Argus, he set her on her feet. "Layla."

She wrapped her hand around his arm and nodded. "I still have a lot of questions." She glanced behind them, though of course she couldn't see Bingham. "I'm afraid someone in the household worked for Bingham, and that's how he managed to poison Mostafa and my parents."

Philip would like to know how, with what poison, but it hardly mattered now. Covering her hand with his, he struggled for words. Argus leaned against Layla, his tail wagging as she scratched behind his ears.

"You don't have to do anything now," he whispered into her hair, holding her close.

She leaned her head against his chest. "If not now, when?" He felt her give a small shrug. "What will happen to Bingham?"

May he rot in the street.

"I suppose I should contact the authorities. No," he added slowly. "Well, yes, them as well, but al-Najjar."

"Him?" She pulled back, surprised. "Why?"

"Not out of any misguided tribute or anything," he assured her. "Once we leave, your family will still be here. If Bingham had associates, which seems likely, even if they knew very little of what he planned, it's best to have the most powerful man in the Damietta underworld owe us a favor."

She watched him for a long moment, openmouthed. Then she grinned. Her grin turned into a laugh, and she leaned her head against his chest again. "I would have never thought of that, Philip. I like the way your brain works."

He snorted. "I'm not sure that's a compliment." Cupping her cheeks, he kissed her softly. "I'm afraid I've corrupted you."

"No," she whispered, holding him tight. Argus tried to butt in, but neither moved. "You've shown me." She kissed him again. "You've shown me love and trust and what it's like to have someone at my side."

"Always."

"Now then." She stepped back, offered Argus the affection he so desired, and nodded at Harry, who looked anywhere but at the two of them. Taking Philip's hand, she grinned. "I think the rest of the family should know what's happened." She offered a sad smile. "And that a traitor might still be working in their midst."

"Ah, yes, well," Harry interrupted, looking abashed, "I did send word round to them, I'm afraid. I'm sure they're on their way to the ship."

Philip nodded, and together he and Layla led the crew back toward *The Lady Kaya*. He had a feeling they made a motley entourage, but then he also had a feeling word had spread quickly through the port town about what happened.

Sure enough, by the time they reached his ship's berth, Philip saw Layla's family on deck. They stood eerily silent, as on guard as the remaining men watching the ship.

He called out the code, and for one heavy beat, as if they waited for a bell to toll, no one moved. Then, as one, the crew breathed a sigh of relief, and everyone sprang into action.

"Where's Lange?" Layla asked, even as her aunts and cousins surrounded her. "I need to thank him."

"He's belowdecks," Reeves said with a quick bob. "Laska and Kaz are seeing to him."

"In a moment," Philip murmured. "We'll gather in the dining room in a moment. Speak with your family first."

"Lange is my family," she said quietly but firmly. "He's your crew, your family, and he literally risked his life so that we had reinforcements."

Love burst through him, and he let out a small laugh, shaking his head. "As my lady commands."

She nodded, then turned and embraced first Augusta then Jomana. "I'll tell you everything, but I need to see to the injured crewmen who saved our lives."

Philip did not roll his eyes. With that sort of praise, there'd be no living with Lange now, not after that.

"Is it true?" Muhammad asked as he, Josiah, Augusta, and Jomana gathered round. Evelyn, Philip noted, had followed Layla belowdecks. "Was it Bingham?"

"Yes." He rolled his shoulders and accepted his khanjar from Harry. "The short version is that he contacted Mostafa with a business proposition, and when it went sour, Mostafa asked Harry Braithwaite for help. Bingham didn't like that and poisoned them both. Mariam Braithwaite, too."

"Over a business deal?" Jomana snarled. In the moonlight, she looked vicious and furious. An avenging angel in her fury. "He killed my son over a business deal?"

"I'm sorry," Philip said, offering a slight bow. "We—he threatened Layla; I don't know how many men he had, and…

and I killed him. We had more questions, Layla had more, but—"

Jomana nodded, tears shining in her eyes as she met his gaze. "Thank you. For avenging my son, my family." She reached out and laid a hand on his arm, which surprised Philip. "And for protecting Layla, my beloved niece."

"I'd do it again." All that and more. He'd protect Layla with his life, until his last breath.

She said he'd opened her eyes, but it was she who showed him that there was more to his own life than he realized. More than the boy trying to salvage his past into a respectable future.

His gaze drifted to the stairs where she'd disappeared. He'd never considered marriage, hadn't wanted his past deeds to taint anyone. But Layla had shown him that their pasts didn't define them. Those pasts made them into the people they were today, and he happened to love that woman beyond words.

EPILOGUE

The sun had barely risen, but they'd only just tumbled into bed. Part of Layla wanted to watch the sunrise, see it brighten a new day, this new part of her life spread out before her.

The other part of her could barely keep her eyes open.

Snuggled against Philip's side, she laid her head on his chest and remained still. This was what she wanted, to be wrapped in his arms.

"The quiet is nice," she whispered, unwilling to break the silence yet also wanting him to know how much she appreciated his presence today. "It's been a haboob."

He grinned, brushing her hair off her cheek. "A sandstorm? That's what you'd call this?"

Layla caught his hand and held it just under her chin. "Wild and unpredictable and messy? Yes."

"The cleanup wasn't so bad, I suppose. The authorities didn't ask too many questions."

"I think that had more to do with what everyone learned about Bingham." She frowned, still puzzling out the whys. "What poison did he use?"

"I'm not the right one to ask about that; my Aunt Cedella knows much about poisons. Whatever it was, it didn't leave a trace. If not for your mother recognizing the changes in your father, no one would've ever realized anything."

"It didn't kill her," she whispered. "Not immediately. Mama suffered for years with skin lesions and nausea and vomiting. There were good days, sometimes good weeks, but more bad ones. She was weak. Even when she rose from bed, she tired easily."

"I'm sorry, Layla. I don't know what that was or how any poison was administered. I'm sorry."

She nodded. She hadn't really expected him to know. No one seemed to, and even if Bingham had said—which she doubted he would've—it didn't matter. What would she do with that knowledge? The only thing that mattered was who he'd hired, or bribed, or tricked, she supposed, into administering it.

"Whoever Bingham had in the house, they were careful. I might not know how they poisoned my parents, but I do know it can't have been easy."

"Food, I'd guess. Drink maybe, but if it had an odor or taste, it'd be more noticeable."

"Aunt Augusta promised they'd let us know if they discovered who poisoned everyone, but I don't know how they could trust anyone again." Perhaps they wouldn't. Perhaps they'd find all new servants, though some of them had been with the family for years, as Evelyn reminded her. "They're looking into everyone. Even Haamid, their former secretary, though he was lost in the invasions."

"I still can't believe Shadi had a shred of honorability in him." Philips lifted her hand and kissed her fingertips. "Or maybe it was the money."

"I'd say the money." She closed her eyes and let the last of the tension she'd carried with her for a decade seep from her shoulders. "Still, he did keep my presence a secret. I don't know why."

"Considering the way he treated you?" Philip trailed off, and she wondered what he was thinking. "Some people like holding things over others' heads. As if they're superior."

"I don't want to talk about him while we're in bed. I don't want to talk about him ever again." No matter how strange it was that Omar had kept her safe, he'd treated her no better than sand on a stoop. For years, she believed her family had abandoned her because of her heritage, because they wanted her well away, the half-English, half-Egyptian wild child.

She'd believed those lies.

"What happens now?" She pushed upright just enough so she could watch him in the slowly brightening room.

"With the business?"

"No. Yes." She sighed and rested her head on his chest again. "With everything, I suppose."

"We can leave whenever you wish," he promised. "Or we can stay for a while longer."

"I think I would like to see England." She smiled and closed her eyes. "Though from what you and your crew have said, it's cold and rainy there."

"It's…yes, it can be." He lifted her hand again and held it over his heart. "I'd like you to meet my family."

She kissed his chest. "I'd love to meet your family. If they're anything like you, they'll be wonderful."

He snorted, and she felt him tense. "They're better than I am. Stronger."

Her head snapped up. "Philip Conrad, you are the strongest person I know!" She kissed him softly. "The kindest one, too."

"I don't know about that." He grinned. "You've shown me how strong I can be. That my past isn't who I am anymore, and the future—our future—is whatever we make it."

"Good." She nodded decisively but hesitated. "What about your great-grandfather in Cairo?"

"I'd forgotten about him," he admitted, sounding surprised

himself. "It's…even if we found him, he may not want anything to do with me. With us. He sent my mother away for her own safety. There was famine and unrest even then."

"We can wait until the messenger returns."

Philip nodded but didn't look convinced. "It was a farfetched hope. It's been thirty years; I'm sure he fought Napoleon's army. From what Mama said, he was a general."

And perished with so many others. He didn't have to say it. She suspected he was correct. "Finding him, or not finding him, doesn't mean you're a failure."

"No," he agreed in that same slow, unconvinced tone. "No, you're right. You showed me that. If you hadn't boarded the wrong ship, had none of this happened and by some chance I did find him, it wouldn't have changed anything."

"Wouldn't have changed you from the strong, confident, kind, persistent man you already are?" She nodded against his chest. "You're right."

His startled chuckle warmed her, and Layla relaxed again, holding him tighter. "Says the strong, confident, kind, tenaciously persistent woman in my arms?"

"Yes."

He rolled over top of her and kissed her. Layla shifted so he could settle his weight more comfortably as she held him close. She might never get enough of this, the warm weight of him, the way even a simple kiss made her want him so desperately.

"I love you," he whispered against her mouth. "More than I have words to express."

"Good." She grinned at him. "I love you as well. So very much." She kissed him softly, that love bubbling up within her. "I cannot wait to see what the future holds for us."

"We'll return to Damietta," he promised, kissing along her jaw. "Perhaps make the ship our home."

She didn't know about that, but she decided that remaining

open to options wasn't a bad idea. "One day at a time," she said, returning his mouth to hers.

"As my lady commands."

STAY IN TOUCH

Thank you for reading, interested in reading more of the Conrad family? https://amzn.to/48ksDOr

IF YOU ENJOYED THIS BOOK, I'd really appreciate it if you helped others enjoy it, too. Reviews are precious and help persuade other readers to give my romances a try.

Sign up to my VIP list for a short story, One Day with You. This story, along 3 additional short stories about Louise and Malcolm, are only available to my list. https://bit.ly/ 3kSzMjI

I send weekly newsletters with things like new releases, special offers, pictures of my dog, recipes, and other exciting news about my stories, preorders, research, and travel that I hope you'll enjoy as much as I do.

STAY CONNECTED
CKMackenzie.com
Facebook.com/ckmackenziebook

instagram.com/ckmackenzieauthor
tiktok.com/@ckmackenzieauthor